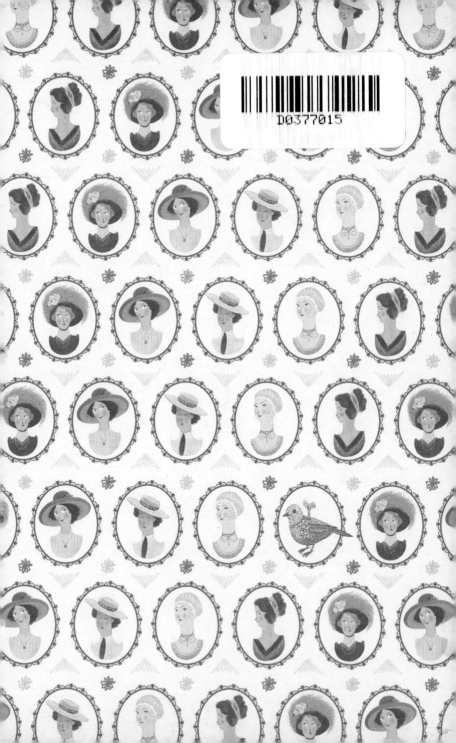

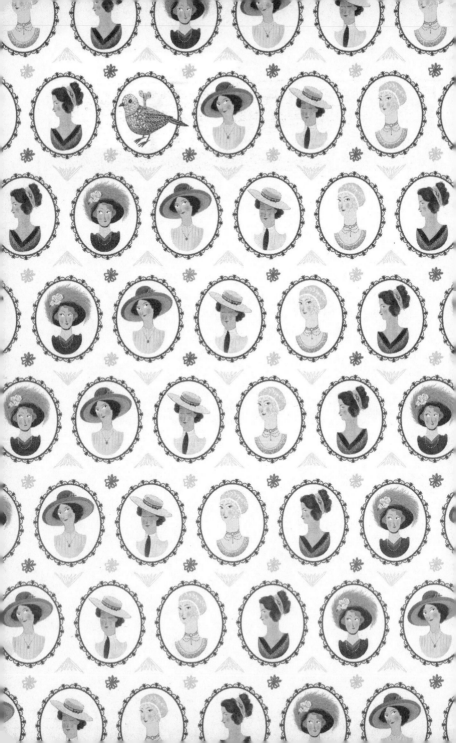

The Mystery of the
CLOCKWORK SPARROW

The Mystery of the
CLOCKWORK SPARROW

Katherine Woodfine

EGMONT

EGMONT

We bring stories to life

First published in Great Britain 2015

by Egmont UK Limited
The Yellow Building, 1 Nicholas Road, London W11 4AN

Text copyright © 2015 Katherine Woodfine
Illustrations © 2015 Júlia Sardà

The moral rights of the author and illustrator have been asserted

ISBN 978 1 4052 7617 7

59339/5

A CIP catalogue record for this title is available
from the British Library

Typeset by Avon DataSet Ltd, Bidford on Avon, Warwickshire
Printed and bound in Great Britain by the CPI Group

MIX
Paper
FSC   FSC® C018306

To Mama and OD,
with much love

was conveyed to the University College Hospital, where life was found to be extinct. It is not known how she received her injuries.

CLOCKMAKER MURDERED, HOXTON

LONDON, March 15.

The body of Mr Daniel Mendel, 52, Clockmaker, was found at his workshop on Hoxton Square on Saturday morning last, his throat having been cut. The discovery was made by his neighbour, Mr Walter Simpson, 37, a Cabinet-maker, who identified the body as that of Mr Mendel. A witness reported seeing a youth and two men loitering on Hoxton Square, close to Mr Mendel's workshop, late on Friday evening. An inquiry has been launched into the circumstances attending his death.

COURT REPORTS

LONDON, March 15.

Henry Walter, a Clerk in the employ of John Steadman, Builder, of Ramsden Road, Balham, was charged at South Western Magistrates' Court yesterday with stealing postal orders to the value of 25s 7d belon-

PART I
'The Straw Sailor'

This dainty straw hat with a ribbon bow is the essence of charming simplicity. Becoming to every face shape, it is a practical everyday choice for the young working lady . . .

CHAPTER ONE

Sophie hung on tightly to the leather strap as the omnibus rattled forwards. Another Monday morning and, all about her, London was whirring into life: damp and steamy with last night's rain and this morning's smoke. As she stood wedged between a couple of clerks wearing bowler hats and carrying newspapers, she gazed out of the window at the grey street, wondering whether that faint fragrance of spring she'd caught on the wind had been just her imagination. She found herself thinking about the garden of Orchard House: the daffodils that must be blooming there now, the damp earth and the smell of rain in the grass.

'Piccadilly Circus!' yelled the conductor as the omnibus clattered to a halt, and Sophie pushed her thoughts away. She straightened her hat, grasped her umbrella in a neatly gloved hand, and slipped between the clerks and past an elderly lady wearing a *pince-nez*, who said 'Dear me!' as if quite scandalised at the sight of a young lady alone, recklessly

3

jumping on and off omnibuses. Sophie paid no attention and hopped down on to the pavement. There was simply no sense in listening. After all, she wasn't that sort of young lady any more.

As the omnibus drew away, she turned and gazed for a moment at the enormous white building that towered above her. Sinclair's department store was so new that, as yet, it had not even opened its doors to customers. But already it was the most famous store in London – and therefore, some said, the whole world. With its magnificent columns and ranks of coloured flags, it wasn't like any other shop Sophie had ever seen. It was more like a classical temple that had sprung up, white and immaculate against the smog and dirt of Piccadilly. The huge plate-glass windows were shrouded with royal-blue silk curtains, making it look like the stage in a grand theatre before the performance has begun.

The owner of Sinclair's department store was Mr Edward Sinclair, who was as famous as the store itself. He was an American, a self-made man, renowned for his elegance, for the single, perfect orchid he always wore in his buttonhole, for the ever-changing string of beautiful ladies on his arm and, most of all, for his wealth. Although they had only been working for him for a few weeks, and most of them had barely set eyes on him, the staff of Sinclair's had taken to referring to him as 'the Captain', because rumour had

4

it that he had run away to sea in his youth. There were already a great number of rumours about Edward Sinclair. But whether the stories were true or not, it seemed an apt nickname. After all, the store itself was a little like a ship: as glittering and luxurious as an ocean liner ready to carry its customers proudly on a journey to an exotic new land.

Somewhere, Sophie could hear a clock chiming. Drawing herself up to her full height – which wasn't very tall – she lifted her chin and set off smartly round the side of the great building, the little heels of her buttoned boots clicking briskly over the cobbles. As she approached, her heart began to thump, and she put up a hand to check that her hat, with its blue-ribbon bow, was still at exactly the right angle, and that her hair was not coming down. She was part of Sinclair's department store now: a small cog in this great machine. As such, she knew she must be nothing short of perfect.

Through the doors was another world. The staff corridors were humming with activity. All about her, people were hurrying along carrying palms in pots, or stepladders and tins of paint, or stacks of the distinctive royal-blue and gold Sinclair's boxes. A smart saleswoman whisked by with an exquisitely beaded evening gown draped carefully over her arm; another hustled along with an armful of parasols, seemingly in a terrific rush; and the strict store manager,

Mr Cooper, could be seen dressing down a salesman about the condition of his gloves. Sophie dived in among them and then slipped into the empty cloakroom to take off her coat and hat.

It still seemed extraordinary that she was here at all. Even a year ago, the thought of earning her own living would never have entered her imagination – and now, here she was, a fully fledged shop girl. She paused for a moment before the cloakroom looking-glass to survey her hair, and pushed a hairpin back into place. Mr Cooper was a stickler for immaculate personal appearances, but worse than that, she knew that Edith and the other girls would be only too quick to notice any shortcomings. Once upon a time she had been rather vain about her looks, carefully brushing her hair one hundred times each night and fussing Miss Pennyfeather to tie her velvet ribbon in exactly the right sort of bow, but now she only wanted to look neat and businesslike. She didn't feel in the least like the girl she had been back then. Her face in the looking glass was familiar, but strange: she looked older somehow, pale and tired and out of sorts.

Her shoulders slumped as she thought of the long week that lay ahead of her, but at once she frowned at herself sharply. Papa would have said that she ought to be thinking about how fortunate she was to be here. There were plenty of others who weren't so lucky, she reminded herself. She had seen them: girls her own age or even younger, selling apples or little posies of flowers on street corners; girls begging for pennies from passing gentlemen; girls huddled in doorways, wearing clothes that were scarcely more than rags.

Thinking this, she shook her head, squared her shoulders and forced herself to smile. 'Buck up,' she told her reflection sternly. Whatever else happened today, she was determined that she wouldn't give Edith any more excuses to call her stuck-up.

She strode purposefully towards the door, but before she had taken more than a couple of steps, she tripped and fell forwards.

'Oh!' exclaimed a voice. As she righted herself, she glanced down to see a boy gazing up at her in alarm. He was sitting on the floor, partly hidden behind a row of coats, and she had fallen over his boots. 'Are you all right?'

'What are you *doing* down there?' demanded Sophie breathlessly, more embarrassed to have been caught pulling faces and talking to herself than actually hurt. No doubt this boy would make fun of her now, like all the rest, and he'd soon be telling all the others what he had overheard. 'You shouldn't hide in corners spying!' she burst out.

'I wasn't spying,' said the boy, scrambling to his feet. He was wearing the Sinclair's porters' uniform – trim dark-blue trousers, a matching jacket with a double row of brass buttons and a peaked hat – but the jacket looked too big for him, the trousers a bit short, and the hat was askew on his untidy, straw-coloured hair. 'I was *reading*.' For proof, he held out a crumpled story-paper, entitled *Boys of Empire*, in one grubby hand.

But before Sophie could say anything else, the door slammed open, and a cluster of shop girls pushed their way into the room, in a flurry of skirts and ribbons.

'Excuse us! Beg your pardon!'

A pretty dark-haired girl caught sight of the boy and smirked. 'Haven't you fetched that tin of elbow grease for Jim yet?' she demanded, sending a ripple of titters through the group.

'Learned to tie your bootlaces all by yourself, have you?' another girl giggled.

A third took in Sophie, and made a ridiculous curtsy in her direction. 'Forgive us, Your Ladyship. We didn't see that you were gracing us with your presence.'

'Aren't you going to introduce us to your young man?' added the dark-haired girl in an arch tone, making the others laugh even more.

The boy's cheeks flushed crimson, but Sophie tried her hardest to look indifferent. She had heard this kind of thing many times already during the two weeks of training that all the Sinclair's shop girls had undertaken. She had realised that she had started all wrong on the very first morning, arriving wearing one of her best dresses – black silk and velvet with jet buttons. She had thought she ought to be smart and make a good first impression, but when she arrived, she realised that every other girl in the room was dressed almost identically, in a plain dark skirt, and a neat white blouse. The rustle and swish of her skirts had made them all look at her, and then begin giggling behind their hands.

'Who does she think she is? The Lady of the Manor?' the dark-haired girl, Edith, had whispered.

The next morning she had come carefully dressed in a navy-blue skirt and a white blouse with a little lace collar, but it was already too late. The girls called her 'Your Ladyship', or if they wanted to be especially mean, 'Your Royal Highness' or 'Princess Sophie'. All through the training, they made game of the way she spoke, the clothes she wore, the way she did her hair, and especially whenever she was praised by Mr Cooper or Claudine, the store window-dresser.

She had tried hard to look unconcerned, and not to let her feelings show. Papa had always said that in times of war, the most important thing was never to let the enemy see that you were intimidated. Remembering this she saw his face again, almost as if he were standing right in front of her with his bright, dark eyes and neat moustache. He would have been pacing up and down on the hearth rug in his study, the walls hung with maps and treasures he had brought back from distant lands, relating one of his many stories about battles and military campaigns. *Keep calm, keep your head, keep a stiff upper lip*: those were his mottoes. But the truth was, the more she ignored the other shop girls, the worse they seemed to become. They said she was haughty and high-and-mighty, and called her the name she hated most, 'Sour-milk Sophie'. Not for the first time, she reflected that perhaps Papa's advice was not *entirely* helpful when it came to dealing with horrid shop girls.

Now, she turned away and went out into the passage, the boy trailing behind her. He looked so miserable that she felt a twinge of guilt for having assumed that he would make fun of her, when, in fact, it seemed that they were in the same boat.

'I shouldn't pay any attention to them,' she said.

The boy tried to smile. 'I really wasn't spying on you – honest, I wasn't,' he said anxiously. 'I just wanted to finish my serial. I didn't even notice you were there. It's the latest Montgomery Baxter.' Seeing that she looked blank, he went on: 'It's about a detective. He's only a boy, you see, but somehow he always solves the crime and outwits the villain, even when no one else can.' He beamed at her enthusiastically and, rather to her surprise, Sophie found herself smiling back. 'I just had to find somewhere out of sight to finish it, so Mr Cooper didn't catch me reading. Anyway, I'm sorry I tripped you up,' he finished.

'It doesn't matter,' said Sophie. She held out her hand politely, like Miss Pennyfeather had taught her. 'I'm Sophie Taylor. I'm in the Millinery Department.' She had already learned that using her full name, Taylor-Cavendish, would do her no favours here at Sinclair's. It was safer to stick to plain old Taylor.

'Billy Parker, apprentice porter,' he explained, accepting her hand and giving it a firm shake.

'Parker? Then are you –?'

'Related to Sidney Parker? Yes. He's my uncle, worse luck,' Billy said, grimacing. 'Oh cripes, and here he comes now,' he murmured in a lower voice, hastily stuffing the creased story-paper into his pocket as a man came striding towards them along the passageway.

Like everyone else at Sinclair's, Sophie already knew exactly who Sidney Parker was. He was Head Doorman, in charge of the whole team of doormen and porters, and Mr Cooper's right-hand man. Tall and handsome in a bullish sort of way, he was impossible to miss in his immaculate uniform. With his hat perfectly brushed, his buttons gleaming and his glossy black moustache always smoothed into place, he couldn't have been more different from his untidy nephew.

'Good morning, miss,' he said, sweeping off his hat with the respectful manner he used for all ladies. Then he turned to Billy. 'Where do you think you've been? Stand up straight, lad – and cheer up, can't you? You look like a wet weekend.'

He winked at Sophie as though they were sharing a joke at Billy's expense and then swung the door that led to the shop floor open for her with exaggerated politeness. Throwing a quick smile over her shoulder to Billy, she walked out of the passageway.

CHAPTER TWO

Billy gazed after Sophie as she vanished through the door. She was the first girl in the whole place who hadn't treated him like he was dirt on the bottom of her shoe. With her golden hair, he decided she looked rather like the heroine of the Montgomery Baxter story he had just been reading. That would, of course, make him the brave boy detective who saves her from deadly peril. He was just beginning to consider exactly what that peril might be when he was brought back to earth by a sharp cuff on the back of the head from Uncle Sid.

'Don't pretend to me that you haven't been larking about again, boy,' he said curtly. 'I know everything that goes on in this place, and don't you forget it. You want to pull your socks up otherwise you'll be out on your ear. Now shift yourself. Go and help George with the deliveries.'

Billy went down the passage towards the door to the stable-yard, muttering the rudest words he could think of under his breath as soon as Uncle Sid was out of earshot. He couldn't believe that just two weeks ago, he had actually been looking forward to starting work and doing a man's job. Now he was here, and all he did was spend each day bored senseless, being treated like everyone's dogsbody, or getting told off. He'd already had his wages docked twice by Mr Cooper – once for being late and once for having dirty boots. Mum was forever harping on about how lucky he was to have such a fine start, but as far as he was concerned, he'd rather be back at school doing sums. At least he'd been half decent at those.

The stable-yard was warm and damp and smelled of horses and hay. George was sitting alone in a patch of sunlight, squinting at a newspaper, his pipe clamped between his teeth. Blackie, the boiler-room cat, was nearby, thoughtfully washing one paw.

'Here you are, young feller,' George said, patting a packing crate beside him. 'Pull yourself up a pew.'

Suddenly, Billy felt better. It was much nicer here in the stable-yard, away from Uncle Sid and those awful giggling shop girls, and he liked George, who never jeered at him.

'You've got good eyes – read us this bit out,' said George, pointing with the stem of his pipe.

Billy sat down on the packing case, took the newspaper that George was holding out to him and read aloud:

NEW YORK TYCOON TO TAKE LONDON BY STORM!

LONDON'S FIRST PURPOSE-BUILT DEPARTMENT STORE TO OPEN ITS DOORS

New York millionaire Mr Edward Sinclair is set to throw open the doors of London's largest department store this week. The new Piccadilly store, which has been a year in construction, stands an impressive eight storeys high, with six acres of floor space, nine state-of-the-art lifts, and over one hundred different departments. As well as a wealth of Ladies' and Gentlemen's Attire and Household Furnishings, the store includes departments dedicated to Photographic Equipment, Cycling and Motoring Goods as well as a Ladies' Lounge, a Gentlemen's Room, an Exhibition Gallery and the fine Marble Court Restaurant.

Mr Sinclair told our reporter: 'Sinclair's is no ordinary department store, but a unique modern emporium open to the world. All are welcome and admittance cards will not be required.'

This extraordinary new store will open to the public at nine o'clock tomorrow morning, with an opening party for Mr Sinclair's invited guests to take place on Saturday night.

Priceless Treasures for Public Exhibition

As part of the opening extravaganza, a very special exhibit will be on display in the store's Exhibition Gallery from tomorrow.

15

Mr Sinclair will be unveiling some of the most prized pieces from his own private collection of jewels to the public for the first time. Highlights from this renowned collection include a priceless diamond tiara, believed to have belonged to Queen Marie Antoinette of France; jewelled eggs created by the House of Fabergé; and some exquisite pieces by some of the world's most celebrated jewellers, among them Cartier, Fouquet, Lalique and Ashbee.

 Pictured is a charming Clockwork Sparrow, originating from the Russian Imperial Court. This delightful bird is encrusted with pearls and pink, yellow and blue sapphires and has a unique talent – each time it is wound, it will play an entirely different song. *Story continued on Page 2.*

Commons debates German dreadnought threat, Page 4.
Curtain up at the Fortune Theatre, Page 6.

'Fancy that,' said George admiringly. 'And to think that all that's going to be coming through here this very morning, jewels that have belonged to queens and the like.'

'Look at the picture' said Billy, and they bent over the paper to squint at the blurry photograph.

'Don't look much like any sparrow I've ever seen,' said George, contemplating it. 'A different tune every time, eh? Now however do you reckon they get it to do that?'

At that moment, a cart loaded with boxes of merchandise rumbled into the stable-yard. 'Shake a leg, George!' called a voice from behind them. 'The gaffer wants this lot unloaded sharpish.'

George winked at Billy and then heaved himself to his feet. 'Come on pal,' he said. 'Let's get on with this and then we'll finish reading later on.'

Saying that was all very well, but Billy found it was difficult to concentrate on boxes and deliveries. He kept picturing immense diamonds glinting in the dark tunnels of an Indian mine. Then there was Marie Antoinette's tiara. How had the Captain come to own it? He imagined a grand Paris auction house, or a furtive transaction with a cloaked stranger in a foreign tavern. Busy with these speculations, it seemed no time at all before the boxes were unloaded, and then two shiny black motor vans were pulling into the yard, each driven by a man in white gloves. George nodded to Billy, who stood staring, fascinated by the thought of the priceless treasures that must be within.

But then Uncle Sid strode up. 'No hanging about, if you please. This isn't a job for the likes of you. Hop it. Find yourself something useful to do.'

Obediently, Billy walked away, but inwardly he was bristling. At the first sign of something exciting happening, he was told to make himself scarce!

He kicked at the ground, feeling bored and irritable. If only there was something *else* he could do instead of being a rotten old shop porter. A police detective, solving crimes; the commander of one of those new submarines, keeping the British Empire safe from her enemies; or even an author, writing thrilling tales like those he read in *Boys of Empire*. Or perhaps he could be a man like the Captain, an adventurer travelling the world, collecting exotic jewels . . . But it was no good even imagining it. Fellows like him just didn't do that sort of thing.

He wandered gloomily into the stables, thinking that he might be able to find a quiet corner to get on with his story. Bessy, the chestnut mare, put her head over the door of her stall as he approached, and he paused to stroke her. Now, being a cowboy, that would be something, he thought vaguely. Riding on his valiant steed across the great plains of America, like Deadwood Dick or Buffalo Bill –

Suddenly, he stopped short. Something was moving under the hay in the empty stall next to Bessy's – something much too big to be a rat, or even Blackie the cat.

He gathered his wits quickly. It was probably just some kid mucking about. Sometimes there were children hanging about the store, waifs and strays begging or hoping to earn a penny. Uncle Sid always ordered them away, threatening to set the law on them if they came near the place again. Well if his uncle could do it, he could too. He puffed out his chest and stood taller.

'Who's there?' he demanded. Nothing happened and he began to wonder if he had imagined the rustling movement. He raised his voice and said clearly, much as he imagined the great Montgomery Baxter himself might speak: 'I know you're there. Show yourself at once.'

To his astonishment, the hay twitched again - first he saw the glint of a dark suspicious eye, and then a form beginning to emerge. But it wasn't just a kid, he saw with surprise and then with growing anxiety. It was a youth - a young man really - probably a few years older than he was himself. Bigger than him, anyway. He looked filthy with a lot of dark, curly hair straggling out from underneath an old cap. But what Billy noticed straight away was that his face was badly bruised, and that he held his arm awkwardly. The young man was injured, Billy realised, but all the same he found himself stepping back. It wasn't that this stranger was threatening exactly, but he wasn't afraid either: his face showed nothing but a sort of sharp-edged curiosity.

'Who are you? What do you think you're doing?' Billy blustered.

The young man said nothing.

'You're trespassing. You're not allowed to be here. I should get the police.'

The fellow gave him a quick, searching look. Then he spoke. 'I'm not doing any harm,' he said in a hoarse voice. 'I'll not take nothing. Let me be.'

'I can't do that!' Billy exclaimed. He couldn't even imagine what Uncle Sid would say if he found that Billy had let some ruffian hang about in the stables. He gathered himself, and said in a voice that was meant to be just as stern as before, except that it *would* wobble in a most irritating way: 'You're to clear off at once, hear me?'

To his annoyance, the stranger suddenly grinned at him. 'Think you're a toughie, don't you, mate?' he said. 'Well, all right then, just for you I'll be off – but I'll be going in my own time. Why don't you get back to your work like a good boy?'

Billy felt his fists clenching. Why did everyone always treat him like he was some sort of stupid, useless kid? This fellow was the worst of the lot of them, looking at him with a silly smirk on his dirty face. Well, he would show him. His fear had fled now, and he stepped forwards boldly, striking out with his fists. But all at once, and more deftly than Billy could ever have imagined, the stranger shot out one foot, and Billy found himself face down on the stable floor in a great pile of dirt.

By the time he had picked himself up again, spluttering with indignation, his jacket plastered with horse muck and straw, the strange young man had completely vanished.

CHAPTER THREE

Stepping on to the shop floor was like stepping inside a chocolate box. Sophie's feet sank into the thick, soft carpet and she sucked in a deep breath of the rich, perfumed air. She had been falling in love with the store since the very first moment she saw it on the day of her interview, when it had still been noisy with the sounds of sawing and hammering, and had smelled of sawdust and paint. Even then, it had seemed more like a place from a fairy story than any dull, ordinary shop.

Now, a reverent hush hung in the air, and she found herself almost tiptoeing as she crossed the shop floor, gazing around her at the immense chandeliers, the glittering looking-glasses, the glossy walnut panelling. It smelled luscious: no sawdust now, but a glorious fragrance of cocoa and candied violets and some other spicy scent, like the cigars that Papa used to smoke after dinner. The ceiling was painted with a mural of cherubs luxuriating upon soft pink clouds, and around her were gleaming glass-topped counters, each displaying an array of beautiful objects for customers to admire, from blue glass bottles of eau-de-cologne to prettily enamelled snuff-boxes. For now, though, there were no customers; the store was deserted. She only glimpsed the occasional salesgirl, whisking to and fro like a ghost as she put the final touches to a rainbow display of soft kid gloves, or ran a feather duster carefully over a collection of dainty rouge and powder boxes.

Sophie wished she had time to linger, but she knew she ought to hurry. She made her way towards the staff staircase at the back of the shop – the grand main staircases and the lifts were, of course, to be for the customers only. But even the staff staircase had the same air of impossible luxury and she couldn't resist dawdling to trail her fingers along the smooth, curving caramel-coloured banister.

The Millinery Department was on the third floor, next to Ladies' Fashions. The room itself looked more like an elegant lady's boudoir than any hat shop she had seen before. The large windows were hung with beautiful draped curtains; chairs with silk cushions were carefully positioned before oval-shaped mirrors in gilt frames; and bowls of sweet-smelling flowers stood on side tables. Mrs Milton, Head of the Millinery Department, was standing by the counter, hustling all the girls together like a distracted hen with a brood of wayward chicks.

'Now where is Sophie? Oh, there you are. Do hurry along, dear! Minnie, keep those sticky fingers off my nice clean counter. And, Edith, take those bracelets off at once. You know as well as I do what Mr Cooper would say. Girls, *really!* We have a great deal to do today.'

As Sophie joined the circle, Edith smirked and whispered something to Ellie. Sophie ignored her, turning her attention to Mrs Milton, who was still speaking: 'This is our last day to prepare before the grand opening tomorrow. Mr Sinclair himself will be walking around before the end of the day to inspect the whole store, so everything must be quite perfect. That includes all the storerooms as well as the shop floor.' She beamed at them all and her tone shifted slightly, 'Now, I have some exciting news. Mr Cooper tells me I may appoint one of you as my assistant. Whoever is chosen will receive an extra five shillings a week, but will also have a great deal of extra responsibility. She will be in charge of the department when I am away, and will help to choose our stock. I shall be watching you work in the next few days once the store has opened, and then I shall make my decision, so mind you all do your best.'

A little murmur of interest ran through the group of girls. Who would be chosen? Surely not Violet or Minnie – they were only apprentices, straight out of school. Ellie was the oldest, but she was rather slow and apt to make heavy weather of any complicated tasks. No, it would have to be either Edith or Sophie – and they all knew that Sophie had been singled out and praised by Mr Cooper during the training. The younger ones gazed at her, but Edith scowled. It was clear she wasn't about to sit by and let Her Ladyship beat her to become Mrs Milton's assistant.

Sophie's mind was racing. An extra five shillings a week! That might even be enough to move out of her awful lodgings and find some nicer rooms somewhere. Of course, it would never be anything like Orchard House – that had gone forever. But at least it might begin to feel something like a home.

Mrs Milton continued: 'I will expect you all to work your very hardest today. So to begin – Ellie and Violet, all of those boxes need to be cleared away. Sophie, you may finish that display over in the window. Edith and Minnie, I want to see those display cases polished until they sparkle. I won't have Mr Sinclair finding so much as a speck of dust in my department!'

Edith looked furious to have been given something as lowly as polishing to do when Sophie had all the fun of arranging a display. As she went to fetch dusters, she shot the other girl a poisonous glance, but Sophie ignored her, determined to focus only on her task. A tower of hat-boxes stood before her, each containing a lovely new spring hat to be removed from its delicate tissue paper wrappings, uncovering a riot of silk flowers, huge chiffon bows, frills of lace and nodding ostrich plumes. Some were topped with artificial birds or fruit, others wreathed in layers of frothy net and tulle like something that might be served up in the store's Confectionery Department. She turned each hat to and fro in her hands, deciding how it might be best displayed, enjoying the soft brush of velvet against her skin, a satin ribbon sliding between her fingers, the crisp delicacy of a net veil.

They were strangely evocative things. A pink organza recalled a frock she had once had for dancing class; a green-striped bow reminded her of one of Miss Pennyfeather's Sunday hats; this velvet was like the dress she had worn when she had first come to Sinclair's. Already, it seemed like a very long time ago, although in fact it was barely two months.

At fourteen, they had said she was too old for an orphanage: she was considered no longer a child, and old enough to support herself. Instead, they had sent her to an employment agency, where two ladies had looked her up and down as she stood there, dressed like a child with a muslin pinafore over her frock, her skirts barely touching the tops of her boots.

'She's very small, isn't she, Charlotte?'

'Undersized. Not much work in her.'

'And look at those hands! Soft as butter.'

'A spoilt little thing, I should say.'

Sophie had wanted to protest that she was *not* spoilt, but they had begun to fling questions at her. Could she cook? Could she launder? Could she work a typewriter? She could only shake her head. It had soon become clear that a girl who had passed no examinations and who had no idea how to begin to set about cooking a dinner or scrubbing a floor wasn't exactly overwhelmed with options when it came to finding a way to earn money. French conversation and dancing were all very well, but they would do nothing to help her now.

It was as she was trailing miserably back from the agency, a few flakes of snow just beginning to fall, that she had first found Sinclair's. Work on the building had still been going on, but the enormous hoarding around it was already plastered in advertisements, and in spite of the cold, people were lingering to read them. But what had made Sophie stop and stare was an enormous sign that read, in scarlet letters, *Staff Wanted*. Almost in a moment, she had known that sign was meant for her.

The next day she had put up her hair and let down the skirts of her most grown-up gown. She had perched on the edge of a hard chair, carefully answering the questions put to her by Mr Cooper – a serious-looking man with a close-trimmed beard and a severe black suit. She had felt almost absurd relief when he had offered her a position as a salesgirl in the Millinery Department, starting at ten shillings a week – just enough to afford bed and board in a cheap lodging house for working ladies.

It was what Papa would have wanted, she had reflected as she toiled back to her lodgings through the snow. She knew that he would have expected her to buck up and make the best of things, just as people always did in the military tales he loved to relate. Perhaps she might not be facing wild beasts or a native uprising in the jungle, but she could be brave and not make a fuss about embarking on this peculiar new life.

Now, with the hat display almost complete, Sophie paused for a moment and gazed down at the street below her, thronged with Hansom cabs and motor taxis, cycles whizzing daringly between them, and omnibuses, bright with coloured advertisements for Pear's Soap and Fry's Chocolate Cream. The pavements were crowded with people and as she watched, Sophie felt a flutter of excitement to see how many of them were casting curious glances up at the huge facade of Sinclair's.

'Now, Sophie, there's no time for dreaming today. That

looks very nice but if you've finished I wish you'd run some errands for me,' came Mrs Milton's voice, and Sophie started guiltily back from the window. 'These hats need to go down to the dressing rooms on the first floor. They're for the mannequins to wear in the dress parade.'

Edith, still busy polishing, looked pleased at the sight of Sophie being asked to do something so menial. 'I'm sure Her Ladyship won't care for that,' she whispered loudly to Minnie.

As a matter of fact, Edith was quite wrong, Sophie thought crossly as she went down the stairs, carefully balancing the stack of hat-boxes. The truth was that she was happy to have any chance to look around the store and felt proud that she already knew almost every corner. The mannequins' dressing room was one place that she had not yet seen, and what was more, she was intrigued by the mannequins themselves – lovely young ladies who had been hired especially for the purpose of modelling frocks and furs and hats. Once the store was open, there would be a dress show once a day, where they would parade before the store's most important customers in a specially decorated *salon* in the Ladies' Fashions Department. The mannequins were called the 'Captain's Girls' as rumour had it that Edward Sinclair had insisted on selecting every one himself. Sophie had heard it said that they were as glamorous as stars of the West End's chorus lines.

She soon found the dressing room in the maze of staff corridors on the first floor, and tapped politely at the door. Hearing no response, she went inside. Like every room at Sinclair's, the dressing room was beautifully furnished, with soft chairs, looking-glasses, bright lamps and several rails of beautiful gowns, but it was otherwise empty – with the exception of one dark-haired beauty, who appeared to be half in and half out of an evening dress. There was no doubt that she must be one of the Captain's Girls. Sophie began to retreat at once.

'I beg your pardon, I didn't know anyone was here,' she murmured, but before she could close the door again, the girl looked up and smiled at her.

'I say – don't go!' she exclaimed in a hearty voice that didn't match her appearance in the slightest. 'Come in, do, and maybe you can help me with this ghastly thing. I simply can't make it fasten.'

Sophie put the hat-boxes down on a table, but as she approached the girl she had to bite back a gasp of amazement. It was as if a goddess had appeared before her, dressed in a white silk petticoat. Tall and statuesque, with a mass of rich, chocolate-brown hair piled on top of her head, enormous, long-lashed dark eyes and a creamy silk-and-velvet complexion, she was by far the most beautiful girl Sophie had ever seen. No wonder Mr Sinclair had chosen her to be one of the Captain's Girls, she thought, trying not to stare.

'I can't seem to get the silly old bodice done up,' the girl was saying cheerfully, clutching uselessly at the evening dress. 'Do you think you could help? Oh thanks awfully. This is the frock I'm supposed to be wearing for the first dress show tomorrow, you see. I'm due to go to see Monsieur Pascal, so he can decide on a hairstyle to complement it, and I don't suppose they'd like it much if I went roaming the place in my petticoats . . . Oh I say, you are doing a good job.'

Sophie had managed to untangle the dress and was looking it over. 'I think maybe your corset needs to be tighter,' she suggested.

'You're probably right,' said the girl with a heavy sigh. Now that they were closer together, it was clear that she was younger than Sophie had first thought – perhaps only about sixteen. 'I can't bear a tight corset. So hateful not being able to breathe properly – don't you think? Oh well, you have to suffer for your art I suppose, not that this is exactly what I'd call art, but you know what I mean. At least I'm only going to be doing this for a little while.' She paused for a moment to gaze at her reflection in the mirror while Sophie tugged hard at the corset strings, and then went on, in a more confidential tone: 'I'm really just doing it to earn a bit of money while I try and get more work in the theatre. You see, what I really want is to be an actress. I've just got my first real part – nothing like proper acting, just singing and dancing in the chorus in a silly show at the Fortune Theatre, but it's a start.'

She stepped into the rustling silk skirt, and as Sophie lifted it up and fastened the tapes, she continued. 'I know acting isn't exactly respectable. My parents absolutely loathe the idea. Father's awfully cross with me about it. As for Mother, she's in a terrible pet that one of her friends is going to come in here and see me modelling frocks. *They* think I ought to be at home doing dreary piano practice and going to tennis parties and waiting for some stuffy fellow to decide to marry me. Could you imagine anything more dull?' She pulled a face so expressive that Sophie couldn't help laughing.

'But then I've always known I was meant to tread the boards. It's just the only thing I *could* do,' the girl went on. Then she added hastily, 'I mean, working here is jolly fine too of course. What do you do? Are you a salesgirl?'

Sophie was doing up the dozens of tiny buttons at the back of the bodice. 'Yes, in the Millinery Department.'

'Hats! How jolly! I love a good hat, don't you? I say, this is rather a nice frock, isn't it?'

Sophie gazed at the girl's reflection in the mirror. If she had looked like a goddess before, she looked even more like one now. The gown was pale gold, with a pattern of peacock feathers on the sweeping skirt and a closely fitted bodice elaborately beaded in blue, green and gold. The girl turned first one way and the other, the rustling skirts swinging, and then gave Sophie a wide grin.

'I think this must be meant for you,' said Sophie, removing a hat from one of the boxes she had brought – an exquisite creation in green velvet trimmed with peacock feathers.

'Thanks awfully for your help. I'm Lil by the way – well, Lilian Rose, if you want to be proper.'

'Sophie Taylor.'

'Nice to meet you, Sophie Taylor,' said Lil, breezing out of the room. Sophie followed her, the empty hat-box under one arm.

'I say –' Lil, who didn't seem to be able to stop talking for more than a second at a time, was just beginning again, when they both stopped suddenly in the passageway at the sound of a voice. It was whispering from behind a clothes rail hung with evening dresses that had been left to one side: '*Pssst! Sophie!*'

To Sophie's astonishment, she saw the young porter from the cloakroom hovering behind the rack of gowns. His face was pink and alarmed.

'What is it?'

He motioned for her to come behind the rack and she

did so, Lil following at once, looking intrigued.

As soon as she saw him, Sophie realised why he looked so unhappy. His smart blue uniform jacket was smeared from neck to waist with what looked like mud, but which smelled distinctly worse.

'Hullo,' said Lil cheerfully. 'Are you a friend of Sophie's? I'm Lil. I say – you're in rather a state aren't you? Whatever have you been up to?'

Billy gaped at her for a moment, evidently confused and horrified to have been discovered looking like this by an impossibly beautiful girl in an evening gown. Then he looked desperately at Sophie. 'I've tried to get it off but it just won't budge,' he said urgently. 'The girls will laugh their heads off if they see me like this – and Uncle Sid'll give me a walloping. And Mr Cooper will sack me for sure. Do you know any way that I could clean it?'

Sophie became serious. Mr Cooper had made it abundantly clear that everything – and everyone – would be expected to be quite perfect before Mr Sinclair carried out his inspection later in the day. She had already seen Cooper dismiss staff who did not come up to his exacting standards. She thought quickly. 'It will come off easily enough, don't worry. But it needs laundering properly. We need to let it dry, then brush it down and wash it.'

The sound of voices passing by made her break off and

for a moment they all crouched down behind the rack, hoping not to be seen. Billy tried his hardest not to brush mud against any of the gowns.

'Gosh, this is rather a lark,' murmured Lil.

'*Ssshhh!*' Billy and Sophie hissed together.

Sophie turned back to Billy. 'We need to find you a spare jacket to borrow, just for a day or two. Then I can take this away and wash it and no one will be any the wiser.'

Billy's face brightened. 'There must be some spare ones somewhere,' he said hopefully.

'In the basement, I think,' said Sophie, thinking quickly. 'I'm not sure exactly where though.'

Lil's eyes lit up. 'I do!' she exclaimed. 'I saw some uniforms in one of the little storerooms down there.'

'Whatever were you doing there?' Sophie asked, looking curiously at their new acquaintance. The labyrinth of twisting passages and storerooms in the basement was one place that even she had not much wanted to explore.

'Oh, just taking a look around,' said Lil, airily. She grinned. 'One of those salesmen – Jim something-or-other – was rather insistent about giving me a tour.'

Sophie laughed, but the sound of Sidney Parker's voice rumbling somewhere not very far away from them made her hurry on. 'Take that jacket off and I'll deal with it,' she said quickly to Billy. 'Then you and Lil can go down the back stairs to the basement and find another one.'

'What – in my *vest*?' demanded Billy, pink-faced.

Distinctly, they heard Sidney's voice calling, 'Billy! *Billy!* Where the devil has the boy got to now?'

'Quickly – go!' Sophie hissed.

Mortified, Billy wriggled out of his jacket and flung it to her. 'But what will you do with it?' he whispered.

Sophie opened the empty hat-box, whisked the jacket inside and put on the lid.

'Perfect! Come on!' said Lil cheerfully, grabbing Billy by the arm, and flashing a grin at Sophie as they disappeared.

CHAPTER FOUR

L il led the way down a dark, echoing passageway. From somewhere behind her came the young porter's uncertain voice:

'Are you *sure* this is the right way?'

She glanced over her shoulder at him. His face was pale and anxious in the dark. Rather a poor show to be frightened by a few dark corridors, she thought; but then he did seem rather a timid sort of chap. For herself, she rather liked this basement underworld; there was something deliciously mysterious about it.

'You're not scared, are you?' she teased.

'No!' he flashed back, a little too quickly. 'It just seems like an odd place to keep uniforms.' He hesitated for a moment, then added suspiciously, 'This isn't some sort of awful *joke*, is it?'

Lil felt a little ashamed of herself. The poor fellow looked exactly the sort who would be forever having his leg pulled.

'Of course not,' she said, heartily. 'I say, there are a lot of rooms down here, aren't there? Dozens and dozens, all of them empty. I suppose they'll be needed eventually, but for now, hardly anyone seems to come down here.'

'I'm glad to hear it,' said Billy, muttering something else almost inaudible about not wanting to be seen skulking around a darkened basement with a *girl*, wearing only his vest.

Lil paid no attention. 'Here we are,' she announced triumphantly, pushing the door open on to a small room containing several racks of Sinclair's uniforms. 'Well, off you go then,' she urged. 'Try them on. One of them will do, I'm sure of it,' she said, perching on the edge of a wooden crate.

Billy eyed her uneasily. 'Are you planning to just sit there and *watch?*'

'Would you like me to cover my eyes?' she asked mischievously.

He ignored her, and wriggled into a jacket that looked about the right size.

'A perfect fit,' she said, pleased, bouncing down from her makeshift seat. 'Now, we'd better get back upstairs before anyone notices we've gone. Come on!'

But they had barely stepped out into the passage again before Lil stopped suddenly in her tracks. She could hear something: not the usual quiet creaking sounds of the basement, but something more distinctive – the sound of regular footsteps, coming closer and closer towards them. She grabbed Billy's arm, and dragged him quickly around a corner, and against a wall.

She could see he was annoyed with her now. 'What d'you think you're doing?' he began crossly, but she put a finger to her lips willing him to be silent. He gazed back at her, confused, then he heard the footsteps too, and understanding, he pressed himself back against the wall. A figure was approaching, shadowy in the dim light. Lil held her breath. Any moment now, they might be discovered. Beside her, Billy squeezed his eyes shut, as if waiting for the moment to come, but she peered round the corner, fascinated, as it approached and then passed by, down the corridor and out of sight.

She let out a long gust of breath.

'Whoever do you think that was?' she whispered, intrigued.

'*Shhhh!*' hissed Billy.

They stood still and waited until the sound of footsteps faded away, before creeping back into the main corridor and up the stairs to the shop floor.

From the very beginning, it had been clear that Edward Sinclair planned to take good care of his staff. They had a far better time of it than their peers in London's other great stores. They were not expected to sleep in cramped dormitories above the shop, nor to work long hours for low pay. They had proper training, decent wages, and sensible working hours, including regular tea breaks and a substantial midday meal, which they ate in shifts in the large staff refectory. Of course, the food on offer wasn't anything to compare with the elegant dishes that would very soon be served in the store's luxurious Marble Court Restaurant, but the smell of mutton stew that day certainly made Sophie feel hungry as she walked into the large dining hall.

On the threshold, though, she hesitated. The staff sat where they liked at the long tables, but there was a rule that the men and boys kept to one side of the room, women and girls to the other. Because of this, although Sophie could see Billy sitting by himself across the room – now looking much tidier, his copy of *Boys of Empire* spread open on the table in front of him – she couldn't go over and sit with him. But equally she knew she would not be very welcome at the table where Edith was holding forth to a cluster of her fellow shop girls. With some relief, she spotted an empty place in a corner where she could sit alone. But before she could make her way over to it, she felt a hand on her shoulder.

'Miss Taylor,' said an unfamiliar voice, and she turned around to see a tall, fair young man whom she recognised slightly – Bert Jones, Ladies' Fashions. He wore his hair sleeked back, and smelled strongly of cologne. Sophie nodded politely, but felt confused. She had barely exchanged two words with Bert before, and all she really knew about him was that Edith had been telling everyone that he had already invited her to walk out with him.

'I hear you're coming up in the world,' he said, in a confidential tone. 'Little promotion on the way? Mum's the word though, eh?' He tapped the side of his nose.

Sophie smiled awkwardly and made to move away, but he put a long-fingered hand on her elbow. 'Look, the way I see it, Miss Taylor, you and I have got things in common. You're obviously a smart girl, and me – well, I don't like to brag, but I'm smart too. Going places, see? Catching the right people's attention. So how about you step out with me on Friday night, after closing time?'

Sophie felt her face flush scarlet. She felt horribly conscious of the shop girls gasping and giggling, and Billy goggling at her from across the room. 'But . . . I thought you were walking out with Edith,' she managed.

Bert shrugged. 'Well, maybe I was. But things change, don't they?' he said with a knowing wink.

Sophie lifted her chin. 'Thank you, but I don't think so,' she said firmly.

Bert eyed her thoughtfully. 'They all said you were stuck-up,' he said. Then he grinned. 'Well, that's all right by me. I don't mind a girl being a bit above herself. Come on, Your Ladyship. I'm a catch, me. On Cooper's good side. Doing his special commissions after hours, so I've got a few quid coming my way. I'll treat you proper – like a lady.'

'Can't you tell she's not interested?' came a clear, matter-of-fact voice from somewhere behind her. To her astonishment, Sophie saw that Lil had appeared at her elbow. She was now dressed in a plain skirt and blouse instead of the green and gold peacock gown, but she still looked as extraordinary as ever. 'Leave her alone and go and eat your dinner.'

One or two people laughed, and Bert stared for a moment, taken aback. Then he seemed to register all the watching faces and a scowl broke over his face. He let go of Sophie's elbow and stalked away towards the gentlemen's side of the room, his hands in his pockets, as if nothing had happened.

'What a bore,' said Lil, leading Sophie towards a couple of empty chairs in the corner, leaving a babble of chatter in their wake. 'You've simply got to put fellows like that in their place.'

Sophie pulled a face, feeling embarrassed. She could well imagine that Lil was used to dealing with all kinds of suitors, but Sophie herself was hardly accustomed to strange young men inviting her to walk out with them.

Lil was staring down at her plate in undisguised disappointment. 'Mutton,' she said with a sigh. 'How dreary. Could you only imagine if it had been roast beef? I'm simply ravenous.'

But Sophie wasn't thinking about stew. 'Edith is going to be even more browned off with me than ever now.'

'Who's Edith?' asked Lil, tucking in. 'Oh, she has a fancy for him, does she? Well, that's hard luck, but it wasn't your fault. Actually it was rather funny. I wish you could have seen your face. And Billy's! He looked like he was about to challenge that Bert fellow to a duel, or goodness knows what!'

Sophie laughed. 'You found a jacket then?' she asked, relieved to change the subject.

'Of course! Though we had a bit of a narrow squeak when we nearly bumped into someone wandering around down in the basement. Billy looked jolly worried.'

'I think he's frightened of getting into trouble with Mr Cooper.'

'I can't think why everyone's so terrified about that,' said Lil. 'Cooper is such an old stick. That stern manner of his is just an act.'

'Doesn't anyone intimidate you?' Sophie asked, shaking her head in astonishment.

'Lord, yes!' exclaimed Lil. 'Miss Pinker, the headmistress

of my old school. Frightful creature. And I have to say, I was rather terrified when I did my audition for the show. I had to get up and sing in front of the director, Gilbert Lloyd. He's simply the tops when it comes to musical comedy – and dreadfully handsome too. I was absolutely quaking in my boots! Anyway, I can't have been that awful because I got the part. Of course I'm only in the chorus. I'm about the least important person there is in the whole place, to tell the truth. But it might be my chance – a real chance to be an actress!'

Behind them, the girls at Edith's table had their heads close together whispering and were casting curious glances over at Lil. Sophie felt a sudden wave of relief sweep over her. When she had arrived at the store that morning she had felt entirely alone here, but at last she seemed to have found a friend. She smiled across the table at Lil, feeling almost light-hearted for the first time in many weeks.

'It sounds marvellous,' she said. 'Tell me all about it.'

CHAPTER FIVE

As the final day of preparations went on, the pace began to accelerate. Men in white gloves were busy in the Exhibition Hall, unpacking crates with mechanical precision. In the Entrance Hall, Mr Cooper and Sidney Parker were engaged in an intense discussion about the best deployment of porters, lift-operators and doormen. In the Ladies' Lounge, bunches of perfect roses were being arranged in crystal vases, and in the Marble Court Restaurant, the waiters smoothed out snowy white linen tablecloths and laid out silverware, the restaurant manager following behind them with a tape measure to ensure that each setting was perfect.

Up in the Millinery Department, the main activities were dusting, sweeping and polishing. Unused to such physical work, Sophie soon found herself weary and aching, but she went on working grimly, determined not to let Edith see that she was tired. All the same, as the afternoon drew on, she was pleased to see Lil appear, giving her a welcome excuse to get up from her polishing.

'So this is where you work?' said Lil, looking around her with interest. 'Gosh, it's all rather splendid, isn't it? They sent me up to collect some more hats for the dress show rehearsal.'

Sophie nodded. 'They're through in the storeroom,' she said, leading the way. 'I'll show you.'

Once the storeroom door had closed behind them, they grinned at each other conspiratorially.

'I was simply bursting for a change of scenery,' said Lil. 'They wanted to send for a porter – Captain's Girls aren't supposed to be running about the store with boxes, and all that, but I insisted on coming myself. Honestly, I can't tell you how fearfully boring it is, just practising walking up and down in different frocks.'

'It sounds an awful lot better than polishing,' said Sophie with a laugh, as she handed Lil the hat-boxes she needed.

'Well, yes, I suppose you're probably right there,' said Lil, grinning ruefully. 'I really oughtn't grumble. And at least tomorrow morning I'll be off to the theatre for rehearsals. We don't have to come in until after luncheon now, you see, because the dress shows will only be in the afternoons, so it's all worked out splendidly.' She paused, and then heaved a sigh. 'Well, I suppose I should go. They'll be waiting for me.'

'And I ought to get on with that polishing,' Sophie agreed, stretching and stifling a yawn. 'Mrs Milton really has our noses to the grindstone.'

They both went towards the door – but when Sophie tried the handle, it wouldn't budge.

'Is it stuck? Here, let me try.'

But it wasn't stuck. No matter how much either of them jiggled at the door handle, it would not open.

'I think it's locked,' said Lil in astonishment.

'This is Edith's doing,' said Sophie, with a slow groan of realisation. 'She must have seen us come in here and then locked the door.'

'But why would she do that?'

'To get us both into trouble, of course,' said Sophie. 'To stop me from finishing my work, and make Mrs Milton angry, and to pay us back for that business in the refectory earlier.'

'Oh I say!' cried Lil indignantly.

Sophie felt her own temper flare. If she didn't finish the tasks she had been set, she could say goodbye to any chance of becoming Mrs Milton's assistant. And now Lil would be in trouble too, and none of this was in the least bit her fault!

But there was no sense in losing her head, she reminded herself. 'Maybe one of the others will let us out. Let's see if we can get their attention before anyone notices we're missing.'

They rattled the door, and called out, but no one came.

'They probably can't hear us if they're on the other side of the shop floor,' said Sophie. 'And I daresay Edith's out there laughing at us right now.'

'What a beast,' said Lil crossly. 'We *are* in a scrape.' Then, in a sudden burst of cheerfulness: 'I suppose at least you get a break from all that polishing, anyway.'

'Oh *bother* her,' said Sophie, folding her arms. 'Well, I suppose if we're stuck in here, we may as well do something useful. Let's bring that ladder over and we can put all those boxes away. We can get the storeroom tidied, at any rate.'

Lil readily agreed, feeling that going up and down ladders and putting away boxes would certainly be no worse than clambering in and out of evening dresses. While they worked, they talked. Lil told Sophie about all the plays she had seen recently, including the plot of a most exciting thriller in which a dashing detective ('So handsome! Simply divine!') had managed to escape from a locked room and foil a dastardly gang of spies, and that of a heart-rending romance in which the young heroine experienced all sorts of trials before finally being reunited with her true love. They ended up sitting on the floor, talking about books that they had read, and laughing about their old governesses. Lil told Sophie all about her parents and how irritating it was that her older brother could do exactly what he wanted ('just because he's a *boy!'*); and how she didn't think she would much like being a mannequin ('Imagine all those beastly old ladies looking you up and down'), but she wanted to be independent and couldn't get by on her meagre earnings as a chorus girl alone.

'But what about you? How did you come to be working here?' Lil asked Sophie at last.

Sophie was quiet for a moment, rubbing at a smudge of dust on her cheek. 'My papa died just before Christmas,' she explained slowly. 'He was a major in the army and he was killed out in South Africa in an accident. There was only Papa and me, you see? My mama died when I was very small. I can hardly even remember her – at least, only little bits. And Papa used to tell me lots of stories about her, of course.'

She broke off for a moment and sighed, thinking that there was so much about her mother that she would probably now never know. 'Anyway, there was a problem with Papa's will. He hadn't left any provision for me – no instructions about a guardian, no money. It was strange because, you see, he was always a very methodical sort of person. But it left me with almost nothing. The house was sold, they sent my governess away, and I had to find work at once – so I came to Sinclair's.'

Sophie didn't dare say more. Somehow, of everything, it was that last day at Orchard House, with the carpets up and dear old Miss Pennyfeather weeping uncontrollably as she got into the cab, that she could not risk thinking about; it was almost the worst memory of all. She gave a small shrug and fell silent.

Sophie might not have said much, but Lil had been able to see the emotions flickering across her new friend's face as she talked: confusion, frustration, sadness. 'Gosh,' Lil murmured quietly, feeling suddenly very conscious of just how flimsy her own troubles sounded by comparison. She felt an unexpected surge of fondness for the family home in Twickenham, with its green lawns mowed to bowling-green smoothness, and Mother entertaining callers to tea in the drawing room. She opened her mouth to speak, wanting to say or do something to comfort Sophie, but all at once she felt unsure of her words.

In the silence that had fallen, they heard a rattling sound, and they both looked up. Then the door burst open and Violet almost fell through into the storeroom. 'The – the door was locked,' she said, confused.

Sophie jumped to her feet at once. 'Quickly – before Mrs Milton sees you!' she urged. Understanding at once, Lil grabbed the hat-boxes she had come for and darted swiftly past Violet, through the door and away, just as Edith's high-pitched voice could be heard approaching.

'I just don't know where Sophie is I'm afraid, Mrs Milton.

She didn't finish that polishing and I haven't seen her for ages. I suppose she's wandered off somewhere. Some people think they're too good to do a proper day's work like the rest of us.'

'Did you want me, Mrs Milton?' called Sophie swiftly.

Mrs Milton came into the doorway and looked around approvingly. 'Oh there you are, Sophie. I knew you couldn't be far away. Well, well, and look at this! You've got the whole delivery tidied away and the storeroom looking perfect. You have worked hard!'

Sophie smiled and said nothing, but heaved an inward sigh of relief as she whisked past Edith's angry face and out of the room.

A few hours later, Mr Sinclair's walk around the store had been completed to everyone's satisfaction, and the clock downstairs in the Entrance Hall was chiming six slow chimes. Sophie's feet ached, her shoulders ached, and she was prickly all over with tiredness. And tomorrow she would have to come back here again to work another long day – and the next day, and the next day, and the day after that . . .

'Well, girls, you've done a fine job,' said Mrs Milton, looking flushed with pleasure. Mr Sinclair had been satisfied with the department and Mr Cooper had given her a few very rare words of praise. 'Mr Cooper has given me a shilling extra for each of you because of all your hard work. Now off you go, and mind you are looking your very smartest and not a moment late in the morning.'

The girls were almost too tired to say goodnight to each other in the cloakroom as they pulled on their coats and hats, and hurried out towards home. Sophie dawdled for a moment, knowing that Edith and Minnie would also be going back to the lodging house, and not feeling at all eager to walk with them.

She thought, with a feeling of great satisfaction, of the extra shilling in her pocket. Not so long ago, a shilling had meant almost nothing to her, but now it spoke to her of all kinds of possibilities: a ribbon, perhaps, to trim her hat; or maybe she could save it and put it towards a new pair of gloves because her old ones were getting so very worn. At any rate, she could treat herself to some buns for tea, she thought.

As she went out on to the street, she caught sight of a rather dirty young man – scarcely more than a boy, really – sitting on a step by the staff entrance. His head was down, and she noticed that his arm was in a rough sort of sling. Vagrants weren't supposed to hang around the store, but it was the end of the day, and he looked ill and exhausted – much more exhausted than she felt herself, she thought, with a stab of sympathy for him.

She considered the shilling in her pocket. In the past, she would have given a shilling to a poor young man like that without even thinking about it. But now, she found herself wrestling with her conscience. Of course she ought to give it to him, she told herself sternly. But a whole shilling! She had worked so hard all day – she had *earned* that money. She made up her mind to walk on, but even as she began to move forward, she turned back again. Papa would never have forgiven her.

Rather reluctantly, she went up to the young man and handed him the shilling. Looking surprised, he took it.

'Thank you, miss,' he said, doffing his cap.

Sophie nodded awkwardly, and went on her way.

It would have been nice to have a new ribbon for her hat, she reflected as she walked down Piccadilly, but she supposed she could do without one for now. Although she still regretted the loss of the buns, she felt she was, after all, walking a little more lightly as she went towards her lodgings.

It had turned into an unexpectedly pleasant evening. The air was still damp, but the last strains of light were soft and warm, the kind of pinkish-grey colour that in the fashion papers they called *ashes of roses*. The street was bustling with people like her, spilling out of shops and offices and making their way home.

She joined the tide, but before she had gone very far, she

stopped abruptly, realising that she had forgotten to bring home Billy's jacket. She turned back at once: there was nothing for it but to return to the shop. She couldn't risk leaving it there for Mr Cooper or Mrs Milton – or worse, Edith – to discover tomorrow morning. Wishing her feet didn't hurt quite so much, she made herself hurry back down the street in the direction of Sinclair's. If she were quick, she would easily get back before the long process of locking up for the night was completed.

The poor young man had vanished from the step now – probably off somewhere buying buns with her shilling, she thought grudgingly. The store was shrouded in darkness, with only a few lights gleaming from the very top of the building, where Mr Sinclair had his own luxurious private apartments. The staff entrance was locked, but as she had hoped, the door that led into the shop from the stable-yard was still open. Hoping to slip in and out without being noticed by anyone, Sophie made her way back inside.

It was strange being in the store after hours. The ground floor was completely silent and still and yet there seemed to be a faint humming sound in the air. The shapes of the counters and chairs looked unearthly in the dark, and little bits of light from the street outside caught and shimmered in the looking-glasses, casting piercing silvery gleams through the shadows. For a moment or two she hesitated, but then she roused herself to hurry forward towards the back staircase the staff used. She wished she had used one of the main staircases instead when she saw how dark it was, but she hastened onwards anyway, trying not to jump at every creak or rustle. It was a relief when she reached the Millinery Department. Rummaging through the hat-boxes, she at last found the one containing the jacket, took it out and bundled it up quickly in a bit of brown paper. On her way back she took the main stairs, running down two steps at a time.

The staircase brought her down into the Entrance Hall, and here she stopped short. Last time she had been here, the doors to the great Exhibition Hall had been closed; now they stood wide open. She could see a great, shadowy room beyond, and down each side of the room was a row of glass cases, gleaming in the shadows. In spite of herself, she tiptoed a little way through the doors to peer inside.

Approaching the first case, she caught her breath in astonishment. An array of exquisitely beautiful objects was laid out on a white velvet cushion, neatly labelled. Forgetting all about wanting to hurry home, she gazed at a sparkling diamond tiara, then a rich purple gemstone the size of a hen's egg, and then at a tiny, ornate golden bird, beautifully enamelled and glittering all over with gold and precious stones. *The Clockwork Sparrow*, she read. It was so small, so richly jewelled, so perfect. She bent to look at it more closely, and for a moment, in the dim light, it seemed almost as if it were looking back at her. Its jewel eye glinted, as if it were winking.

A hand fell heavily on her shoulder, as sudden as a thunderclap. She started up and gave a little yelp of terror, but fell silent when she saw Mr Cooper's face looming out of the dark.

'Miss Taylor – what are you doing here?' he demanded, frowning sharply.

'I beg your pardon, sir, but I left something behind and I wanted to run up and get it before everything was shut up for the night,' she said quickly, pink flooding her cheeks. She clutched her parcel close to her, hoping that he wouldn't ask what was inside it. 'I thought it would be best not to trouble anyone.'

'Get on home,' said Cooper sternly. 'Quick, quick, be off with you.'

'Yes, sir,' said Sophie. She fled in relief through the darkened store, and then out into the stable-yard.

'Well, well, and what have we here? Why, it's the high and mighty Lady Sophie, running around after hours. And all alone without your *friend* this time, I see.'

It was Bert Jones, she saw in surprise, standing half-concealed in the shadows. He seemed different out here in the dark: there was a look in his pale eyes that she didn't like. What was he doing here, so long after all the others had gone?

'Excuse me, please, I'm going home,' she said briskly, but Bert just laughed and stepped in front of her, blocking her way. A sudden prickle of fear ran over her.

'Always in such a hurry to get away, aren't you? Well there's no need. Whatever it is you're up to, you don't have to worry about me. I won't split on you. I'm good at keeping secrets, me.'

He laughed again, as if the thought pleased him, and Sophie's heart began to beat more rapidly. What would Lil do, if she were here? 'Let me pass at once,' she said, trying to keep her voice steady. If only Mr Cooper would come out of the door!

But he didn't come and Bert still stood there, grinning at her. Then he reached towards her and instinct took over. She darted past him as fast as she could and ran, not stopping to look back. In a moment, she was out into the street and away, still clutching the bundled jacket.

Left behind, Bert smirked to himself as the distant sound of Sophie's feet skittering on the cobbles faded to nothing in the settling dark.

Sophie kept running, her feet clattering, her heart bumping. She was conscious of attracting curious looks from passers-by: after all, young ladies didn't generally go racing down the city streets. But at that moment, Sophie didn't care in the least about what young ladies generally did.

It had begun to rain, and everything seemed darker now. The last few shops were shutting, and the bursts of music and voices that spilled out of the public houses seemed louder and more menacing. As she turned the corner she ran blindly into a young man carrying a big portfolio, which at once crashed to the ground, spilling out papers. 'Hey! Look where you're going, can't you?' he demanded, but too agitated even to pause and apologise, Sophie kept her head down and ran for home, leaving him calling angrily after her.

By the time she reached her lodgings, pink-cheeked and out of breath, she had missed supper. The lodging house was not an attractive place, and as usual the hall smelled like overcooked cabbage. As she started up the creaking stairs towards her room, a trio of girls spilled out on to the landing. Edith was at the centre of the little group and gave her a sneering look, taking in her red face and damp hair, which was now most definitely coming down. There was a bubble of laughter and then they breezed past and the door slammed abruptly behind them.

Sophie trudged upwards to her room. It was small and shabby. There was a damp patch on the ceiling, and the sound of a baby crying could be heard through the thin walls, but at least it was her own. There wasn't much in it: only a narrow, iron-framed bed, a washstand squeezed into a corner, and a chair wedged in the space between the bed and the tiny fireplace. But her old china doll sat on the chair smiling a glassy-eyed welcome, and on the mantelpiece were a few treasures she had been able to save from Orchard House: a jug with cowslips on it, one or two books with pretty morocco bindings, and a walnut box that held keepsakes – a hatpin shaped like a rose that she wore often, a string of green beads that had once belonged to her mama, and her papa's medals. Most precious of all was the photograph of Papa, which she kept at the very centre of the mantelpiece. It was a rather stiff, formal portrait in which he stood very upright and gallant in his military uniform, and yet somehow he seemed to be looking at her with the barest hint of a smile. It gave her a strange sort of comfort to fancy that he might almost be watching.

She dropped the parcel containing Billy's jacket on the floor, lit the lamp and then sank down on to the bed to ease her boots from her aching feet. In the warm glow of the lamplight, everything troubling – the dark streets, the empty store, the girls' laughter, and even the looming figure of Bert – seemed to fade away. There would be no buns for supper, but bread and butter would do just as well, she thought decidedly, pulling the shabby curtains firmly closed against the darkness outside.

He sat still in the shadows of the stable-yard, watching. It was a risk staying here after that lad had spotted him earlier, but he felt it was a risk worth taking. He'd stay tonight and be on his way again tomorrow. It was a shame, for this was a good place, safe and quiet. He felt sure that no one would ever think of looking for him here. Besides, he was fond of horses, always had been, and they were fond of him.

There was a light burning high up in one of the top windows of the big shop building – a little point of yellow light in the grey dusk. It made his thoughts flash suddenly back to that awful night, to looking in through the misted window as the watchmaker held up a pocket watch, like a gleaming gold star in the dark. He remembered how still the old man had been, motionless, but for the delicate movements of his long fingers as he bent over the bench, all scattered with the parts of clocks and watches. Something about the way he sat there had made him think of his old grandad. Suppose the watchmaker had been someone's old grandad too? He had known then that he couldn't do what they wanted. He couldn't do it, and so he'd have to run.

He pushed the memory away and wiped the rain off his face. He had to forget all that. He had to stay sharp, concentrate on the here and now. He'd been watching since the store closed. Soon, he'd be able to find a quiet corner to kip for the night, well away from the nightwatchman's beat. Not that he'd been getting much sleep since he left the Boys behind. The wound from Jem's knife ached, and the pain left him wakeful. Besides, what little sleep he managed to snatch was tormented by dreams. He dreamed of his own treacherous hands, shaking as they gripped the blade; the small, defenceless figure of the watchmaker behind the window; Jem smiling his jagged smile; and always the unknown figure of the Baron, lurking somewhere beyond, a faceless monster from a child's nightmare. 'Know why they call him the Baron?' he remembered Jem saying to him once. 'Cos he's the tops when it comes to villainy. There's no one who can touch him for that.' He'd heard some people say that the Baron was no more than another tall tale surfacing from the slums of the city, but he knew they were wrong. The Baron's Boys and the things they did were real enough, that was for sure.

There was hardly anyone left in the store now. The big fellow with the black moustache had long gone, heaving himself on to his bicycle and pedalling strenuously off into the evening. One or two others had followed, but still the thin young fellow remained, standing just beside the door smoking a cigarette. He wished that young fellow would sling his hook. There was something about him that he didn't trust – the curl of his lip, the glint in his eye, or perhaps just the way he'd tried to bully that girl, the one who had given him the shilling. It had been a relief to see her dart past him and hurry away.

A shilling, that was something. For the dozenth time, he felt for the reassuring circle of it in his pocket. Once or twice before he'd got a penny or two, but he didn't set himself up to go a-begging. The old fellows and the kids, they might do all right, but he didn't reckon that anyone would want to give a farthing to someone like him. But that girl, she'd just given him that coin, right out of nowhere. A whole shilling, just like that.

His ears pricked at a new sound. The door was opening and someone else was coming out. Another man, his collar turned up, a cap pulled well down over his eyes. The young fellow looked surprised, but then an expression of interest broke over his face and he opened his mouth as if to speak. Somewhere, close by, there was the splintering tinkle of glass shattering, and the yowl of a cat.

Then all at once, as if the sound had sparked it off, everything happened very fast. There was a glint of metal in the dim light; a sudden, heart-stopping explosion of sound. He started and shrank back into his corner, but the thin young fellow had fallen. He was on the ground. His body was crooked, slumped face-down. The other man turned smoothly, soundlessly away, and a moment later he had melted into the dark.

The yard was empty but for the black shape of the young fellow's body. He stole forward and hesitated, seeing the dark pool blooming on the ground. The young fellow had been shot.

There was a crumpled piece of paper lying beside the body. He picked it up instinctively and shoved it into his pocket with the shilling. Already he could hear the sound of a whistle: the police, the nightwatchman? He couldn't stay to find out which it was. He had to get away.

He slipped into the shadows by the wall, where he blended with the darkness and became invisible. It was something he knew only too well how to do. Silent and swift as a fox in the night, he padded away down the alley. Once again, he had to disappear.

This elegant crinoline straw, with velvet on the crown and bunches of violets under the brim, is a smart choice for spring. Bringing elegance and grace to even the most modest costume, it will serve excellently for any town occasion – from a tea party to a tour of the shops . . .

CHAPTER SIX

A new day was breaking over London. It was Tuesday morning, and chimneys were puffing out smoke again; boats were surging up and down the river and the church bells were sounding out the start of another day.

Sophie walked along the Embankment, the air rushing cold and clear against her face. She clutched her hat as the wind whirled against her skirts and set her ribbons streaming out behind her. Above her, birds dipped and soared, and below, the river sparkled, transformed by the clear morning light to glitter as brilliantly as any of the jewels she had seen in the Exhibition Hall last night.

She had awoken early, surprised to find a prickle of excitement in the pit of her stomach before she remembered that today was the day that Sinclair's would open its doors for the first time. She had decided to walk to the store along the river, and through the park, where already a couple of nursemaids were taking out babies for the morning air in enormous black perambulators, and a footman accompanied an absurd little lapdog on its pre-breakfast trot.

'Good morning, miss,' the footman said, doffing his hat politely.

'Good morning,' Sophie replied, and walked on.

The park smelled sweet with rain, the fountains were playing and the flowerbeds were full of wind-blown crocuses and daffodils. She was wearing her spring hat and her favourite blouse with the mother-of-pearl buttons, and she was almost looking forward to the day ahead of her – or at least, to seeing Lil and Billy. The thought gave her a sudden tingle of cheerfulness. Not so long ago, she had thought she would never be able to feel cheerful again.

Lost in her thoughts, she didn't notice the newsboys or hear the headlines they were calling, but simply drifted onwards, carried by the morning's current towards Sinclair's.

'Break-in at Sinclair's! Robbery at London's new department store, due to open this morning! Priceless jewels stolen! Read all about it! Read all about it!'

By half past eight, a large crowd had gathered on the steps outside. Whether they were waiting for the store to open or whether they were curious about the robbery was unclear, but there were certainly plenty of newspapermen amongst them. Children darted through the crowd, trying to peep into the windows; men smoked pipes to pass the time; soberly dressed ladies stood still, their gloved hands clasped. Many of those that waited were reading the morning newspaper. Indeed, the boy who sold papers on the corner had had such a profitable morning's trade that, as he yelled out the headlines, he inwardly blessed Mr Edward Sinclair – yes, and the burglars too, whoever they might be – and thought with satisfaction of the meat pie he would be able to take home for dinner.

As time passed, conversations began to strike up amongst the waiting crowd. Some had heard that Mr Sinclair was in a raging fury and had cancelled the grand opening entirely. Others said that the police had forbidden him to open the store as the whole place was under investigation. Still others said, with confidence, that the store was going to open exactly as planned – it would take more than the likes of a few petty criminals to stop Mr Sinclair in his tracks. They had heard the great man himself would be appearing on the steps at nine o'clock to make a formal address. The crowd settled in for the wait. Ladies of fashion found themselves chattering enthusiastically to one another about the latest Paris styles; an elderly gentleman handed round a bag of mint humbugs; and a young man turned shyly to talk to a girl with roses in her hat about the novel she was reading to pass the time.

As the hour of nine approached, the crowd became larger and ever more restless, drawing closer to the great doors. Whispers ran through the throng: once or twice, someone thought they saw one of the silk curtains twitch, or felt sure they glimpsed a figure moving somewhere inside, but then all was still and silent once more. The church bells chimed nine, and the crowd rumbled with anticipation – but all remained quiet. There was no sign of Mr Sinclair, and it began to seem certain that the shop would not open at all that day. But just as they had all but given up hope, as if on the signal of some invisible conductor's baton, the curtains in all of the store windows rose with a single movement, revealing the most marvellous window displays any of them had ever seen.

A gasp went through them, like a jolt of electricity. Children ran forwards, gaping at the great mounds of confectionery, the brightly coloured wonderland of toy soldiers and Noah's ark animals and dolls. The ladies pressed closer, sighing in delight at the exquisite frocks, the ravishing hats, the impossibly elegant shoes. But there was no time to stare any longer, for now the great doors themselves were swinging open, each one held back by a handsome doorman wearing a blue and gold uniform.

There was one moment of breathless anticipation, and then the crowd surged forward. Young newspapermen, keen to be the first with the scoop, elbowed their way to the front. Eager shoppers forced their way through the crowd and the young lady with the book was almost pushed over in the crush. Feeling rather daring, the man who had spoken to her moved closer and took her arm. Together they went forward, and in a moment, found themselves standing inside Sinclair's department store.

As they swept past the doormen into an immense marble entrance hall, the first thing they noticed was the delicious smell, like bonbons on Christmas morning. The next was a magnificent fountain in which white-marble mermaids basked in a sea-green pool. The silvery tinkling of the water mingled with the tick of an enormous golden clock that stood against the wall. Some of the crowd paused to admire the clock and the fountain, whilst others made at once for the sweeping marble staircase. Still others came to a halt before a row of doors, each painted dark blue with a pattern of silver stars, and a lamp in the shape of a crescent moon suspended above it. Each door was manned by a young lift operator in the same blue and gold uniform who bowed and asked: 'Which floor, sir?' or 'Which floor, madam?' But most of the crowd pushed forward through the Entrance Hall and flooded into the maze of rooms and passages that opened up beyond.

Through one archway was a rose-coloured room, in

which elegant shop girls offered scent in pretty bottles. A display of coloured parasols dripped down from the ceiling, like a waterfall of exotic hothouse flowers. Whole walls were covered from the floor to ceiling with sparkling mirrors, stretching the room on forever into the distance until at last it seemed to bend around a corner and disappear. In another direction lay the Confectionery Department, papered in violet silk and powdery with the scent of sugar and cocoa. Girls in frilled white aprons stood behind glass counters laden with pyramids of Turkish Delight sprinkled with a snowstorm of icing sugar, and chocolates scattered with crystallised flower petals. Another archway led into the sunshine of the Flower Department, decorated in the pale greens of early spring and filled with a rainbow of blooms. Real blossoming trees reached up leafy boughs towards a glass roof, through which it was possible to glimpse snatches of blue sky.

There were no floorwalkers to hurry them. In fact, customers were encouraged to linger: soft armchairs were placed in corners, so they could take a moment to rest whenever they wished. There was so much to discover. A pianist in a white waistcoat played a grand piano on the fourth-floor landing, the melody drifting down the stairs as the eager crowds ventured upwards towards Ladies' Fashions and Gentlemen's Outfitting. The China Department, on the sixth floor, was papered entirely in blue and white: stepping inside felt like entering the landscape of a willow-pattern plate. The concierge – whom, rumour had it, could get you anything from tickets to the latest West End show to a steamship passage to New York – sat behind a desk swathed in fringed velvet curtains like a master magician, a red rose in his buttonhole. Everywhere uniformed porters and doormen bowed and smiled, and swung doors open.

There was only one door that remained firmly shut: the door to the Exhibition Hall. Here, a large sign read: *Closed to the Public.*

But the burglary was the last thing on any of the customers' minds now – for they were, of course, customers already, having been quite unable to resist the allure of a perfect cone of sugared almonds, a bunch of yellow roses, a pair of butter-soft kid gloves, a delicious new scent that smelled like bluebells. Now, they were beginning to grow weary, but almost as if by magic, they stumbled upon places to revive themselves. In the fifth floor Marble Court Restaurant, courteous waiters ushered customers to tables gleaming with silverware. Following a spiral staircase, gentlemen found themselves standing in a wood-panelled smoking room furnished with leather armchairs, and already thick with a fug of cigar-smoke. Tea and cakes were being served on dainty white and gold plates in the Ladies' Lounge, and the journalists found their way to the private Press Club Room, fully equipped with typewriters and telephones and intended specifically for their own use.

Glancing through the door of this Press Club Room, Miss Atwood, Mr Sinclair's private secretary, was rather astonished. More than anyone, she felt she had understood the scope and ambition of Mr Sinclair's plans for the store, but all the same, she had not expected the sense of palpable excitement that buzzed around her. Every journalist in London seemed to be here. To one side, a young fellow was enthusiastically barking something down a telephone receiver; to the other, two more were clattering on typewriters; and in one corner, she saw the editor of the *Express* smoking a cigar at the centre of a noisy group. If anyone had thought that the burglary would damage the sensation of the store's opening, they couldn't have been more wrong.

'It's very busy, sir,' she reported, slipping away to Sinclair's secluded penthouse apartments situated high on the eighth floor, far from the crowds. 'Busier than we could ever have expected,' she added, hovering at his elbow and nervously twitching the silk necktie she always wore.

Mr Sinclair was seated at his enormous mahogany desk. He nodded briefly. 'Good,' was all he said, his eyes fixed on the morning's letters.

Miss Atwood felt she knew her employer better than most

people, but even she was baffled by the calm expression on Mr Sinclair's face. Surely today of all days he might have been expected to show some feeling – anger at the theft of his jewels, perhaps, concern about young Mr Jones's condition, anxiety about the store's opening, even excitement at the sensational success of the first morning. But not a ripple of emotion betrayed him. Instead, his routine had proceeded exactly as it did every other day. The assistant from the store's barber shop had given him his scalp rub and hot-towel wrap; his valet had delivered his freshly laundered cream-silk shirts; he had carefully selected an orchid *boutonnière* from the selection offered by the store florist; and he had sipped his customary weak China tea quite coolly whilst discussing the lunch menu with the restaurant manager. Now, he was sitting at his desk, looking through the day's correspondence, his black pug, Lucky, squirming on his knee. He hadn't even been down to see the crowds surging into the store.

'Everything seems to be running extremely well, sir,' she added uncertainly, smoothing out yet more invisible creases in her necktie.

'Yes, Cooper has everything in hand.'

Miss Atwood did her best not to look nettled by this remark. There was a certain rivalry between herself and Mr Cooper. As store manager, technically Cooper was her superior, but as private secretary, Miss Atwood had more opportunities to ingratiate herself with Mr Sinclair. She had been sure that last night's incident would constitute a black mark for Mr Cooper, but it seemed this was not so. She swiftly changed the subject away from her rival. 'The gentleman from Scotland Yard has arrived, sir. We're making sure he has everything he needs.'

Mr Sinclair still did not look up, but he nodded. 'Send McDermott up to me as soon as he gets here,' he said. 'And I want all the papers today. See to it that I don't miss an edition.'

'Very good, sir,' said Miss Atwood.

'Oh, and, Miss Atwood,' he said. 'Take Lucky out for her morning air, would you? My little girl does need her outings.'

With a resigned expression that did not entirely conceal her distaste, Miss Atwood accepted the pug's lead and chivvied her towards the door.

'And come straight back up when you're done. I want to dictate an advertisement for tomorrow's *Post*.'

Looking harried, the secretary hurried from the room, leaving Sinclair to lean back in his chair, light a cigar, and then turn back to his letters.

CHAPTER SEVEN

'I say! What a terrific lot of people!' exclaimed Lil as she came galloping towards the staff entrance, rather late to prepare for the first dress parade, she knew, but not in the least concerned about it. 'Isn't it marvellous?'

A few of the staff were standing in a solemn, whispering huddle on the steps.

'You haven't heard, then?'

'You'll never believe it!'

The shock of the robbery had broken up all the usual store hierarchies, so it was a strange group that stood mixed up together on the steps: a delivery driver, a salesgirl, one or two porters, a kitchen maid.

'Whatever is the world coming to?'

'It's a disgrace, that's what it is.'

'What is?' demanded Lil, completely forgetting that she was supposed to be getting ready for the dress show. 'Whatever has happened? *Do* tell me.'

Billy detached himself from the circle and came over to her. 'Didn't you hear? There was a big robbery. Here, at the shop. Last night. Thieves broke in and most of the stuff in the exhibition has been taken.'

'Golly!' exclaimed Lil, her eyes round with surprise.

Billy gave her a very solemn look. 'And the robbers – they *shot* Bert. You know, Bert Jones from Ladies' Fashions? He's been taken to the hospital. They aren't sure if he'll pull through.'

Lil's mouth dropped open in amazement.

'It's true. Right over there, in the yard, it happened. Edith's already been taken home in hysterics.'

'But whatever was Bert doing here at night? And what about the nightwatchman?'

'The nightwatchman's all right, just a bump to the head. They knocked him out. Poor fellow didn't even get a look at them.'

'Have they caught who did it?'

Billy shook his head. 'There's a policeman here now. Scotland Yard,' he added, in awestruck tones. 'He's upstairs with Cooper.'

'*Golly*,' said Lil again, shaking her head in astonishment. 'But the store's opened just as planned? I say! Where's everyone else? Where's Sophie?'

Billy looked even more troubled. 'That's the worst

of it,' he said, lowering his voice. 'She's upstairs with the policeman, too.'

Mr Cooper's office seemed full of sombre, black-clad men. He ushered Sophie in brusquely and pointed her to a low chair.

'This is Sergeant Gregson of the Metropolitan Police. He works out of Scotland Yard,' he said, his clipped tones sounding even more curt than usual as he gestured to a fatherly looking older man with small round spectacles and a drooping moustache. 'And this is Mr McDermott, an inquiry agent working for Mr Sinclair, who is helping Sergeant Gregson with his enquiries.' An inquiry agent meant a private detective, Sophie knew, although the grizzled person standing in the corner didn't look in the least like one of the gallant heroes from Billy's stories.

She was still struggling to make sense of what she had been told. The store had been burgled . . . the jewels stolen . . . Bert *shot* by the burglars.

'Gentlemen, this is Miss Taylor from our Millinery Department . . .' Mr Cooper's voice faded away into nothing, and he straightened the collar of his neat black suit with an uncharacteristically nervous gesture. In spite of the feeling of dread that was beginning to creep over her, Sophie felt a sudden stab of sympathy for the store manager. After all, he was the one ultimately responsible for security, always so determined to keep everything running in the most perfect order. And this had happened on the very evening before the store was due to open for the first time.

All at once, she became conscious of Sergeant Gregson's eyes fixed on her, now cold and serious over the rims of his spectacles.

'Miss Taylor, I want you to answer some questions about what happened yesterday,' he began. 'Please listen carefully and answer as fully as you can.'

Sophie realised with some irritation that he was talking especially slowly, as if he thought she would have difficulty following him. Her cheeks flushed with annoyance as he continued.

'Omit no details, but stick to the facts only, please. We don't want any shop girl gossip here. A man is gravely injured: I am sure you realise this is a very serious matter. Do you understand?'

'Yes, sir,' she replied shortly.

'You have been working here, in the Millinery Department, for how long?'

'Just two weeks, sir. The same as the other salesgirls.'

'You were working in your department until around six o'clock last night, is that correct?'

'Yes, sir. The same time as all the other girls.'

'And you left the building as usual?'

'Yes, sir.'

'Did anyone actually *see* you leave?'

Was he suggesting she wasn't telling the truth? 'Yes, I think so. The other girls from my department left just before me. There were other people still there though – Uncle S– I mean, Sidney Parker. And I think Dot – Dot Baxter from Ladies' Fashions. And –' she broke off, uncertainly.

'*And?*'

She wasn't sure if she should mention it, but perhaps it might be important. 'As I came on to the street, there was a young man there – a vagrant,' she said hesitantly. 'He looked unwell. I stopped to give him some money.'

Sergeant Gregson raised his eyebrows slightly, but made no comment. He seemed less and less fatherly with each second that passed. 'But having left the shop as normal, you later returned?' he went on.

'Yes.'

'Why exactly was that, Miss Taylor?'

'I had forgotten something,' she explained as briefly as she could, hoping that he would not ask for any details. 'I went back to fetch it.'

'It couldn't have waited until the morning?'

'No,' she said simply.

'And what exactly was it, this vital object that you could not leave until the next day?'

'I would rather not say,' she said carefully. 'It has no bearing on . . . what happened. It has nothing to do with it.'

The man called McDermott smiled grimly at her from his corner, and spoke for the first time. 'You would be surprised, Miss Taylor, how often the things you might think would be the most irrelevant are in fact the most important.'

'Thank you, Mr McDermott,' said Gregson, sounding rather irritated by this interruption. He turned his stony gaze back to Sophie. 'Well?'

Sophie sighed. She would simply have to tell the truth: this was the police, after all. 'It was something belonging to another staff member. A jacket. He had given it to me to have it laundered.'

Gregson gave her a stern look. 'Laundry? That doesn't sound particularly urgent to me, Miss Taylor. Can you explain to us exactly what you mean?'

'It was his uniform jacket. It had got rather dirty, owing to a mishap. He didn't want anyone to see it. I forgot it and I didn't want him to get into any trouble.'

Gregson took off his spectacles and put them sharply down on the table. 'Miss Taylor, this all seems rather silly. Why exactly would a *jacket* cause trouble?'

Mr Cooper interjected at this point, to Sophie's relief:

'We have rules here about appearances, Sergeant. Mr Sinclair is particularly keen that employees are always well turned out. It is an important principle of the business. There are small penalties – fines and so forth – imposed for untidiness.' He turned to Sophie, 'I believe I know who you're talking about. One of our apprentices, gentlemen – a bright young lad, but unfortunately a little slapdash. I had cause to have a few words with him yesterday and no doubt he was nervous about this incident coming to my attention. Is that right, Sophie?'

Sophie's heart was beginning to thump apprehensively. 'Yes . . .' she said reluctantly, hating the thought that she might have got Billy into trouble.

Gregson shook his head, as if the whole situation was quite incomprehensible to him. 'Very well. Cooper, what is this boy's name?'

'Billy Parker.'

'Any relation to Sidney Parker?'

'Yes, indeed. His nephew.'

Gregson nodded curtly and turned back to Sophie, fixing his gaze upon her once more. 'So you went back to the store. How did you get in?'

'The staff entrance was locked but the side door in the stable-yard was still open. I went in that way.'

'And what time was this?'

'I'm not sure exactly. I don't have a watch. I should

say around half past six, maybe a little later.'

'Hmmm. And then what happened?'

'I went in, got the jacket from upstairs in the Millinery Department and came straight down again. I saw Mr Cooper on my way out and then I left and went home.'

Gregson leaned back in his chair and contemplated her coldly. 'What do you know about the exhibition of Mr Sinclair's jewels?' he asked, suddenly.

'Very little. I didn't have anything to do with it. I'd only read what was in the newspaper. I didn't have a chance to go and look at it. We were very busy getting everything ready for this morning.'

'But Mr Cooper here tells us that you were in the Exhibition Hall last night.'

'Yes, but only for a moment, on my way out of the shop.'

'That's not usually the way staff come in and out of the building, is it?'

'No,' Sophie said, keeping her head held high. Sergeant Gregson's eyes seemed to bore into her. 'The back stairs were rather dark. I was a little nervous, so I went the other way.'

'But you weren't too "nervous" to go and look at the exhibition?'

'It caught my attention for a moment, that was all. It was the little bird – the clockwork sparrow. But then I saw Mr Cooper and I left.'

'The sparrow, eh? That interested you?'

Was he trying to trip her up? She shook her head vigorously. 'Not especially. It just happened to catch my attention for a second or two. I thought it was pretty.'

'I'm sure you did,' said the Sergeant witheringly. 'Now tell me, Miss Taylor: what exactly is your relationship with the injured man, Albert Jones? I understand you are, er . . . *romantically* involved. Is that the case?'

'No!' Sophie exclaimed, half rising in her seat. 'That is not the case! I barely know him!'

'Please, Miss Taylor. There is no need to upset yourself. I am simply repeating what I have been told. Several people have reported that you spoke with him earlier that day in the refectory.'

'He spoke to me – yes. But before that, we had barely exchanged two words!'

'And yet it was a conversation of a personal nature?'

'He asked me to walk out with him,' she said tightly, her cheeks flushing with embarrassment. 'But I made it perfectly clear that I didn't want to. That was all – and you can ask anyone who was there, and they will tell you that's all that happened.'

'And you mean to say that this was the only time you spoke to him?'

'I suppose we might have spoken once or twice during our

training; I don't remember. And I did speak to him again when I left the shop that evening,' she added, reluctantly.

'Ah. The first time you left, or the second?'

'The second.'

'Most interesting. Where did you speak to him?'

'He was standing in the yard when I came out of the shop.'

'What was he doing there?'

'I don't know. He seemed to be waiting.'

'For you?'

'No – at least I don't think so. He seemed surprised to see me. He couldn't possibly have known I would be there.'

'And what exactly did you speak about, with Mr Jones, as you left the shop? Please tell us exactly.'

Reluctantly, Sophie dragged her mind back to the darkness of the stable-yard the previous evening. Her stomach felt hollow as she remembered. 'I said I was going home, but he wouldn't let me pass.' The men around her were watching her, passing judgement on her, she thought angrily: 'Then I managed to get away, and I ran off. That was all. I went straight home.'

'I see. And what time was this?'

'I don't know. It was about half past seven when I got home, so perhaps around seven o'clock?'

'You can't be any more precise?'

'I'm afraid not. As I said, I don't have a watch.'

Gregson glanced down at a paper in front of him. 'And you reside in "digs", is that correct?'

'Yes, at Mrs MacDuff's boarding house. Several of the girls that work here live there too.'

'Did your landlady see you that night?'

'No – I was too late for supper. But Edith and Minnie and one or two of the other girls saw me as I was coming in.'

Gregson nodded, but his face gave nothing away. 'Thank you, Miss Taylor,' he said gravely. 'That will be all for now – you may go back to your duties. But I believe we have more to talk about, so we will want to speak with you again very soon.'

The sergeant did not rise as she turned blindly to leave the room. To Sophie's surprise it was the quiet, grim-looking detective McDermott who put a hand on her shoulder and guided her out of the door. Outside, she stood still, unsettled.

'Don't be alarmed, Miss Taylor,' said Mr McDermott crisply before he turned back towards the office. 'He simply needs to know exactly what you saw. It's very important because if all you say is true, you may have been the last person to see Bert Jones before someone made a serious attempt on his life.'

He disappeared back through the office door, leaving Sophie standing in the passageway bewildered and alone.

CHAPTER EIGHT

By lunchtime, Sinclair's was electric with speculation. There were whispers down the corridors, murmurs in the cloakroom, lowered voices in the refectory.

'Did you hear that Cooper saw her lurking around the exhibition after hours?'

'You know she left at the usual time, but then came back to the store later? She says she forgot something, but it sounds fishy to me.'

'I heard that Bert was working for a gang, and they planned the robbery. She was helping them!'

'They were in on it together. They were going to run off with the loot.'

'No, you've got it all wrong. I heard that he saw the gang break in and tried to stop 'em. That's why they shot him. He's a hero!'

'But what about her? What's she got to do with it?'

'She was with that policeman for hours this morning.

He must suspect her of something.'

Outside in the yard, Billy was loading the deliveries. Moving fast and angrily, he heaved a succession of boxes into the van for delivery to customers one after another. *Thump, thump, thump, thump, thump.*

'More haste, less speed,' said George. 'There could be porcelain china in there, for all you know.'

But Billy felt too furious to do anything slowly. He couldn't believe all the rubbish those idiots were talking about Sophie. As if she could have had anything to do with that awful fellow Bert! As if she could be mixed up in a burglary! The worst of it was, it was all his own fault. If only he hadn't got into that stupid fight with that boy in the stables and ended up on his face in the muck. If only he had just taken what was coming to him like a man and not gone looking for help. It was all because Sophie had been looking out for him – going back to fetch his stupid old jacket – that this had happened. He heaved another box on to the wagon with an ominous crunch.

There was nothing he could do to help her, either. As soon as he had heard what everyone was saying, he had gone straight to Uncle Sid, but his uncle had said the same thing as always: 'Keep your nose out! The Law are in charge now. It's not for the likes of you to go sticking your oar in.'

After that, Billy had decided that the only thing for it was to go directly to Mr Cooper himself. It didn't matter what the consequences were: he felt it was a matter of honour. But Cooper had been even chillier than usual. Almost before Billy had even had a chance to open his mouth, the store manager had put a finger to his lips, looked at him pointedly, and said 'Thin ice, Parker,' before sending him straight back to work.

And so here he was. But every time he heard one of those chumps say something about Sophie, he felt awful all over again. He'd even heard some of them talking to that sneering policeman who wrote down every word they said in his black notebook. All Billy could really do now was to hope that the policeman would soon find out what had really happened. But it was hard to have much faith in him. He didn't seem to have done anything so far, other than keep Sophie holed up in Cooper's office for half the day.

'Calm down, lad,' said George soothingly. 'Don't pay any attention. A bit of talk is only human nature. It'll settle down soon enough.'

'But it's not fair. I know she didn't have anything to do with it.'

'And I daresay you're right. A bit of a girl like that isn't likely to be mixed up with the likes of this. It'll all come out in the wash, you'll see. The Old Bill know what they're doing. You just let them get on with their job, and we'll get on with ours.'

'I just wish there was something I could do to prove that she's innocent,' said Billy. 'Or to find out who the burglars really were.'

'Well, how about you help me instead, eh?' said George, wiping his forehead. 'What do you reckon you turn driver and take this delivery out? You can manage old Bessy all right, can't you?'

In spite of himself, Billy couldn't help a small smile. He hadn't expected to be allowed to take out any deliveries by himself for a while yet, and he saw this was George's way of trying to cheer him up. 'All right,' he said.

Bessy plodded forwards out of the yard, her harness jingling. Out on the street, amongst the throng of Hansom cabs and shiny new motors, the light seemed clear, the air was brisk and the blue sky arched above him. He saw one or two people pointing and nodding as they saw the blue and gold Sinclair's livery, and he began to take pleasure in being in charge of the van and the glossy well-groomed horse. He shook the reins and clicked his tongue to Bessy. This was a whole lot better than mucking about with boxes. He turned towards Hyde Park, keeping Bessy at a steady, surefooted pace, careful to give the motor buses a wide berth because George had told him that they made her nervous.

The deliveries were mostly for Mayfair: the first was a lot of boxes for a mansion on Belgrave Square, one of London's most fashionable and elegant addresses. He pulled up neatly in front of the house, hopped down from the seat and pulled down the running board – and then he stopped short.

'*What – are – you – doing here?*' he managed to burst out at last, almost speechless with surprise and anger.

The young man he'd found hiding in the stable-yard was crouched at the back of the van, curled up in a shadowy corner behind a pile of boxes. Now, he scrambled to his feet and hopped out.

'Here – listen a minute – keep yer hair on,' he began awkwardly. 'I'm sorry for cadging a lift. I didn't mean to make you jump like that. It's just that I wanted to talk to you.'

Billy snorted. 'Why on earth would I want to talk to *you?*' he demanded. 'Give me one good reason why I shouldn't go for you, here and now. You knocked me down, you nearly lost me my job and now you've stowed away in the van! Do you have any idea how much trouble I'd be in if anyone found out you were there? And it's all thanks to you that Sophie is in this mess!'

'But that's what I want to talk to you about,' the strange young fellow said eagerly. 'I was there, see. I know what really happened last night!'

Billy laughed disbelievingly, but the young fellow went on:

'You want to help that young lady, don't you? The one they said did the burglary?'

All of the anger of the day seemed to boil up inside Billy, and snapped out of him like a taut elastic band that had suddenly been released. 'I'm telling you, she didn't do it!' he yelled. Startled by the sudden noise, Bessy whinnied anxiously, but Billy went on. 'Now shut up and get away from me! Scram! I don't want anything to do with you!'

He found himself giving the fellow a sharp shove. Knocked sideways, the young man grabbed for the shafts of the van with his good arm to steady himself. Jostled and frightened now, Bessy reared up with a great neighing sound, sending parcels spilling out into the street, and almost overturning the van. Horrified by what he had done, Billy made a grab for the reins – but to his surprise, the young man was there before him, hanging on to the bridle, forcing the horse's head back down again. The young man's body crashed against the shafts, but he hung on valiantly until at last the horse was still again, though blowing and rolling her eyes wildly. Billy gaped at him for a moment, and then opened his mouth to speak, but before he could say anything a long shadow fell across them.

'Well then, fellers. What have we got here?'

They looked up into the face of a tall policeman, who was swinging his truncheon threateningly. He had a black moustache and looked rather like Uncle Sid. Visions of what his uncle would say – and worse, do – if he were brought back to the store by a policeman, having failed with his very first delivery, swam in Billy's head. Opposite him, the young man had stiffened, his eyes flooded with terror like an animal caught in a trap.

'This your vehicle? This your horse?'

Billy thought on his feet. 'Yes, sir. That is, they belong to Sinclair's department store,' he replied. 'We've a delivery for . . . er . . . a Mrs Whiteley,' he added hastily, glancing down at the bill of delivery, which was now crumpled in his hand. 'We were just . . . er . . . discussing which was the right house, but a motor horn startled the horse.'

'I didn't hear no motor horn,' said the policeman, suspiciously.

'Could you direct us to the house, Sergeant?' asked Billy, quickly.

The policeman looked rather pleased to be addressed as 'Sergeant', but it didn't stop him sounding sharp as he said: 'You're right in front of it,' gesturing with his truncheon. 'Get on with it then, young shavers. This is a fine part of town, not somewhere for kicking up a racket in the street.' He stood back and watched, his arms folded.

Luckily the young man seemed to be quick on the uptake: he picked up a couple of the boxes and trotted after Billy up towards the house, quite as if he did it every day. Billy rang the bell at the tradesman's entrance and a pert maid in a frilly apron and mob cap answered, wrinkling up her nose at the sight of his companion's tatty clothes.

'No begging here,' she began.

'We're not begging,' said Billy, crossly. 'We have a delivery for Whiteley, from Sinclair's department store.'

She looked doubtfully at them, and then out at the policeman standing watching on the street, but the sight of the boxes seemed to reassure her. To their relief she took the delivery inside, and they went back to the van and made as if to drive off again. Billy had to admit that the young man was a pretty good actor, nodding to him as if Billy were the boss, and then going round to the horse's head, adjusting her bridle and calming her down in quite a professional manner. She stood quietly now and, apparently satisfied, the policeman strode off down the street. As soon as he turned the corner, they both heaved a sigh of relief.

'Thanks for covering for me, mate,' said the young man, running a finger around the inside of his grimy collar.

'I'm *not* your mate,' said Billy shortly.

'All right, all right. You're not. But thanks for it all the same – I don't need no trouble with the rozzers. And I'm sorry I tripped you the other day, I mean it. But listen. I heard what you were saying to that old feller. You're angry on account of they think that young lady – your friend – had something to do with what happened at the shop. But you know she didn't. You want to know who really done it. Well, I can tell you. I was there in the yard last night.'

In spite of everything, Billy felt a tingle of excitement, but he didn't want to give anything away. 'Go on,' was all he said, crossing his arms.

'I was staying out of the way. Waiting for 'em to all go home and then I'd find a quiet corner to kip for the night. And they all left, except that young feller what got shot. He just kept standing there, like he was waiting. And then someone did come out. Another geezer.'

'Who was it?'

'I dunno. Just a feller. I couldn't see his face; he had a cap on and his collar up. But he had a shooter. Shot that feller down, as quick as winking, and then disappeared. But before he went, he dropped this.'

He held out a dirty piece of paper, and Billy took it, still doubtful. 'What's it say?' he asked.

'Dunno. I can't read. But you can, can't you? I've seen you reading.'

Billy unfolded the paper quickly. It had got wet, so the words were difficult to make out, but it looked like a page from a ledger, and he began to feel a thrill of anticipation. He looked up to see the young man watching him intently.

'What's it say?' he asked eagerly.

'It's a list of some sort,' Billy began, then stopped. 'Why are you giving me this?' he asked, suddenly suspicious. 'Why don't you take it to the police?'

The young man gave a short laugh. 'I ain't talking to the rozzers. No chance. The thing is, I'm in a bit of hot water. There's some fellers after me, and I've got to find a place to lie low for a while. I was going to move on – but then I thought that if I help you with this, maybe you might see your way to help me out too. I know you want to look out for that young lady, and you're right about that. She ain't got nothing to do with it. She's all right,' he added, awkwardly.

Billy felt himself wavering at this. 'But I don't know how I'm supposed to help you,' he said reluctantly. 'I haven't a brass farthing.'

'It's not chink I'm after.' The young man shrugged. 'All I'm looking for is a place to hide out. Somewhere quiet like, somewhere that no one can find me. Just for a while, till they've forgot about me. If you help me with that, I'll do anything I can for you – I swear it on me old grandad's grave.'

Billy glanced down at the young fellow's arm. 'Did they do that to you?'

He nodded, shamefaced.

Billy looked back at him through narrowed eyes. He wasn't at all sure he ought to trust him. But something made him say, 'Fair enough,' letting out a long breath. 'We'll call it a truce for now. But no funny business,' he added hastily. 'I think I know somewhere you can hide out for a bit, but you'll have to toe the line and help me find out who he is, that man you saw.'

'All right. You're the boss.'

'I'm Billy – Billy Parker.' He held out a hand, and the stranger looked confused for a moment, but then took it rather gingerly in his dirty paw and gave it an uncertain shake.

'Joe,' he said.

'I've got to finish the deliveries now. You'd better get out of here. But meet me later . . .' He struggled to think of a place that they could meet, with Uncle Sid's eye on him at work and Mum's at home. 'Meet me at the store, in the stable-yard, after closing time,' he suggested finally.

Joe nodded. 'I'll find you,' he said, and disappeared so quickly it was almost as if he had never been there at all.

Billy glanced at the piece of paper again. The tattered note seemed to glow with mystical properties: he felt as if he had suddenly been transformed into Montgomery Baxter himself. The writing was smudged and not easy to read, but he felt certain that with time, he would be able to decipher it. This could be it – the evidence he needed to prove what had really happened. For a moment, excitement overwhelmed him, but then he remembered his task. Folding the note carefully and putting it into his inside pocket, he turned back to the now quiet Bessy, and the next batch of deliveries for the store.

CHAPTER NINE

'The rehearsal went off far better than I could have hoped for. And Gilbert Lloyd – he really is an absolute *dream* –' Lil broke off mid-sentence, her bright face suddenly solemn. 'Oh Sophie, do have something to eat. You look as white as a sheet.'

The two were sitting opposite each other at a little table in the ABC teahouse on Oxford Street at the end of the long opening day. They had already discussed all the events of the first day of business in the store: the proceedings of the first ever dress show; Sophie's hectic day of selling dozens of hats to over-excited ladies; and Mr Sinclair's tour of the store to greet some of the most important customers. Now, Lil was busily relating the story of her rehearsal at the Fortune Theatre that morning.

All around them were other girls like themselves: office girls, shop girls, telephone operators, released from work and chattering over cakes and buns. Going out to supper had been Lil's idea, something to take Sophie's mind off the gossip that had been surging around the store, and Sophie had been touched by the suggestion. She had been half-wondering whether, given everything that had happened, Lil's friendship might fade away again as quickly as it had appeared. If anything, though, Lil seemed friendlier than ever. She was now pushing the plate of crumpets towards Sophie, a concerned expression on her face.

Sophie took one. 'I'm sorry I'm being such a bore,' she said. 'It's just that I can't stop thinking about the burglary. The whole thing seems so extraordinary. I haven't known them for very long, but I can't believe that people at the store really think I could be some sort of a criminal.' She couldn't help thinking about what Papa would say if he could see her being questioned by the police.

'It's all rot,' said Lil, through a rather unladylike mouthful of cake. 'I can't imagine what the duffers are thinking of. But I'm sure it will all soon blow over. I mean, once Bert comes round, he'll be able to tell everyone what really happened.'

'If he does come round,' said Sophie bleakly. She was still struggling to take in the fact that just a few minutes after she had seen him in the yard, Bert had been shot.

'It's just idiotic gossip, that's all,' said Lil firmly. 'Actually, I'm rather astonished that Mr Cooper hasn't nipped it in the bud already.'

Sophie shook her head. 'I think he half suspects me himself,' she said. 'He's watching me, I know it. He was the one who told Sergeant Gregson that I'd been there, in the Exhibition Hall, after hours.'

'Oh, I'm certain he doesn't *really* believe you had anything to do with it. Or that policeman, either. How could he? I think he's simply asking you all these questions because he wants to know absolutely everything that went on last night – and you just happened to be there. He probably thinks that you might have seen or heard something that will help him find out who the thieves were,' suggested Lil.

'That's like what Mr McDermott said,' Sophie mused. Lil looked at her questioningly and she explained: 'He's Sinclair's private detective. He's working with the police.'

'Well, there you are then. And the Sergeant has talked to other people too, remember – Cooper and Billy's uncle and even Edith, I think.' Lil made a face, as if to suggest that anything Edith would have to say couldn't be much worth listening to.

'The problem is that he doesn't really understand why I went back to the store. It doesn't make the least bit of sense to him that I'd gone back to fetch Billy's jacket. I just wish there was some sort of proof I could give him.'

Lil almost upset her tea in her excitement. 'But there is!'

she exclaimed. 'The jacket itself, of course. Didn't you take it away to clean?'

'Yes.'

'And did you actually clean it?'

'No!' Sophie's eyes lit up as she realised what Lil was driving at. 'I was going to – I hung it up to dry overnight, and then I was going to launder it today.'

'Well let's go and get it now and take it to this idiotic policeman. I'll back you up, and I'm sure that Billy will too, and with the jacket as proof he'll just have to believe that you're telling the truth.'

Sophie's spirits began to rise. Of course, Gregson would probably still be rude and suspicious – but at least she'd have something that she could show him that might make him take her story seriously.

Lil insisted on accompanying her to the lodging house, but when they arrived, Mrs MacDuff, the landlady, was waiting for them. She had a strange expression on her face.

'So here you are at last,' she said as they came through the front door. 'Strolling in as if you haven't got a care in the world. Well, let me tell you, this is a decent, respectable house. I won't stand for this kind of thing.'

Sophie stopped abruptly. 'Whatever do you mean?' she asked.

'What do I mean? What I mean, young lady, is that I'm

not accustomed to having policemen turning up on my doorstep, asking questions and poking about. No indeed!' Mrs MacDuff bridled angrily. 'I don't know what you've been up to, my girl, but you'd better mend your ways or you'll be out on the street.'

Sophie felt cold. Policemen had been there? Did she mean Sergeant Gregson? What could he have been doing at her lodgings?

'Tracked mud all up my clean carpets going to your room, they did.'

'Policemen?' repeated Lil, but Sophie had already turned and was running up the stairs. On the threshold to her room, she stopped motionless and stared inside.

The room that she had left neat and bare that morning was now almost unrecognisable. The bed had been tipped over on to its side, the scanty covers pulled off and muddled on the floor. The washstand was smashed, and the closet door stood open, hanging drunkenly on one hinge. Her clothes were scattered in disordered piles, some of them ripped or torn, and her dear old doll lay face down in the midst of it all. Her trunk had been pulled out from under the bed, the lid forced open. Worst of all, everything had been swept off the mantelpiece: books spilled pages and her precious cowslip jug was shattered into a dozen fragments. For a moment, she couldn't move.

Lil came running up behind her. 'Oh, Sophie . . .' was all she said.

'What's all this?' Mrs MacDuff entered the room, red-faced and panting. She looked around in high indignation. 'Well this is a fine way to treat your room, I must say!'

'*I* didn't do this!' cried Sophie. 'It must have been those policemen you let in!'

Mrs MacDuff scowled. 'I don't care who did it – it's got to be cleaned up. And anything damaged or broken will be paid for. It looks more like a pigsty than a young lady's room! I'll be back up in an hour, and I want to see it spick and span by then.'

The door shut behind her with a bang.

'Ugh, what an awful old witch,' exclaimed Lil in disgust. She heaved the bed back upright with a heavy crash, and began to pile the bedclothes on to it. 'Oh, Sophie, this is perfectly ghastly. Do you think Gregson sent some policemen here to search your room?'

Sophie was crouching on the floor amongst the chaos of her belongings. 'I suppose they must have been,' she said flatly. 'I wonder if he thought they'd find the jewels,' she added, shaking her head in disbelief.

'What about Billy's jacket?' Lil asked suddenly, remembering their original purpose.

Sophie glanced up at the back of the door where the

jacket had hung. 'Gone,' she said. 'As are one or two other things, by the looks of it.'

'Do you suppose they took them away as – as evidence?' Lil said, her eyes widening, even as she bent down to pick up clothes from the floor. She shook out Sophie's good velvet dress, now creased and dirty, and then paused to try and collect a handful of green beads, broken from their string and scattered all about. 'I don't understand. Why would the police make a mess of everything like this? How could they?'

Sophie picked up her doll and smoothed down its tumbled hair. 'I don't know,' she said slowly. 'Perhaps this is what they do.'

'But it isn't *fair*,' said Lil.

Sophie took up the precious photo of her Papa from where it was lying on the floor. The glass had been smashed, the cracks fracturing right across his face. She felt hollow. 'No. No it isn't fair at all.'

CHAPTER TEN

'I tell you what, this is a bit of all right, this is,' Joe said. He was looking around as if quite delighted with the place, Billy thought. It was after closing time and the two of them were seated on upturned crates in a small storeroom in the basement of Sinclair's. High windows let in the fading light: a candle stuck in an old ginger-beer bottle would provide Joe with a light for later. They were sharing a hastily prepared picnic of a bit of bread and cold mutton that Billy had managed to pinch from the refectory at lunchtime. Joe had fallen on it as if he hadn't eaten for weeks.

'Sorry,' Joe said apologetically, after Billy had watched him wolf most of it down. 'I ain't had much to eat these last few days. Been trying to keep a low profile. I don't want word to get back to the Boys that I'm about.'

'Who are the Boys?' asked Billy, watching Joe intently. He was still not at all sure whether he had done the right thing by helping this strange young man sneak into the store basement. Joe's penitent attitude had gone: he seemed cheerful now, and that in itself made Billy feel nervous. What if all this was some sort of a trick – a set-up? Something to do with the robbery, perhaps? His imagination jumped back to stories he had read, but then he reminded himself that this was not, after all, a Montgomery Baxter tale, where there was always someone trying to pull the wool over the young hero's eyes. Besides, there was surely not much harm that Joe could really do, shut up in an empty basement storeroom.

'You ain't ever heard of the Baron's Boys?' Joe was saying, his eyes widening in surprise even as he stuffed the last bit of bread in his mouth.

Billy shrugged and shook his head.

'Blimey,' said Joe, chewing and swallowing. 'Well, I suppose you'd call 'em a gang of sorts,' he began, and then fell silent.

The truth was Joe was struggling to think how he could start to explain the Baron's Boys. Even calling them a gang was wrong because they weren't really – not like the rowdy families of Irish fellows or the East End Jewish clans, the ones who banded together to protect their own. The Baron's Boys were different. They were the lost ones, the ones without homes or families or anything of their own left to stick up for. He fought to explain this, found that words failed him, went on anyway. 'They work for the Baron. You know who the Baron is, right?'

Billy shook his head again. Joe was astounded. 'But *everyone* knows about the Baron. He's famous in London. You've really never even heard of him?'

'No, never,' Billy said.

'My eye,' Joe said slowly, shaking his head. 'Where've you been hiding?' He heaved an enormous sigh and went on. 'The Baron . . . well, I dunno exactly who he is. No one knows his real name. That's one of the things about him. But he's the top Johnny in the East End. He's the man in control and the others all have to answer to him.

'You don't want to know the stories about what's happened to them that's got on the wrong side of him. Give you nightmares, they will,' he went on. 'But you see, the thing that's really funny about the Baron' – and here, Joe lowered his voice to little more than a hoarse whisper – 'hardly anyone's ever set eyes on him. There's all sorts of stories about why. Some people say he's got these terrible scars and burns all over his face, and that's why he won't let no one see him. Some people say he's a black magician what made a pact with the devil and it turned him invisible. Some people say he ain't a man at all . . . Some people say . . . well they say all kinds of things.'

Billy was sceptical. 'But that can't be right,' he remarked, trying to shake off the strange feeling that had been creeping over him as he listened to Joe's tale in the dark basement. 'I mean, *someone* must have seen him.'

Joe shrugged. 'Those that have ain't saying nothing,' he said in a grave voice.

Billy saw to his astonishment that Joe looked genuinely unsettled. Surely he didn't really believe that this Baron fellow was some sort of monster?

'There's a feller who runs the show for him and gives all the orders,' Joe explained. 'The Baron's Boys, they do his business. You know, collecting the rents, keeping folks in line. Shutting up folks he needs shutting up. Doing whatever he wants, no matter how much it makes you sick to your stomach. There's no choice, see? I used to be one of 'em. That's about all a fellow like me can do, I reckon.'

'What do you mean?' asked Billy, beginning to feel intrigued.

Joe shrugged. 'There ain't exactly a lot of ways to get by,' he said, rubbing a hand over his forehead. 'No flash jobs in posh shops like this place, anyway. My old grandad, he was a cabinet-maker. Made a few bob so we could pay the rent, keep a roof over our heads. But he died when I was just a kid and I ain't got no one else. I've not got much schooling and I never learned a trade. You got to have a bit of tin to go in somewhere as an apprentice, and anyway, they'd rather have a proper British lad, wouldn't they.'

Billy frowned, confused, and Joe explained. 'Grandad came over from Russia. Anyway, a feller like me can only make a few pence here and there. Carrying luggage for the swells at Liverpool Street, selling papers, that sort o' thing. Or if you're smart you might pinch a wallet now and then. But that won't keep a roof over your head and there's no way I want to get stuck in the Spike.' He must have seen Billy's questioning look, because he added, 'The workhouse. Rotten dump.

'So I got in with the Baron's Boys. It's not much of a life, though.' Joe sighed. 'I'll level with you: I hated every second of it. Don't reckon they ever thought much of me, either. Jem, he always said I hadn't got enough bottle for it. But I was useful to them on account of I'm good with animals – horses especially. You got to have someone good with horses about, so you can get away sharp when you need to. But they wanted me to do more. They wanted me to . . . well, never mind what it was they wanted me to do, but I didn't want to do it.'

Joe was silent for a moment. His thoughts had run back to the alleyway, the knife, the watchmaker behind the window. He shook his head and then went abruptly onwards: 'So I said I wouldn't, and I ran away, but they don't like that. Once you're one of the Baron's Boys, then you're in for good. And if you leave, well then you're a stinking turncoat. That's why I couldn't stick around – I'm a marked man now. But they'll never find me here. That's why I came: they don't come out West, and I bet they'd never dare come to a place like this. I reckon if I stay out of their way long enough, I might be lucky. Maybe they'll forget about me.'

Billy had listened to all this with great interest, and found himself looking at Joe with new respect. All the same, he still felt anxious. 'Well, you'd better be careful down here,' he said warily. 'Stay put. Remember there's a nightwatchman on duty. Don't go wandering about or anything, will you?'

Joe shook his head earnestly. 'Don't worry, mate,' he said. 'I'll be on my best behaviour. This is a cracking good kip, this is. Ever slept rough? No I didn't reckon you had. Can't get more than a few winks before the rozzers have you up and move you on again. But this place is diamond.'

'Well, there shouldn't be anyone down here much. As long as you stay out of sight in one of these rooms, you ought to be safe enough for a day or two,' said Billy.

Joe looked unconcerned. 'There's plenty of places I can get out of the way, if I've got to,' he said airily. Then he added, more awkwardly, 'Thanks. For helping me out, that is.'

'We're helping each other, remember?'

The light was almost gone now, so Billy grabbed his cap and jacket and got to his feet. Mum would be mad as hops with him if he was late home, but after everything that had happened that day, it didn't seem to matter any more.

Night fell over London. In the bedroom of the lodging house, barer than ever now, Sophie looked out of the window over shadowy streets and back alleys, the darkness broken only by the faint gleam of the street lamps. In the basement of Sinclair's department store, Joe slept, undisturbed by vigilant policemen, but still troubled by the phantom figure of the Baron, who stalked him through his dreams. Not so very far away, Lil sat by the red glow of her bedroom fire, patiently threading a handful of green beads one after another, back on to a string. And across the water, on the south side of the river, Billy lay awake in his narrow bed, staring up at the familiar map of cracks in the ceiling by the flickering light of the candle.

He took the note out once more, and carefully traced the letters with his fingers. It was really something, having a proper clue like this. He'd already started trying to decipher it, but with just a candle it was too difficult to make out the smudged letters: he'd have to be patient until the morning. Carefully, he tucked it inside one of the books he kept stacked beside his bed. He didn't want to risk Mum seeing it and throwing it away, thinking it was just some old bit of rubbish.

He knew it was late, but sleep seemed impossible. He still had a good inch of candle left, so he pulled a copy of *Boys of Empire* from under his pillow, nestled down under the blankets and began to read.

PART III:
'À La Mode'

With fine ostrich plumes and rosettes of tulle, this delightful
chapeau in café au lait silk is graceful in shape, and fine enough
to catch the eye at a dressy luncheon party . . .

CHAPTER ELEVEN

It was the second day of business at Sinclair's, and the store was busier than ever. On the ground floor, a group of ever-so-slightly scandalised customers were gathered round an elegant saleslady who was demonstrating some of the daring new cosmetics: *Blanc de Perles*, *Baton au Raisin Lip Rouge* and *Veloutine Powder*. Up in Sporting Goods, several gentlemen were admiring a new display of golf clubs; in the Pet Department, a little girl was choosing a white kitten with a green ribbon around its neck as her birthday present from a doting grandmama; and in the Marble Court Restaurant, none other than the Countess of Alconborough could be observed, drinking tea and daintily nibbling a scone. Upstairs in the office, the telephones shrilled and the typists' fingers hammered at the keys; whilst below, Sidney Parker threw open the door with an especially theatrical flourish, to admit yet another crowd of excited shoppers who had heard talk all over London of the marvels they could find inside

117

Edward Sinclair's wonderful department store.

For the first time, Sophie felt overwhelmed by it all: the endless rush of the lifts going up and down, the constant hum of voices, the relentless tinkling of the grand piano. Even the rich, sweet scent that hung in the air seemed suddenly stifling.

It was true that she had been relieved to hear, on her arrival at the store that morning, that there was better news of Bert Jones. He was showing signs he would certainly recover from the gunshot wound, but he was not yet well enough to tell the police anything about what had happened. Store gossip excitedly reported that a police guard had been placed at his bedside night and day.

But any small comfort Sophie could take from knowing that Bert would soon be able to tell the truth about the burglary was quite spoilt by Edith's return to work. Mrs Milton had been called to Mr Cooper's office first thing, and Edith had taken advantage of her absence to sit in the storeroom at the centre of a cluster of sympathising shop girls, alternately dabbing at her eyes with a lace-edged handkerchief and throwing venomous looks in Sophie's direction.

Sophie fought to remain calm and keep her head, but she could not stop the horrible sick feeling that swept over her as she struggled on alone on the shop floor. It was only her second day of serving customers, and the hustle and bustle of the busy store still felt very new, and now, she was obliged to deal with the growing crowds of customers all by herself.

'Do you have this in pink?' a customer was demanding.

'One pound nine shillings!' scoffed another. 'Why I declare I saw the very same model at Huntington's yesterday for only a guinea! This Sinclair fellow must think we're all fools!'

'Miss – Miss! I need some assistance at once!'

'One moment, please, madam,' said Sophie breathlessly, diving back into the storeroom to find the hat with the pink ribbons.

'Look at you,' spat out Edith as she entered. 'Acting just as if nothing had happened! You're as hard as nails.'

Sophie rifled through the hat-boxes. 'Violet – could you come and help me on the counter please? There are customers waiting.'

Violet dropped the sewing she was doing. She had been listening wide-eyed to Edith for most of the morning. Now she looked up at Sophie with a half-afraid expression on her face.

'Oh, for heaven's sake!' exploded Sophie. 'Don't tell me you actually believe all this nonsense?'

Violet gaped at her, and then glanced back at Edith. She looked as though she might be about to burst into tears.

'I suppose you've been stuffing her head with rot,' said

Sophie, tartly. Exasperated, she pushed past them both out of the storeroom. She would rather deal with all the rude, bad-tempered customers in the world than her fellow shop girls, she thought angrily, if they were all so certain of her guilt.

Away from the bustle of the shop floor, the farthest reaches of the basement were peculiarly silent and still. Hoping that his absence would go unnoticed, Billy slipped down to the storeroom with the high windows, taking with him a large hunk of seed cake, and the morning's newspaper tucked under his arm. He had been wondering whether Joe would still be there when morning came, and he felt relieved when the young man appeared, looking quite pleased to see him. Close at his heels trotted Blackie, the boiler-room cat.

Joe noticed Billy glancing in surprise at the cat, and gave a small, embarrassed shrug. 'He just . . . turned up,' he said. 'I ain't been encouraging him, honest – but he seems to like it down here.' He sat down on a crate and the cat wound itself round his ankles, purring enthusiastically, before leaping into his lap.

Billy handed over the cake he had brought. 'Sorry I couldn't bring any more. Mum keeps a pretty sharp eye on her larder. But I'll try and bring you something else later on.'

He took a seat on a crate opposite Joe, who was already

tucking in with obvious appreciation. 'Aren't you bored down here?' he asked, curiously, looking around at the empty room. 'I could bring you some magazines, or something, if you like?'

'No point, mate. Can't read, remember?' said Joe, through a mouthful of cake. 'Anyway, I don't mind telling you, I'd rather be bored out of my skull than worried about my skin.' He gestured at the newspaper that Billy was holding. 'What's all this, then?'

Billy's eyes lit up. 'I wanted you to hear this,' he said, and he read aloud:

£100 REWARD
OFFERED FOR THE RETURN
OF PRICELESS STOLEN GOODS

A sum of £100 is hereby offered to any person, or persons, who return, undamaged, the Jewels and other Articles recently apprehended from Sinclair's department store. Of particular interest is the Clockwork Sparrow: a separate sum of £50 will be paid for its safe return. Signed: Mr Edward Sinclair.

The Clockwork Sparrow

'A hundred quid! You're having a laugh!' Joe's eyes were wide with disbelief.

'That's what it says, right here in black and white.'

'But that's a fortune, that is!'

Billy nodded eagerly. Ever since he had seen the advertisement, he hadn't been able to stop thinking about how marvellous it would feel if he could be the one to discover the stolen goods – and win the reward. He imagined coolly strolling into the Captain's office, and placing the missing jewels casually on his desk. He would be able to prove that Sophie didn't have anything to do with the burglary; the Captain would be delighted; Uncle Sid and Mr Cooper wouldn't be able to treat him like a useless kid any longer; and everyone would admire him – Sophie, most of all.

'What is this clockwork thing anyway?' asked Joe, stroking Blackie absently.

Billy screwed up his face, trying to explain: 'It's like a little musical box in the shape of a bird. Like a toy, but stuck all over with jewels and stuff. It has some special workings inside it that make it play a completely different set of notes each time you wind it – it's the only one like it in the world that can do that. That's part of what makes it so special. I think it must have been one of the most valuable things on display.'

Joe let out a long, slow whistle.

'We'll have to act fast, though, if we want to be the ones to find out what happened,' Billy went on. 'Now this reward has been offered, I expect every fathead in the store will be trying to get it. But we've got the message you found. That's one thing.'

'Did you figure out what it says?' asked Joe.

'I'm working on it,' said Billy, a little evasively. 'But I've thought of something else too. Something Montgomery Baxter always does in his cases.'

Joe listened, his brow furrowed. He still wasn't completely clear on who this Baxter fellow actually was.

'He *examines the scene of the crime*,' Billy went on triumphantly. 'Of course, the police have already done that. But it's just possible there could be some clue there that might help us. As soon as I get the chance, I'm going to scout around the Exhibition Hall and see what I can find – before anyone else starts sniffing about.'

'The police turned your room upside down?' Billy repeated, in astonishment. 'But why would they do that? Do you think they were looking for the jewels?'

'I suppose they must have been,' said Sophie. It was just after the midday meal, and she and Lil had come to find Billy in the stable-yard to tell him about what had happened the previous evening. She leaned back against the wall, taking in a deep breath of the cold, fresh air, rich with the scent of horses and hay.

It was a relief to be here, out of the suffocating atmosphere of the store – and especially to be away from the other staff. Sophie couldn't help but notice that the staring and whispering was growing worse and worse. Even Claudine, who had always been quite cordial, had hurried away without meeting her eyes when they passed each other on the stairs. For a moment, she found herself thinking almost nostalgically of the days when all she had to worry about was the girls calling her 'Sour-milk Sophie'. Now, she had Sergeant Gregson to think about too. All morning, he had seemed to be lurking close by, and after what had happened last night, she found his presence oddly sinister.

'It was perfectly horrid,' Lil was saying, with a sympathetic shiver. 'But tell us more about this young man you met, Billy. Did he really witness the shooting? Let's see this note he found.'

Billy had been eager to tell the two girls about meeting Joe, and what he had seen, but he had decided to skate quickly over the part of the story where he had agreed to help Joe hide. He wasn't at all sure whether the girls would approve of him helping a strange young man who was, after all, not merely a vagrant but apparently a sort of criminal himself. Now, he carefully took the piece of paper from where he had been keeping it folded safely in his jacket pocket. He handed it to Sophie. 'Here it is. It had got all wet, so it wasn't easy to read, but I worked out what it says, and I've copied it out here.' Sophie read the list aloud.

3 organdie nightgowns
Ivory gloves
Handkerchiefs 10s
Driving-gloves £8
Ladies ivory velvet evening robe
Silk petticoat
All red ribbons
1 white undershirt
Navy dress, embroidered
Ready-ordered gown, ruffles £1
Umbrellas 19s
Dressing-gown
Ballgown, yellow taffeta £8 9s
Boots and raincoat
1 necktie

'Why, it's just a list of clothing!' she said, with a laugh. 'A page from a ledger from the shop, probably.'

'Was he sure that it was the man with the gun who dropped this?' asked Lil, reaching over to take it from Sophie and scrutinise it herself.

'Maybe Mr Cooper or someone else – even Bert himself – dropped it in the yard, and he just assumed the thief dropped it,' suggested Sophie.

Billy shook his head. 'No,' he said firmly. 'Joe was quite certain that it belonged to the man who shot Bert.'

'So maybe he *was* someone from the store,' said Lil, and they looked at each other uncomfortably.

'It's a strange kind of list though, isn't it?' Sophie went on. 'It doesn't seem like an order, or an inventory of stock, or anything like that. It's just a jumble of all sorts of things, from all sorts of different departments. I mean, *handkerchiefs* – which handkerchiefs? Sinclair's must stock dozens of different kinds. And some of the prices look odd too.'

'That's what I thought,' said Billy. 'It doesn't make sense.'

Lil was squinting at the original note, wrinkling up her nose. 'What's this, here?' she said curiously, pointing to a dark squiggle at the top right-hand corner of the page. 'It's a bit like a snake. Or then again, I suppose it could just be a funny ink blot.'

'*All red ribbons*,' continued Sophie. 'What does that mean?'

'It's almost as if it's just . . . made up. Any old words, scribbled down anyhow,' said Lil.

'But what for? Why would anyone make up a list of clothing like that?' Sophie wondered.

Billy sucked in his breath. 'They might if it isn't really a list of clothing at all,' he burst out.

'Whatever do you mean?'

'Maybe it isn't a list,' said Billy. 'Maybe it's a coded message. You know, like in *The Adventure of the Dancing Men*, or *Journey to the Centre of the Earth*. A secret code. The thieves wanted to keep their communications secret, so they disguised them.'

Sophie laughed in spite of herself. 'A secret code! That's a little far-fetched, isn't it?'

Billy folded his arms. 'Well, how else do you explain it?' he shot back.

Sophie shrugged. 'I don't know. I just can't imagine anyone making up a secret code about . . . handkerchiefs and nightgowns, and so on.'

'But that's the point, isn't it?' said Lil. 'I mean, it's supposed to look completely ordinary.' She turned to Billy, suddenly excited. 'I saw it in a play once. The villain was sending all of these postcards that sounded perfectly innocent - you know, *Weather is fine, Aunt Mildred expected in Brighton on Tuesday* - and actually they were coded messages giving instructions to his accomplices!'

'And that's what you think this is?' said Sophie, glancing down at the list doubtfully.

Billy nodded emphatically.

Lil clapped her hands, looking elated. 'Now all we have to do is work out what it says!'

CHAPTER TWELVE

Billy frowned and scribbled down a few words in the exercise book that was resting on his knees, then crossed them out and started again, feeling irritable. He was supposed to be collecting boxes from Gentlemen's Outfitting and taking them down to the stable-yard for delivery, but instead he was perched on his secret window ledge, staring at the list Joe had found and trying to recall everything he had ever read about cryptograms and ciphers.

He had been keeping a sharp eye out for any quiet corners where he could read in peace, out of sight of Uncle Sid, and this was the best of the hidey-holes he had found so far, much better than the staff cloakroom or the stables – an out-of-the-way store cupboard where surplus stock from the Sporting Goods Department was kept. It had a small rectangular window with a conveniently wide window ledge, which made the perfect place to sit and read. Now, however, the story he had been engrossed in earlier that day was all but forgotten as he squinted at the list, determined to decipher any hidden meaning it might conceal.

The horrible thing was that he was beginning to have an unpleasant feeling that Sophie might be right. There was certainly nothing suggestive about any of the things in the list: he couldn't see any connection to the events of the burglary at all. Worse still, he wondered uncomfortably, what if Joe had just pretended to see the shooting? He could easily have picked up any old rubbish off the ground and made up the story of what he had seen, knowing that he could use it to convince Billy to help him.

He rubbed his head. He didn't want to believe that Joe had set out to trick him, and he wasn't ready to admit defeat, not yet. He just needed to be systematic about it, he told himself. It was really no different from an arithmetic problem on the blackboard at school, and he'd always been good at solving those. He sucked the end of his pencil thoughtfully, scribbled down a few more letters and stopped again. No, that couldn't be right. He scowled, scribbled, crossed out and started afresh.

'Hullo!' said a brisk voice, close beside him. He jumped so violently that he nearly fell off the window sill. 'What are you doing here? How did you find me?' he demanded.

Lil smiled, rather pleased with herself. 'I followed you, of course,' she said, hopping neatly up on to the window ledge beside him. 'I know how it's done. You're not the only one who likes detective stories, you know. I saw this simply wonderful mystery once, all about –'

But Billy cut her off before she could say any more, not feeling at all in the mood to hear Lil raving about a play. 'Listen, I'm trying to work out this code,' he said curtly. 'It's important.'

'I realise that,' said Lil, impatiently. 'That's why I'm here. I thought I might be able to help. Two heads are better than one, and all that.'

Billy glanced up at her doubtfully. Somehow he couldn't imagine that code-cracking was exactly Lil's strong suit, but she looked so earnest that he couldn't refuse. 'Very well then,' he sighed, moving the note over so that they could both see it.

'So what do you think so far?' she asked, with interest.

'I don't know yet. There are all sorts of different ciphers. Transposition ciphers. Substitution ciphers. It could be a really tricky one. They could even have used invisible ink.'

'Well let's start with a simple one,' said Lil promptly. 'What's the easiest kind of cipher?'

Billy wrinkled his forehead. 'I suppose something like just writing the words backwards. Or using the first letter or the last letter of each word to conceal the hidden message.'

'Well, let's try those then.'

'But it's bound to be something much more complicated,' protested Billy.

'Oh go on, let's just try it.'

Sighing heavily, Billy quickly began to write out the words backwards, starting at the end of the list. *EITKCEN 1 TAOCNIAR DNA STOOB*, he wrote. 'See? Useless.'

'Well, what about that other one you just said? The first letter of each word?'

Billy jotted down the first letter of each word and then tapped the page: *ONIGHDG*. 'It's just nonsense.'

Lil shrugged. 'Well maybe, but at least we've tried it.' Then she leaned over and pulled the piece of paper closer towards her. 'Wait a minute, though, what about the numbers and the prices?' she asked, suddenly. 'We have to take them into account too.'

She snatched the pencil from Billy's hand, scribbled for a moment, paused, and scribbled again. Then Billy grabbed the pencil back and added a few swift pencil marks. Suddenly, three quite recognisable words had appeared on the page:

TONIGHT/DELIVER/SPARROW

'Oh my goodness . . .' said Lil, slowly.

Billy gazed at the paper, and then up at Lil once more.

A moment later, they had both leaped down from the window sill, Billy upsetting a box of shuttlecocks and Lil almost tripping over a stack of tennis rackets as they hurried out of the room.

In the Millinery Department, Sophie was serving a customer – a very fashionably dressed young girl, with an even more fashionably dressed lady beside her. They were sitting comfortably in velvet armchairs, whilst Sophie trailed to and fro from the storeroom, fetching one hat after another as the girl tried them on, admired her reflection in a gilt-framed looking-glass, and then discarded them carelessly again. Lil and Billy hovered impatiently just out of sight, watching Sophie nod and smile to each new request, focused on her task, just as if it were a perfectly normal day.

After what seemed like an impossibly long time, the young lady finally seemed satisfied, and the customers departed. They watched Sophie pick up the enormous plumed hat that had finally been chosen and head towards the storeroom, presumably to pack it for delivery. Seizing the opportunity, they darted forward.

'We've done it!' Lil said, her voice shrill with excitement. 'We've cracked the code!'

Sophie jumped in surprise. '*What?*' she exclaimed.

'Look,' said Billy, steering her behind a potted palm, feeling shivery with the thrill of the discovery. 'Just look. Remember how you said that there was something funny about this list – how the prices didn't sound right, and so on? Well *you were right*. It's a secret message. Look.'

'It's so simple really,' said Lil, as they all bent their heads over the piece of paper. 'Just the first letter of each word,' and she gestured to where they had underlined, on the first line, 'organdie' and 'nightgowns'. 'And you turn the figures into words. So the number "3" becomes the word "three" and then you apply the same rule.'

'Three organdie nightgowns,' read Sophie carefully. 'T-O-N . . . Ivory gloves . . . I-G . . . Handkerchiefs 10s . . . H . . . and then I suppose the ten is T. *Tonight*,' she concluded. 'That's incredible,' she breathed. 'It really does say something! However did you do it?'

Lil's cheeks were red with pride. 'It's awfully simple really,' she said.

'Go on – what does the whole thing say,' said Sophie, her face flushed with excitement too.

Lil read the message out in full. '*Tonight. Deliver sparrow underground by ten. Baron.*'

three
3 organdie nightgowns   T O N

Ivory gloves   I G

           one
Handkerchiefs _10s_   H T

          eight
Driving-gloves £_8_   D E

Ladies' ivory velvet evening robe   LIVER

Silk petticoat   S P

All red ribbons   A R R

   one
1 white undershirt   O W U

Navy dress, embroidered   N D E

                    one
Ready-ordered gown, ruffles £_1_   RGRO

       nineteen
Umbrellas 19s   U N D

Dressing-gown   D

             eight nine
Ballgown, yellow taffeta £_8 9s_   BY TEN

Boots and raincoat   BAR

one
1 necktie   O N

TONIGHT. DELIVER SPARROW
UNDERGROUND BY TEN.
BARON.

'Baron?' Sophie repeated, confused.

'*The Baron!*' Billy's eyes widened as he suddenly recalled Joe's strange story from the previous evening. He had been so excited about the code that he hadn't made the connection with what Joe had told him until now.

But even as his thoughts raced, Sophie's face became anxious. Mrs Milton could be seen gathering all the girls together by the counter. She was looking around for Sophie, a frown on her face.

'Oh dear – you'd better go,' Sophie said hurriedly. 'Come and find me later.'

Sophie hastened over to the circle of girls. Mrs Milton smiled at her as she came up, but it did not escape Sophie's notice that her smile did not reach her eyes, and she was quick to glance away again. All the excitement Sophie had felt about the coded message immediately rushed away, like the air out of a burst balloon. Apparently now even Mrs Milton was suspicious of her.

'Well, my dears,' Mrs Milton began briskly. 'I know that the opening days have been rather upsetting. But we must try very hard to all pull together. Pull together – and do our best. That's what Mr Sinclair wants. We have the opening party coming up on Saturday, which as you know, will be a very special occasion: everything must be absolutely faultless for Mr Sinclair's guests.

'Now, I have an announcement to make. As you know, I have been thinking carefully about who should be appointed as my assistant. This morning I have been discussing the matter in detail with Mr Cooper, and I'm pleased to say that we have decided that my new assistant will be . . . Edith!'

One or two of the girls gasped in surprise, and though Violet began to clap, she soon faltered awkwardly and let her hands drop. Astonishment flooded Edith's face, but was swiftly replaced by a look of triumph.

'Well done to Edith,' said Mrs Milton, rather hurriedly. 'Her new role will be in effect as of today. And now I see we have customers coming, so we must get to work.' Some of the girls were still whispering and staring, and she flapped at them with her hands, suddenly cross. 'Come along, Ellie, don't dawdle.'

She hurried back to work, the girls following obediently behind her. Sophie came last of all, feeling sick at heart.

Leaving Lil to return to the mannequins' dressing room to prepare for the afternoon's dress show, Billy ran back down the stairs, his heart thumping. He had been right – it really had been a coded message – and they had cracked it! Of course, it had actually been Lil who did the cracking. He shook his head for a moment, feeling slightly disgusted with himself. He was the one who knew about codes, yet it had been she who had used her brain and worked out the solution to the puzzle. *Deliver sparrow underground by ten. Baron.* He murmured the words over to himself again as he reached to the ground floor.

He had planned to go straight down to the basement to tell Joe what they had discovered and to ask him more about this Baron character, but he stopped suddenly in his tracks, remembering his earlier idea of examining the Exhibition Hall. Perhaps he could find some other clue, which, together with the coded message, would prove that the man known as 'the Baron' was beyond any possible doubt the one responsible for the burglary. After all, Lil might be quick when it came to working out that code, but he bet she didn't know anything about examining a crime scene. Full of enthusiasm now, he swerved in a different direction, going quickly through the door that led on to the shop floor, and cutting through the crowded Entrance Hall.

The door to the Exhibition Hall was still hung with the sign that read *Closed to the Public*. The door was probably locked, he thought, but when he touched the handle, he was surprised to find that it swung open quite easily. For a moment, he hesitated. He was quite sure of what both Uncle Sid and Mr Cooper would have to say about him going into the Exhibition Hall, when it had been made clear that it was out of bounds. But surely this was too important to be worrying about rules? He took a deep breath, looked swiftly around him to be sure that no one had noticed what he was up to, and then slipped quickly through the door.

The Exhibition Hall was completely empty. The big glass cases with their printed labels and velvet cushions were all standing empty: several were broken, and shards of shattered glass crunched underfoot. It looked as though it had been left exactly as it was immediately after the burglary. Moving as quietly as he could, he began to examine the cases, working his way slowly from one side of the room to the other. The only problem was that it was difficult to know quite what he should be looking for. There certainly weren't any of the usual things that Montgomery Baxter found when he was investigating: no little shreds of tobacco, no bullet holes or smears of paint. He carefully collected a tiny piece of black cotton he found snagged on a sharp edge of broken glass, but he couldn't help feeling that it wasn't very promising. Perhaps examining the scene of the crime hadn't been such a very good idea, after all.

Just outside, he heard the great clock in the Entrance Hall striking. He had been away from his duties for a long while, he realised – he ought to hurry back to work, before Uncle Sid noticed his absence and kicked up a fuss about it. All the same, he couldn't resist turning back one final time to examine the big cabinet where the clockwork sparrow had been displayed. He used the copy of *Boys of Empire* that was folded in his pocket to gently sweep away some of the shards of glass on the floor in front of it, and then caught his breath. There was actually something down there. Something so small, so insignificant that it must have been overlooked, caught in the narrowest of cracks in the smooth parquet floor.

Carefully he pulled it out and examined it, holding it delicately between finger and thumb. It was a long, narrow silver pin, its head fashioned into the unmistakable shape of a rose. He had done it – he had actually done it – he had found a clue!

Bursting with excitement, Billy turned and ran out of the room.

CHAPTER THIRTEEN

The pin with the silver rose lay in the palm of Sergeant Gregson's outstretched hand, and Sophie felt her heart drop to her boots. 'Well?' he asked again, a note of triumph in his voice.

'It's mine,' said Sophie, grimly.

Mr McDermott was watching her gravely. Of course, they must already know that the hatpin belonged to her. It was no use pretending that it didn't. She knew precisely what Sergeant Gregson would make of this. No matter that the pin could have fallen from her hat at any time, under perfectly innocent circumstances. The fact that it had been discovered in the Exhibition Hall, right beneath the cabinet where the clockwork sparrow had been displayed, would be more than enough to secure her guilt in his eyes.

'I see,' said Gregson, with satisfaction. 'I thought as much. And how exactly do you propose to explain this, Miss Taylor?'

'I don't attempt to,' said Sophie. 'I don't have any idea how it came to be there, but I don't believe it proves anything.' She was determined not to let Gregson intimidate her. 'I wear it often. I could have dropped it any time. You already know that I saw Mr Cooper in the Exhibition Hall on the way out of the store. Perhaps I dropped it then. It could easily have fallen out of my hat without me even noticing.'

Gregson contemplated her steadily. Beside him, Mr Cooper looked on with a solemn face, whilst in the corner of the room, Mr McDermott's expression was impassive.

'It seems odd that your men didn't notice it when you searched the Exhibition Hall before,' Sophie went on. 'Perhaps someone put it there.'

'Miss Taylor, please,' Gregson snapped. 'Are you seriously suggesting that someone intends to frame you?'

'I don't know. All I do know is that when my lodging-house room was searched – by your men – some of my things went missing. It seems rather convenient that my hatpin has now been found here, don't you think?'

Gregson's face clouded over. 'I am not sure exactly what you are implying, but I don't care for your tone, Miss Taylor. And what is all this about your lodgings being searched?'

'I'm sure you already know all about it, Sergeant.'

'On the contrary.'

'It was yesterday evening,' said Sophie, suddenly

disconcerted. 'Some policeman came to my rooms when I was out and they turned the place upside down. I assumed you had sent them.'

Gregson was staring at her. 'There has been no search of your lodgings authorised by me,' he said shortly. 'I can assure you of that.'

Sophie looked back at his stern face, confused. 'But – my landlady said they were policemen.'

'Did she really?' said Gregson sarcastically, looking as if he was entirely convinced the whole story was no more than her own ridiculous fabrication.

Awful fingers of cold dread began to sweep over her. It was clear that they didn't believe a word that she was saying. Gregson was writing notes; Mr Cooper wouldn't even meet her eye. What if they actually arrested her? Surely they couldn't do that – surely they wouldn't, not without any real evidence? Visions of dank police cells swam suddenly before her eyes. *Keep calm, keep your head, keep a stiff upper lip*, she told herself.

'Please listen to me – I didn't steal anything. I had nothing to do with this,' she said, trying to keep her voice steady. 'But – but I think I can tell you who did,' she finished, a note of desperation creeping in.

Gregson looked up suddenly from the notes he was writing. 'What?' he barked out.

'We were going to wait until we had found out more, but – well, we discovered something. A note, written in code.' She turned to Mr Cooper. 'It was in the stable-yard. Right where Bert was shot,' she added. 'It mentioned the sparrow and seemed to be from someone called "Baron".'

Mr Cooper glanced away, as if embarrassed. Gregson stared at her for a long moment. Then he suddenly began to laugh scornfully. 'Nonsense!' he said, finally. 'Utter poppycock! Coded messages – really Miss Taylor, this is beneath you. A man has been shot – this is a very serious matter. Please do not waste our time with this sort of bunkum. I have had quite enough for one day.'

Sophie's cheeks burned scarlet with mortification, but the sergeant wasn't even looking at her any more, instead he was blotting his paper with fastidious care. He nodded briskly to Mr Cooper, and the two left the room. Sophie could hear the buzz of their voices outside the door, but not what they were saying. The room was completely silent, but for Mr McDermott coughing once, a low, hollow sound.

After what felt like an eternity, the two men returned, but Gregson did not sit back down. 'That will be all for today, Miss Taylor,' he said shortly. 'But do not be deceived. We are watching you closely.'

He picked up his papers from the table and went out of the room again. McDermott nodded briefly to Sophie and

Cooper and then made his exit too. Sophie was trembling, but she knew that it was more from anger than it was from fear. How dare he speak to her like that – and dismiss what she had to say with such contempt? Mr Cooper was still sitting watching her gravely and she struggled to keep her composure.

'May I go now, sir?' she asked. She began to rise, but Cooper shook his head and gestured for her to sit back down.

'Sophie,' he began, placing his hands together, and her heart fell again at the sombre tone of his voice. 'I hope you realise that all this puts me in a most difficult position. You have already shown you are a very capable member of our staff. But all this suspicion is not good for the store. It is not good for the other staff. Sinclair's is the finest store in London: we simply cannot have this kind of atmosphere.' His voice dropped lower. 'If I could make an exception for you, I would. But the standard cannot be allowed to slip. I must be able to trust all my staff completely. I'm sorry, but I'm afraid I am going to have to let you go.'

Sophie gazed at him, dumbfounded. Of everything that could have happened, she had never expected this. 'But I didn't have anything to do with it, Mr Cooper! You must know I didn't! It's just . . . silly speculation, that's all!'

'I'm sorry, Sophie,' said Mr Cooper again. 'It's probably

best that you leave at once. Here are a week's wages.'

Sophie gazed disbelievingly at the long envelope he had placed in her hand, addressed to her in neat copperplate handwriting. After everything she had done to work hard and do the best she possibly could – all it came down to was this envelope. She was suddenly filled with a fiery desire to rip it into a million pieces in front of him.

Finally, as if conferring a great favour, Mr Cooper added: 'Perhaps I could send a letter of recommendation to Huntington's store?'

Huntington's! Sophie felt ill. She had heard that the salesgirls there were expected to work fourteen-hour days and to sleep in communal dormitories above the shop, but were paid only a few meagre shillings a week.

'You can go now,' said Cooper, rising from his chair. 'We shall be in touch if the police need any more help with their enquiries.'

Sophie was speechless. Somehow she found herself out of the office, still holding the envelope crumpled in her hand. Billy was there, catching hold of her arm, saying something to her in an urgent voice, but she couldn't distinguish any of his words.

'It doesn't matter,' she managed to mumble. 'They've let me go.'

All she could think was that she had to get out of the store as fast as possible, before anyone could see her. She hurried down the stairs, taking the most direct route through the shop. Everything seemed to blur around her: the looking-glasses, the palms, the cloud-painted ceiling. The light from the chandeliers fragmented and smeared before her eyes, but she didn't stop, elbowing her way past shoppers, muttering 'excuse me please,' dodging a porter with a stack of boxes, and finally pushing through the door that led to the cloakrooms. She put on her hat and coat and gloves and picked up her umbrella as if she were walking in her sleep. As she hurried towards the staff entrance and went down the steps, the shocked whispers of the shop girls and the salesmen, the porters and the drivers, seemed to boom and resound in her ears.

'They've dismissed her!'

'They've given her the old heave-ho!'

'Blimey, do you reckon she really *did* do it, then?'

It was only as she joined the crowds out on the street that Sophie realised she would never go back to Sinclair's again.

CHAPTER FOURTEEN

'**B**illy! *Billy!*'

Billy could hear Uncle Sid cursing him out in the yard, but he didn't move from the stable. He knew he would be in trouble when his uncle finally tracked him down, but he stayed where he was, close beside Bessy's comforting warmth as she quietly crunched sugar lumps from his palm.

'I thought you might be here,' said a voice behind him. Lil came up to stroke Bessy's nose too. 'Your uncle's making a jolly big row out there, looking for you.'

'He can chuck it,' said Billy furiously.

Lil looked at him keenly. 'It wasn't your fault, you know,' she said. 'You couldn't have had any idea that pin belonged to Sophie.'

'I should never have taken it to them.'

'How could you have known they would dismiss her? It's perfectly ghastly of them,' Lil shook her head, as if in disbelief. 'I wish I'd been able to see her before she left.

I'm going to go round to her lodgings just as soon as I've finished with the dress show and make sure she's all right.'

'I tried to go after her, but she just rushed off,' Billy went on, sounding rather mournful now. 'I just . . . really thought I could do something to help.'

'Well maybe you still can,' said Lil. 'You mustn't give up now. You're the one who knows about this sort of thing, aren't you? You're the one who guessed that message was a code. So buck up, and help me think. What do we do now?'

Billy looked up, surprised to hear the purposefulness in her voice. For a moment he looked unsure, then the wisp of a smile came over his face. 'All right,' he said. 'I will. We ought to go and talk to Joe.'

'Joe?' Lil's brown eyes flamed with interest. 'The one who saw the shooting? Is he still nearby, then?'

Billy had forgotten that Lil and Sophie didn't know he was hiding Joe in the basement. If he told Lil, she might want to go and report him to Mr Cooper. He hesitated for a moment, unsure of whether or not to trust her. Then he made up his mind.

'He's in the basement,' he said briefly. 'He's hiding there.'

'Why?' asked Lil.

'Nowhere else to go. He was in a gang and now they're after him. I found a place for him to hide out – just until his arm gets better, you know.'

'Gosh – but what if Cooper finds him down there?'

'I don't think he will. Joe's good at hiding.'

Lil took this in for a moment. 'Can I come and meet him?' she asked.

Billy shrugged. 'If you want,' he said.

Once again, they descended into the basement, and went along the deserted corridors towards the empty storerooms. Lil was following Billy this time: it was obvious that he knew his way much better now. He led the way down a couple of long, snaking passages, until they came to a room with two high windows that let in slanting rays of light. It looked deserted, so Lil was startled when Billy gave a low whistle and a boy appeared, as if he had materialised out of the shadows. He looked equally surprised to see her standing beside Billy, and immediately took a step backwards.

'This is Lil,' said Billy, gesturing to her in an awkward attempt at an introduction. 'She's a friend of Sophie's. This is Joe.'

Coming closer, Lil took in the young man. He was probably about sixteen, her own age, tall and square-shouldered, but very gaunt and thin. His dark hair was messy and tangled, and his dark-shadowed eyes slid quickly away from hers. His injured arm was bound up with a dirty cloth, and the rest of his clothes looked old and shabby. He glanced at her uncertainly, and sensing his discomfort, she sat down on a box in the corner of the room, letting Billy talk. He was already telling Joe about all that had happened in the last few hours: the hatpin, Sophie's dismissal and the coded message. As Billy related what it had said, Joe looked astonished, and all at once, his wariness seemed to fall away.

'I don't believe it!' he exclaimed. 'I don't blooming believe it! I came all the way over here to be rid of him, and blow me if the Baron ain't here too.'

'But who is he – this Baron?' asked Lil, finally losing her struggle to stay quiet.

'He's the man that Joe used to work for,' said Billy. 'He's the boss of a big East End gang.'

Joe snorted. 'Not just any boss. *The* boss. The Baron's the biggest fish there is – finger in every pie. I suppose he's got a finger in this one too. I should've known.' He gazed at them both for a long moment, then shook his head. 'I can't believe that neither of you has ever heard of the Baron.'

'This must have been his instructions,' Billy was saying, taking out his piece of paper again. 'A coded message, telling someone to steal the sparrow that night.'

Lil gazed at it, intrigued. 'I wish we understood what the instructions mean. It's so jolly mysterious. Do you think *underground* might mean the underground railway?'

'What I really want to know is why it's the sparrow that is so important,' said Billy slowly. 'There were heaps of other

151

valuable things taken that night. But this only mentions the sparrow.'

'Sophie said that Sergeant Gregson – that's the policeman – was awfully keen on talking about the sparrow,' Lil remembered. 'It's special, isn't it? Not only because it's worth a lot, but because it's so unusual.'

'And there's a separate reward for finding it, too. It was mentioned particularly in the Captain's advertisement,' Billy remembered.

Lil looked up at Joe. 'Are you absolutely sure you didn't recognise the man who dropped this? If it was someone working for this Baron person – and if you worked for him too – then maybe it might have been someone you'd seen before.'

Joe shook his head. 'I couldn't get a good look at his face,' he explained. 'It was dark and he was just wearing normal clothes – a cap and a jacket with the collar up, nothing to make him stand out. I tell you what, though, he weren't one of the Baron's Boys. I reckon I'd have recognised any of them right enough.' He paused for a moment, scratching his head thoughtfully. 'But the Baron's got all sorts of folk in his pocket. It could've been anyone.'

They all sat in silence for a moment, letting this sink in. Lil found herself staring hard at the message, as if she could will it into giving up the answers they were searching for.

'I just can't believe that they've sacked Sophie,' said Billy at last.

Lil shook her head. 'I don't think it makes the slightest bit of sense,' she said again. 'Why would they sack her? Surely they can't be such idiots as to really believe she could be involved in this. She's a shop girl, not some sort of . . . master jewel thief.'

'It was the pin – that's what convinced them,' said Billy, sounding rather mournful.

'That silly old pin didn't prove anything at all!' said Lil crossly. She paused for a moment and then went on, more hesitantly. 'I know it sounds a bit potty, but don't you think it's all been rather convenient? I mean, Sophie was at the scene on the night, and then Gregson interviews her, and everyone suddenly believes she was involved, and then her hatpin just happens to turn up at the scene of the crime.'

'You mean maybe someone put the hatpin there? On purpose?'

'Perhaps. Maybe someone is going out of their way to make it look like Sophie is guilty – or at least to keep everyone's attention on her, instead of on what really happened. On this fellow the Baron, or whoever else was behind it all.'

Joe considered this. 'You might just be right about that. There's something fishy about this whole business, I reckon. I tell you what, I'd be watching them coppers. Gregson and that other fellow too, the detective. The Baron's probably straightened 'em up.'

'Do you mean *bribed* them?' asked Lil, fascinated.

Joe gave an experienced nod. 'Given them a few quid, got them to look the other way when he wants them to. He does it all the time. Half the coppers in London are as crooked as they come. They'll do more or less anything for a bit of bread and honey.'

'Hang on a minute,' said Lil, her eyes widening. 'Sophie knew what the message said, didn't she? She knew about the Baron.'

'Yes, but she didn't know who he was,' said Billy, frowning.

'But when she was being interviewed, maybe she told them what we found out.'

'That's it then!' said Joe, realising what Lil was getting at. 'That's why. If she told them what she knew – and if they are working for the Baron – she'll have put the wind up them good and proper, won't she? I reckon they'll have told your Mr Cooper she wasn't to be trusted and to give her the push. Get her out of the way before she sends anyone sniffing around in the Baron's direction.'

Billy's brow was furrowed. 'So what on earth do we do now, then?' he said after a moment. 'I mean, if the police can't be trusted – then who do we go to with what we know? Should we tell Cooper?'

'I don't think Mr Cooper will listen to us,' said Lil, shaking her head. 'He obviously trusts the police, and we would need real proof, something more than the message. After all, Sophie's already told him about that, and if Gregson has told him not to believe her, he's bound to be suspicious. For all he knows, we could have written it ourselves.'

'You want to get some dirt on those coppers,' said Joe. 'If you can prove they're being paid off, I don't reckon the high-ups would be too pleased with them.'

'There's something in that,' said Billy thoughtfully. 'But how?'

Lil shrugged. 'Well, we know exactly where Gregson is working,' she said. 'In Cooper's office. We could wait until he's out of the way and then have a good poke about and see what we find.'

Billy looked at her in alarm, not at all liking this suggestion. His last bit of investigation had, after all, ended in disaster. The Exhibition Hall had been one thing, but Cooper's office was quite another – and if the last few hours had proved anything to him, it was just how easy it could be to be dismissed from Sinclair's. 'I'm not sure that would be a very good idea,' he said warily.

'Well, what else can we do?' said Lil, looking impatient. 'I'm going to go and look, even if you're not.'

'All right, all right,' said Billy hastily. 'I'll do it. But let's not just rush off. We need to find the right moment, when we shan't be spotted.'

From high above them, outside in the yard, they dimly heard a familiar voice yelling: 'Billy! I don't have time for this! Get here, you little skiver, or I'll tan you till you can't sit down!'

Billy heaved a deep sigh. 'I'd better go and get it over with,' he said. 'The longer I stay away the worse he'll be.' He gave Joe a quick nod. 'I'll be back later on with some grub, if I can get away.'

To Joe's surprise, Lil didn't immediately follow Billy out of the room, but instead sat still, contemplating him with her long-lashed brown eyes. It had been one thing when there were three of them talking together, but now they were alone, he felt as awkward as when she'd first walked in. He'd never seen a girl anything like her before.

'What happened to your arm?' she was asking.

'Chap went for it with a shiv.' His voice came out sounding rough and brusque.

'A shiv? What's that?'

'A long blade. Like a razor.'

'Gosh,' she said lightly. 'Mind if I take a look?'

Without waiting for him to say yes or no, she took hold of his arm and rolled back his sleeve briskly. Her fingers felt warm: her touch was light. Joe was very conscious of how close she was, and felt disorientated for a moment, but then she peeled back the rough bandage, and the sudden stab of pain brought him back to himself.

'Sorry,' she said. 'It doesn't look so good. I think it ought to be properly cleaned. I'll bring some stuff to dress it for you tomorrow.' She rolled his sleeve briskly back into place. 'You look like you could do with a decent meal, too,' she said. 'Billy's a good chap, but I don't believe he's exactly what you'd call practical. I'll bring you some proper food – and some old clothes of my brother's, if you like?'

Joe shrugged uneasily. Lil smiled at him, and for a moment he was dazzled.

'All right then. I'd better go.' But as she stepped towards the door, Joe heard something. Acting on instinct, he pulled her quickly back, motioning to her to be still and quiet. There came the sound of swift, decided footsteps, passing the door of the little room.

'Wasn't that Mr Cooper?' whispered Lil, after they'd gone.

'The starchy looking chap with the beard? I reckon so. He's been down here half a dozen times. Always goes off down that way towards where those furs are kept. Must be keeping a careful check on them, I reckon. But it's no trouble to me to stay out of his way.'

He came to a sudden stop, as if exhausted by such a long speech. But Lil was hanging on to his words.

'The fur storage room?' she asked. 'How funny. I wonder if there's something really special down there. Or maybe Cooper's got some sort of sordid secret he's hiding amongst the sables.' She laughed, and Joe stared at her, fascinated and confused. I really must go,' she said. 'I'll see you later.'

He stood and watched as she slipped out into the passage, peering around carefully for any sign of Cooper before she went. He fingered his arm uncertainly: it felt different where she had touched it. He settled back down in his hidden corner again, but the room seemed suddenly very empty now that she had gone.

'I'm still not sure about this, you know,' Billy said doubtfully. It was nearing the end of the day, and he and Lil were hovering outside the door to Mr Cooper's office.

'Don't bottle it now. We're doing this to help Sophie, remember?'

Billy couldn't help feeling annoyed. 'Yes, but we won't be able to help Sophie much if we both get caught and get the sack too.' Lil was actually enjoying this, he realised, seeing how her eyes were sparking with mischief.

Now she huffed a small sigh of impatience. 'We aren't *going* to get caught. I heard Gregson say he'd be gone for at least half an hour. Come on . . . we haven't got all day. I want to go and see Sophie on my way to the theatre, remember?

And I really mustn't be late for the rehearsal.'

With that, she slipped quickly through the door and inside Mr Cooper's office. Billy followed reluctantly. Like everything that the store manager touched, it was neat as could be: books ranged in perfect rows on the shelves, an upright, rectangular clock ticking on the mantelpiece, and nothing at all, not a plant or an ornament was out of place, Billy thought ruefully.

Lil was already at the desk, rapidly turning over the papers that lay across it. From the way that they had been left, there was no doubt that they must belong to Gregson: Billy couldn't imagine that Cooper would ever leave things spread about like that.

'Don't make such a mess,' he whispered to Lil. 'He'll know someone has been in here.'

Lil rolled her eyes, but began to look through the papers in a more orderly fashion. For several minutes, there was silence but for the sound of rustling paper.

'There's nothing here,' she said, after some time had passed.

'Keep your voice down!' hissed Billy in alarm. 'Cooper could be nearby for all we know.'

'It's all just terrifically boring paperwork,' said Lil, only a touch more quietly. 'Mind you, what were we really expecting to find? I mean, he was hardly going to leave out a nice juicy cheque, signed *Baron*. If he really is being bribed, I suppose he wouldn't be fool enough to write it down.'

Billy was trying his best to decipher a pile of notes in an almost illegible handwriting. 'We have to look through everything carefully,' he said. 'The evidence might be anywhere. It could just be something very small.'

'I don't think any of this is going to tell us anything,' said Lil. 'If there is evidence, they're bound to have put it safely away out of sight.'

Billy glanced up at the clock on the mantelpiece and started. 'Look at the time! We should go.'

'Wait a moment,' said Lil, gesturing to a small mahogany bureau that stood against the wall. 'Look at that – all those drawers and cubbyholes. That's exactly the sort of place you might hide something.'

'We don't have time,' Billy urged. 'They could be back any minute. Come *on*!' He quietly pushed the door open, glanced along the corridor to make sure no one was there, and then slipped out.

Paying no attention to Billy, Lil stayed where she was, examining the bureau. Most of the drawers seemed to contain only stationery, ink-bottles, pen-nibs and blotting paper – and the rest were carefully locked. How like Mr Cooper, she thought in frustration. She was just about to give up, when she came across a folded piece of paper. It was a telegram. She gazed at it for a moment, but just then she heard the door open, and she jumped back from the bureau in time to see a strange man enter the room.

Lil was never flustered. She gave him a dazzling smile. 'Oh – hello,' she said blithely. ' I was waiting for Mr Cooper.'

'Sergeant Gregson is using this office at present.'

'I'm so sorry, I didn't know,' said Lil, a little taken aback that her smile didn't seem to be having its usual effect on this person – a tall, greying man who she didn't recognise. 'Please pardon the intrusion. I don't suppose you can tell me where I might find Mr Cooper?'

'You'll find him in the office just across the way, Miss – er . . .'

'Rose. Lilian Rose. Thank you very much.'

With a final smile, Lil strolled out of the room, the crumpled telegram balled in the palm of her hand. As soon as the door was shut firmly behind her, she raced off round the corner, where she found Billy waiting looking very agitated.

'I *told* you we had to leave! That was Mr McDermott – the private detective! He didn't find you in there, did he?'

Lil grinned. 'He did. But it didn't matter. I simply told him I was waiting for Mr Cooper, and he believed me. I'm an *actress*, remember? This is what I do. I promise you, he didn't suspect a thing.'

CHAPTER FIFTEEN

Sophie put on her hat without bothering to check whether it was at the right angle, or whether her hair was tidy. She had spent a restless night reliving every second of yesterday's terrible interview with Sergeant Gregson. And even when she had at last fallen asleep, her dreams had been troubled.

Now, in the hazy morning light, yesterday seemed like the memory of a nightmare. She could still scarcely believe it had happened. The thought of what the other staff at Sinclair's must now be thinking and saying about her made her feel sticky all over with hot shame.

The strange thing was that what she minded most was being sent away from Sinclair's itself. She was surprised to realise how much the store had come to mean to her. All that beauty ... There was nothing beautiful here in the bare lodging-house room, she thought, looking around at the peeling walls, the empty mantelshelf, the bed with its faded eiderdown. Once again she had been torn away from a place she loved and people that she cared about, she thought bitterly.

She struggled to swallow the lump that was threatening to rise in her throat. She had to pull herself together. She would simply have to look for another job, that was all.

But she would not be looking for work in another shop, she thought soberly. No ordinary draper's shop, nor even another of the big London department stores like Huntington's could ever compare with Sinclair's. She would have to find something else to do. Perhaps she could be a music teacher, she thought. Miss Pennyfeather had always said she had a good ear. But she hadn't been near a piano for months, not since she left Orchard House, and surely she would need a good deal of practice before she could approach the standard that would be expected of a teacher. Drawing, perhaps? Her Papa had often praised her drawings, and unlike dear old Miss Pennyfeather, he wasn't in the least given to exaggeration. But she would be expected to have references – or at least the names of other pupils she had taught. It was no good – she was just too young and inexperienced to teach anyone anything.

A nursery-maid then? That couldn't be too bad? Or maybe she could become a paid companion to some wealthy elderly lady? She couldn't possibly need any special experience to do that. There was bound to be something she could do, she said to herself as she put on her gloves, noticing as she did so that the finger-ends were wearing thin. She would place an advertisement in *The Lady*. '*Reliable young lady seeks respectable employment.*' She concentrated on how she would word it as she went down the stairs and out into the early morning rain.

The truth was that she had not wanted to go out at all that morning. What she had wanted to do more than anything else was to stay inside, far away from everything and everyone that had anything to do with Sinclair's. But Lil had turned up at her rooms the previous evening, running late for a rehearsal and in a tearing hurry, but so terribly insistent that Sophie must come and meet her first thing the next morning, that she simply hadn't been able to refuse. She had been surprised and pleased that Lil had come at all. Anyway, she could call at the offices of *The Lady* and place her advertisement while she was out; and besides, surely anything was better than having to endure breakfast at the lodging house, putting up with the girls' scandalised whispers.

She found Lil sheltering from the rain in the bandstand where they had agreed to meet in the park not far from Sinclair's. Sitting beside her were Billy and a shabby-looking young man that she guessed must be Joe, the one who had seen the shooting. All three were tucking into what looked like a bag of buns and, in spite of everything, a smile crept on to Sophie's face at the thought of what Miss Pennyfeather would make of her eating buns out of a bag in the park in the company of a chorus girl, a shop porter and a youth who, as far as she had been able to understand from Lil's garbled explanations yesterday evening, was on the run from some sort of an East End gang.

'Sophie!' called Lil, grinning a welcome and waving a bun in her direction. 'Come and meet Joe.'

'I'm ever so sorry about what happened at the shop,' Billy plunged in, before anyone else could say anything. 'I never even thought – it's all my fault –' He broke off, looking upset.

Sophie took a seat beside Lil, accepted a bun from the bag. 'It wasn't your fault,' she told Billy. 'You were only trying to help.'

'We're all sorry about what happened,' said Lil.

Sophie tried to smile, but she began to feel uncomfortable with all of their eyes on her, so full of sympathy. Even Joe looked as though he felt sorry for her. She remembered now that she had seen him at Sinclair's just a few days ago – yes and given him her shilling, too! Then, she had been the one who had felt sorry for him: now she was suddenly the one that everyone pitied. 'You need to hear about everything else we found out yesterday,' Lil was saying. 'You tell her, Billy.'

His anxiety seemingly forgotten now, Billy began to relate the story of the previous day, with Lil interrupting often, and Joe weighing in to explain about the Baron. 'So,' Billy wound up, 'what we believe is that the Baron orchestrated the burglary. He's paid off the police to help him cover it up, and they've used you to distract attention from what really happened.'

Sophie had been listening intently, still holding the bun, which she had quite forgotten to eat, her forehead scrunched into a frown. Could it possibly be that an East End gang and some corrupt policemen were trying to set her up? It sounded more like something from one of Billy's story papers or one of Lil's plays than the truth.

Feeling rather as though she were pouring cold water on their excitement, she said: 'I can see that it perhaps makes sense that this man, the Baron, was involved in the burglary. After all, we have seen that message, and from what you say, Joe, it sounds like the sort of thing that he might do. But I can't believe that Gregson could be working for him. I mean, I know he's been awfully unfair – but that doesn't necessarily mean that he's crooked. And what about Bert? Someone tried to *kill him*. Surely the police wouldn't cover up an attempted murder?'

Joe rolled his eyes, but before he could say anything, Lil took a paper from her pocket, with the air of a magician producing a white rabbit from a hat. 'Look at this,' she said, handing it over.

Sophie took the flimsy, creased piece of paper: a telegram addressed to Sergeant Gregson.

'I found this yesterday in the office,' Lil explained. 'We went to have a look around to see if we could find anything that would point to them working with the Baron. It looked awfully funny to me, and I thought it might be another code. Billy took it home with him and worked out what it said.'

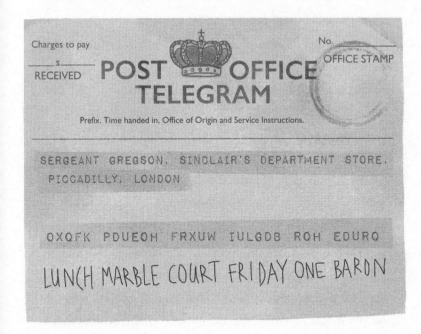

Charges to pay

s

RECEIVED

No.

OFFICE STAMP

POST OFFICE TELEGRAM

Prefix. Time handed in. Office of Origin and Service Instructions.

SERGEANT GREGSON, SINCLAIR'S DEPARTMENT STORE, PICCADILLY, LONDON

OXQFK PDUEOH FRXUW IULGDB ROH EDURQ

LUNCH MARBLE COURT FRIDAY ONE BARON

'It's from him,' said Sophie slowly. She glanced keenly up at them. 'How on earth did you work it out?' she asked, shaking her head in astonishment.

Billy shrugged, his face growing rather pink. 'I don't know. When I started looking at it, playing around like last time, I realised that he'd used a method called the Caesar cipher – I read about it once in *Pluck* magazine. Julius Caesar used it in his letters to keep their contents secret, you know. It's quite straightforward: you just replace each letter with one three letters further on in the alphabet. So an "A" becomes a "D", you see?'

Sophie sat still, not saying anything for a moment, holding the telegram. Then she said: 'So it's true. The police really are involved in this.' She sounded calm, but her eyes were blazing. 'Gregson had me sacked on purpose. He's used me as a scapegoat.'

'That's what it seems like,' said Billy quietly.

'But listen, Sophie,' said Lil, leaning forward. 'We aren't going to let them get away with it. Lunch Marble Court Friday One? It's Friday tomorrow. By the sounds of it, Gregson is going to be meeting the Baron in the Marble Court Restaurant at Sinclair's for lunch at one o'clock. We have a real chance to actually go and find out who the Baron is – or at least what he looks like – and maybe to prove that Gregson is in his pay!'

Joe had been sitting silently for some time. Now he shifted uneasily and spoke up: 'Hang on half a minute,' he began. 'Begging your pardon, miss – I don't want to be rude, but you're off your nut if you're thinking of going after the Baron like that. It's not that I don't reckon you're right – course it ain't fair that you lost your job,' he said, nodding to Sophie. 'But I don't think you've got a notion of who you'd be taking on. The Baron – he's not one of your soft-handed shop fellers. He's a villain: he's dangerous and he's clever. You'd never get near him – and if you did, you'd never be able to pin anything on him. Even if you could, it'd be more than your life's worth. You want to prove that you had nothing to do with this robbery – or even that this copper is bent, you go ahead. But don't go meddling with the Baron. You'd best steer well clear of him, else you'll be up to your necks in it.'

'In what?' asked Lil.

'Trouble, that's what,' said Joe, his face serious. 'Look at that bloke that got shot, for starters.'

'But you must see that we jolly well can't just ignore this,' said Lil more coaxingly. 'The Baron is going to be at Sinclair's tomorrow, and we have the chance to actually get a *look* at him. What harm could there be in just looking?'

'It's an intelligence mission,' said Billy, grandly. 'We aren't going to actually do anything. We're just going to go and see him and – and gather information,' he finished.

'No, Joe's right,' said Sophie. 'Look what has happened to me, just through being in the wrong place at the wrong time. If they know you're watching them, it could be really dangerous. I won't risk anyone else losing their job – or worse – because of this.'

Lil shook her head. 'They won't know that we're watching them. We'll be careful.' She gazed at Sophie seriously, her dark eyes clear. 'We can't sit back and do nothing; you must see that. It just wouldn't be right.'

Sophie looked back at Lil, seeing the resolve on her face. 'No, I suppose not,' she said at last, feeling acutely grateful for Lil's friendship. The lump was threatening to rise in her throat again, and it was a moment or two before she felt able to say, in an ordinary voice: 'Well, in that case you'll just have to make sure you draw no attention to yourselves whatsoever.'

'You'll need a blooming good reason to be in this restaurant place, as well,' added Joe, still looking doubtful.

'Well, we shan't be going there to have lunch, that's for sure,' muttered Billy, half to himself. He had recently seen the prices on the restaurant menu and was still faintly disgusted by the discovery that a single Dover sole cost almost as much as his full week's wages. 'Not unless one of you has recently come into a fortune, that is.'

'That's it!' squealed Lil suddenly.

'What?'

'I've got the *perfect* reason to be there,' she said, looking very pleased with herself. 'I'm going to be a fortune hunter!'

'I beg your pardon?' demanded Sophie.

Lil gave a little wriggle of excitement. 'There are lots of fellows who hang around the theatre after rehearsals, waiting for the chorus girls to come out. Stage Door Johnnies, they call them,' she explained. 'Some of the older girls love it – the ones who are looking for a rich husband who we call the fortune hunters. Anyway, there's this one young fellow, Mr Pendleton, who has been pestering me ever since I started at the theatre, always wanting to take me out or some stuff and nonsense. The other girls told me he's frightfully rich – the son of some factory owner, I think. Plenty of spare cash to splash around. So perhaps I might relent and let him take me to lunch tomorrow – but only if we dine at the Marble Court Restaurant, of course!'

Sophie laughed suddenly. 'Lil, you can't possibly ask a strange young man to take you to lunch so you can spy on someone,' she said.

'Why ever not? I was thinking that I might say yes anyway. He's only a silly boy really – but just think of the food! It's bound to be an awful lot better than that rotten old refectory.'

'Wait a minute, though,' said Billy, his mind moving

quickly on to practical matters. 'The restaurant is enormous. What if they seat you right on the other side from Gregson?' He smoothed out the bag that had contained the buns, and sketched out a floorplan with the stub of a pencil. 'Look. Two main entrances: one where the lifts come up, and one where the main staircase is.'

'Three,' said Sophie, leaning over. 'There's the smaller flight of stairs that comes up in that back left hand corner too.'

'And there are four different sections,' Billy went on. 'You might not even be able to *see* Gregson from wherever you are. How could you possibly watch the whole place?'

'Well it won't just be me there, will it? You'll be there too.'

'And what possible reason would I have for being there?' said Billy impatiently. 'I can't go there for luncheon!'

'You're a porter,' said Sophie, thinking it out. 'You've got reason to be almost anywhere. There are porters all over the place at Sinclair's. No one will take a bit of notice of you, as long as you seem to be busy. If anyone questioned you, you could always say you'd been sent up with a parcel or a message.'

'You could even say it was a message for me,' added Lil, her eyes glinting at the thought of this new plan.

Sophie had crumbled her uneaten bun and was now

feeding a couple of sparrows that had hopped on to the steps of the bandstand. 'I just wish I could be there too,' she said, sounding frustrated.

Joe shook his head. 'You're better off out of it,' he said, shortly. 'And the pair of you better make sure he doesn't set eyes on you.' He found himself unable to repress a slight shiver. The very idea of the Baron actually being in the same building as him – even if it was five floors above – seemed unreal, like one of his nightmares coming to life. *Rather them than me*, he thought grimly. He still couldn't help thinking they were a set of fools.

They went their separate ways not long after that: Billy and Joe to go back to Sinclair's, whilst Sophie and Lil strolled out of the park together sharing an umbrella.

'I say – you are going to come to the first night of my show on Saturday, aren't you?' Lil asked suddenly. 'I'll get you a ticket, of course.'

Sophie almost laughed. With all that had happened in the last few days, it seemed bizarre that she was being asked to attend a musical comedy.

But Lil seemed quite serious. 'Do say you'll come,' she pleaded, looking uncharacteristically anxious. 'Otherwise I won't have anyone in the audience. My brother's away, and I can't invite my parents. They'd die a dozen deaths to see me part of a chorus line. But I can't bear to be the only one of the girls without anyone watching. I'm certain I'd do much better if I knew you were there.'

Sophie was touched. 'Of course I'll be there,' she said, feeling that she couldn't let Lil down.

She was rewarded with a beaming smile. 'Marvellous! I would say come round to the Stage Door afterwards and we could do something jolly, but I've got to go straight to Sinclair's afterwards for this beastly opening party. Apparently the Captain wants all the mannequins there.' She pulled a face, although Sophie suspected that really Lil thought the party would be anything but beastly. And who could blame her? Everyone knew that Mr Sinclair's opening gala would be one of the social events of the year, and Sophie realised with a stab of disappointment that now she wouldn't have the chance to see it for herself. But Lil was still talking: 'Anyway, I'm awfully glad you can come to the show. I'll get you the absolute best ticket I can!' Her enthusiasm was infectious, and somehow, in spite of everything, Sophie found herself smiling as they left the park.

CHAPTER SIXTEEN

'That's the last lot, Tom!'

'About time too,' complained one of the porters, wiping his forehead with a handkerchief after filling yet another van with an enormous load of boxes. It was mid-morning on Friday, and already it had been a hectic day for the drivers and porters, as they tried to keep pace with the ever-increasing volume of deliveries, as more and more customers surged through the store.

'They'll be needing to take on more fellers, I reckon, if it keeps on at this rate,' said George.

'The Captain must be making a mint,' said Tom.

'Wish he'd send a bit more of it over my way,' grumbled another porter. 'I reckon we deserve a few bob extra, the pace we're going at.'

George called out, 'Billy! Tea!'

Billy came hurrying over from where he had been packing another van, just as one of the kitchen maids appeared with their morning tea. As they had taken to doing when the weather was fine, the drivers and porters drank their tea all together in the yard, standing about in little groups, or leaning against the wall, smoking. George usually sat on a chair and read the paper, commenting on whatever was in the news that day. This morning he had already covered Russian refugees and the British Navy's new warships, which he was sure would prove to that Kaiser who was boss, and he was now shaking his head over the theft of the Captain's jewels. Although the story was no longer making front-page news, the papers had not yet tired of speculating about who was behind it.

'Now they're saying it was immigrants. Or one of them criminal gangs,' he said, scratching his chin pensively. 'There's a lot of that going on out east around the docks these days, or that's what I hear.'

Billy wrapped his hands around his mug of tea, made very strong and sweet, and sipped appreciatively. 'Have you ever heard of a gang run by someone called "the Baron"?' he asked suddenly.

George nearly dropped his mug in astonishment. He pushed back his chair. 'Blimey, what d'you want to go saying things like that for? Give me a heart attack, why don't you?'

'Wherever did a shrimp like you hear about the Baron?' asked Tom, with a laugh.

Billy shrugged, trying to seem casual. 'Oh, I just heard someone talking about him, and I wondered who he was.'

'Listen, son, you don't want to know nothing about the Baron,' said George in a low, serious voice.

'Oh, come off it, George,' snorted one of the porters, flicking a cigarette end to the ground. 'The Baron? He's nothing but an old tale.'

'There's some good yarns about him though,' said Tom. 'Remember the one about the Limehouse Lads? That was one to make your hair stand on end, all right.'

'Or the Bride of Hoxton? And what he did to her? Stuff of nightmares, that.'

'All right, not in front of the boy,' said George sharply. 'You can keep your filthy stories for after hours. Come on, let's get back to work. You come with me, lad,' he said to Billy, who trailed after him obediently. 'I'll tell you the only thing you need to know about the Baron,' George muttered as he did so. 'You want to stay as far away from him as you can get.'

Billy headed back to work, an anxious feeling rising in his stomach as he realised that in just a couple of hours' time, he and Lil were planning to do exactly the opposite.

Sinclair's Marble Court Restaurant was a picture of perfect elegance. Waiters in white coats glided to and fro between the marble columns that gave the restaurant its name, bearing silver dishes and trays of crystal glasses. Beneath a ceiling adorned with a pattern of golden swirls and flourishes, there was the civilised buzz of conversation, the clinking of glasses, a pop as a champagne bottle was opened. The few faint rays of sunlight that crept in at the stained-glass windows sparkled on the diamonds of the American heiress who was holding a luncheon party for twenty on one side of the restaurant.

A handsome waiter bowed to Lil as she came through the door looking nervously around her for any sign of Gregson. She felt suddenly very conscious that her lawn tea-gown, and her best hat with the crimson poppies, which had seemed pretty enough in her own bedroom, were far too plain and ordinary for her surroundings. At least her frock was new: she had bought it at the store with her first pay packet, at the generous discount afforded to all the Captain's Girls. And young Mr Pendleton certainly did not seem to object to her appearance. As a matter of fact, he leaped to his feet as soon as he saw her approaching, almost knocking over a vase of flowers in his eagerness.

As she took her seat, she glimpsed Billy across the room, very nearly hidden in a corner behind a large arrangement of hothouse flowers not far from the restaurant entrance. She guessed by the way he was glancing around that he hadn't seen any sign of Gregson yet, either. She looked quickly away in case she drew attention to him, and flashed a charming smile at Mr Pendleton, whose face went purple with gratification. But even as she accepted the menu card from the waiter, she felt uneasy. Whether it was because they were watching for Gregson, or because she was worried about Sophie, or simply because of the opening night of the show that evening, she felt suddenly tense and twitchy with nerves.

All around her was a flurry of chatter:

'Oh, Mama, must I really have that dreary mauve? The pink taffeta was so much prettier!'

'Herbert Gladstone needs to come to his senses. This is an out and out threat! We are an island nation, for heaven's sake – Germany is not. What possible reason could there be for them to have a naval force to match our own?'

'Do try the oysters, old boy – they're simply splendid. I say, waiter, more champagne, please.'

'Well, you see, then the poor beast went lame, and I had to change horses, and –' Pendleton was talking too. He had begun telling an incredibly long story about a recent hunting party. Lil nodded and smiled, as if she was listening, but really her attention was fixed breathlessly on the figure that was even now striding past Pendleton's shoulder. It was Sergeant Gregson – she recognised his round spectacles and bushy moustache. He was really here!

He settled himself at a table just out of her eyeline, and she leaned slightly to one side to see him a little better. He was sitting alone, fiddling with the menu card nervously. She had never really thought of someone like Gregson being nervous, but then, being secretly on the Baron's payroll was probably a rather worrying business. She leaned over a little further and accidentally knocked her butter knife off the edge of the table, sending it skittering across the floor.

'Are you all right, Miss Rose?' asked Pendleton anxiously as a waiter swiftly whisked away the knife and replaced it with a clean one.

'Oh yes, of course. I'm so sorry Mr Pendleton, I was so busy listening to you that I didn't notice what I was doing!' she laughed, her cheeks flushing, trying to conceal her annoyance. Now she'd have to pay attention to this tedious hunting story and she wouldn't be able to get a decent look at Gregson. But even as she turned back towards Pendleton, there was a sudden bubble of movement and noise by the lifts. Across the room, heads swivelled to look, and all at once she realised why: it was none other than the Captain himself who had strolled into the restaurant, elegant in his morning suit, a cream-coloured orchid in his buttonhole.

'So that's Edward Sinclair?' said Pendleton, a little too loudly. 'He's quite a fellow, isn't he?'

Lil watched with interest as Sinclair nodded to several of

the gentlemen diners, gave a gallant bow to a lady in furs, and paused to say a word to the head waiter. There were two men with him who must be journalists, she realised: one was scribbling in a notebook, the other, a rather jolly-looking chap, was manoeuvring a big camera. Behind them was the prim young woman who she recognised as Miss Atwood, Sinclair's private secretary. Lil remembered her from her interview with Mr Sinclair. She'd sat to one side, reluctantly holding the Captain's little dog on her very rigid knees.

'I've never imagined Sinclair's as merely a store,' Lil heard Sinclair saying to one of the journalists as he passed by, lines of waiters bowing on all sides. 'It's not just a shop – it's a cathedral, a museum.' He made a sweeping gesture that encompassed everything around him, whilst the young journalist scribbled faster in his notebook, evidently determined to capture every word. 'Sinclair's is a monument to style and elegance, beauty and charm. It is . . . a civic centre. Somewhere people can meet and mingle. An escape from the humdrum, the everyday. A place to *dream*.'

'Mr Sinclair, if I could just ask you . . .' the journalist was saying, his voice fading away as they passed out of their earshot, whilst the photographer struggled behind him with his bulky camera equipment. As they went by, Lil glanced up and caught her breath. Whilst everyone had been looking at Sinclair, a man had appeared across the table from Sergeant

Gregson, although from where she was sitting, there was no way she could get a proper look at his face.

She took a deep breath. 'Would you please excuse me for a moment, Mr Pendleton?' she asked, and without waiting for a reply, she got up from her chair and went quickly across the room towards the Ladies' Cloakroom. Once there, she doubled back and ducked behind the hothouse flowers beside Billy. He was holding tight to an envelope with her own name on it, which they had agreed he would bring in case he needed to explain to anyone what he was doing in the restaurant.

'I say – do you think that's him?' she demanded at once.

'What are you doing here?' he hissed furiously, spinning around.

'I couldn't see properly from our table,' she shrugged. 'Anyway I needed a break from Pendleton. He keeps going on and on about hunting. Deadly dull.' She peered around the flowers once more. 'I tell you what, though, the roast chicken with truffles looks tremendous. Well, is that really him, do you think?'

They both gazed across the room towards Gregson's table. The man they could see sitting opposite him certainly looked nothing like the East End criminal Joe had led them to expect, although there was no doubt that he stood out amongst the other gentlemen who were lunching in the restaurant. Tall, powerfully built and dressed with careless extravagance, he cut an imposing figure. He had a thick mane of black hair streaked with white. From across the room, they caught the gleam of a silver-topped cane, the glint of several heavy rings on his fingers and the sheen of a violet silk scarf. He was leaning over the table, his dark eyes fixed firmly on Sergeant Gregson, who was listening to him in what was evidently respectful silence. But looking at the expression on Gregson's face, Lil felt certain that the Sergeant wasn't just being respectful – he was frightened. His eyes never left the Baron's. He looked as though he was being hypnotised.

'He's really bending Gregson's ear, isn't he?' she said, fascinated. 'Do you think we could get any closer? It's jolly infuriating not being able to hear what he's saying.'

'We're not supposed to be doing anything to draw attention to ourselves, remember?' said Billy, sternly.

'Oh very well. But if we're not careful this will have been an awful waste of time. We haven't heard a word of their conversation.' She fell silent for a moment and then said: 'I suppose I ought to go back before Pendleton starts wondering where I've gone.'

'All right,' said Billy, not really listening, his eyes still fixed on Gregson.

Lil slipped out of his corner and strolled back casually in

the direction of Mr Pendleton's table. Billy watched as she passed close by the photographer, who had now set up his camera and was taking some pictures of Mr Sinclair sitting at his table. He saw Sinclair look up and point to her as she approached. For a moment Billy felt horrified that she had been discovered, but then, as the photographer beckoned to her, he relaxed. Before he knew it, Lil was posing beside one of the statues and smiling prettily for the camera. *So much for not drawing attention to herself*, Billy thought. As he watched, she laughed at something the photographer said, and then struck another pose. Across the restaurant, Mr Pendleton was watching too. His soup had arrived and he was spooning it glumly into his mouth.

The Baron was on his feet now, addressing a final pointed word to Sergeant Gregson. Then he turned and stalked away, leaving Gregson looking uneasily after him.

On the other side of the room, the photographer was shaking Lil's hand. 'Thank you, Miss Rose, you've been a tremendous help,' he said with a grin. 'Those shots are just what I needed. We can't have a picture story about Sinclair's without one of Sinclair's famous mannequins, after all. Look out for the story in the next day or two.' He paused for a moment, then added, more seriously: 'You've a real talent for photographic work. I don't just work for *The Daily Picture* you know – I've my own studio and I do postcards, that sort of thing. I'm always on the look out for good models. It's paid work, of course, perfectly above board and respectable.'

'Is that so?' asked Lil, grinning back.

The photographer reached into his pocket. 'Look, here's my card,' he said, handing it over. 'Why don't you drop into my office tomorrow morning, and I'll show you the pictures when they're developed? Perhaps we can talk about whether you might do some other photographs for me sometime soon?'

As Lil made her way back towards the table where Mr Pendleton was waiting, she glanced down at the photographer's card, and then over to the empty table where Gregson was now sitting alone. It was just possible, she thought, that their visit to the restaurant might not have been such a waste of time after all . . .

PART IV
'Evening elegance'

No evening toilette would be complete without a bandeau, the
perfect finishing touch for a young lady's coiffure. This elegant
beaded creation is ornamented with a jewelled pin, and is certain
to impress at even the most stylish evening occasions, whether a
first night at the theatre or a society ball.

CHAPTER SEVENTEEN

Thick, dark clouds rolled in over London. Wind surged up the river, turning the water dark and turbulent, and whisking the first of the spring blossom from the trees. Fingers of marsh-scented fog began to creep out across the city, and by Saturday morning Piccadilly was a sea of glossy black umbrellas.

Outside Sinclair's, doormen braved the storm to flag down motor taxis for ladies of fashion, who were anxious about the effect of the rain on their new spring hats. People moved faster than usual, tutting and shaking their heads at the weather. Inside the store, though, all was warm and bright. Sinclair's was crowded with damp shoppers, taking refuge from the rain and gossiping about the grand opening party that would be taking place that evening. As the hour of noon approached, a little cluster of people gathered in the Entrance Hall in front of the enormous golden clock. It had already become something of a tradition for children to be

189

brought here by their nurses to see the hour sound, clapping their hands in delight as the figure of a lady and gentleman, each holding an umbrella, appeared from small doors on either side of the clock, and bowed to each other gravely before retreating once more. The sight of so many muddy footprints stretching across the marble floor of the Entrance Hall caused Sidney Parker to shake his head and send Billy running for a mop and bucket.

'Just as long as it clears up in time for this evening,' Miss Atwood muttered to herself, gazing out of the office window at the damp street below.

She didn't really believe that a little rain would put off the guests attending Mr Sinclair's much-anticipated opening gala, but she did feel that it might hamper the mood. How would the guests be able to enjoy strolling on the magnificent roof terrace in this awful drizzle?

'Mr Sinclair doesn't have all day, you know!' she snapped abruptly to the typewriter girl who was finishing the latest version of the list of guests expected to attend the evening party.

'I – I'm sorry, Miss Atwood, ma'am,' she squeaked nervously, as the private secretary whisked the finished list from between her trembling fingers and strode off in the direction of the Captain's office.

*

In the basement, the rain drummed rhythmically against the high windows. Billy, Joe and Lil perched on boxes, sharing a packet of sandwiches, Blackie the cat prowling around them. He had all but abandoned the boiler room, and seemed always to be in the basement, spending most of his time snoozing behind a warm pipe in Joe's usual corner. Now, he curved himself around Lil's ankles, purring loudly.

But not one of them was paying him any attention. They were all gazing at the photograph that Lil had brought back from the photographer's office that morning.

'That's him, all right,' said Billy, trying not to drop crumbs on the picture.

Joe squinted through narrowed eyes at the face of the man who could be seen in the background of the photo. 'That can't be the Baron,' he said dismissively. 'He looks like a proper dandy – a toff.'

'He met Sergeant Gregson exactly like the message said,' Lil argued. 'And there's no question that Gregson was frightened of him.'

'Was this the only picture?' Joe asked her.

'I think so. I pocketed it when he went to make me a cup of tea. I don't think he'll even miss it. It isn't anything like the best of the photographs. But it's the only one you could see *him* in.'

Joe stared at the image. Was this really the Baron? He

didn't look anything like the monster that was whispered about on the streets of the East End. Instead, he was simply an expensively dressed, but otherwise ordinary man: he could have been almost anyone.

But as he looked, this initial sense that here was just an ordinary man began to dwindle. There was something in the shape of his shoulders, the intensity of his eyes, the fierce lines of his face that spoke to Joe of menace. He had seen those qualities too many times before not to recognise them clearly – and the Baron, for all his fancy clothes, suddenly seemed a powerfully threatening figure. He repressed an abrupt desire to shiver.

'It's a shame you can't really see Gregson, only the back of his head,' Lil was saying, leaning her chin on her hands as she looked over Joe's shoulder at the photograph.

'We're going to need more than this if we're going to prove that he's working for the Baron,' Billy agreed. 'But all the same, it's a good start.'

As he headed back towards the stable-yard, Billy's thoughts were racing. He felt sure that having an actual photograph of the Baron – a man whom hardly anyone had ever seen – must be tremendously important, but what could they do with it?

He pulled on a mackintosh cape and went out into the

rain to help unload cases of champagne for the party that evening, his mind running over the scene in the restaurant yet again: the man leaning over the table talking, and Gregson's tense face as he listened. What had they been talking about? The Baron had the jewels already, but was there something else he was planning? And if so, why had he come to the restaurant at Sinclair's, of all places, to tell Gregson about it?

The questions ran through his mind at a hectic pace, but for once, no one seemed to notice that he wasn't paying much attention to the task at hand. They were far too distracted themselves: the store was buzzing with excitement about the party that evening.

Even for Sinclair's, this would be an unusually luxurious affair. The maid who had brought down their morning tea had spoken in lip-smacking detail of the delicacies that were being prepared in the kitchen: smoked salmon and caviar, lobster and stuffed snipe. There would be desserts like something from a fairy tale: pastries fluffy as clouds and powdered with sugar; lighter-than-air castles spun from meringue and cream; ice-cream cakes smothered with strawberries.

But the refreshments were not all – there would be spectacular entertainments too. London's finest orchestra would be playing in the Entrance Hall, where mannequins dressed in the store's most exquisite Paris gowns would give a dress parade. Unexpected performances would be taking place throughout the shop: a renowned opera star would sing; a *prima ballerina* would dance; and a master illusionist would perform. There would be dancing in the Exhibition Hall; cards in the Gentlemen's Smoking Room; and an immense supper would be served in the Marble Court Restaurant. Amidst all this, Mr Sinclair's specially invited guests would be free to sip champagne and explore the store at their leisure. The staff were required to stay on and work throughout the entire evening. They would have an extra meal in the refectory from six o'clock, and they would all work until two o'clock in the morning, when the party would at last come to an end. It would be an exceedingly long and tiring day, but the staff felt that they could put up with that, when it meant they would have the chance to witness all the sights of Mr Sinclair's opening gala.

Most of all, everyone was excited about the party guests. All of London's finest would be attending: aristocrats and West End stars; intellectuals and famous beauties; politicians and celebrated artists and writers. Most exciting of all, the typist from Miss Atwood's office had whispered of a Very Important Royal Personage who was expected to be in attendance. More than one shop girl found her attention wandering that afternoon, as she dreamed hopefully of a rich, eligible young man coming to her counter that evening and falling head-over-heels in love.

The only person who seemed unaffected by it all was Mr Cooper. Striding about the store, dressed exactly as usual in his habitual severe black, his keen eyes did not miss a single smear on a brass doorplate, or a single scuff on a salesman's shoe. As the afternoon drew on, a rumour began to travel around the store that Sinclair was planning a surprise inspection to ensure that everything was perfect in advance of the party.

'Best make sure it looks tip-top,' said Bill from Sporting Goods, warningly, to Claudine. 'Sid reckons the wind's in the east.'

Claudine looked alarmed. Sinclair's staff had taken to using the phrase 'an east wind' to indicate that the Captain was in one of his rare tempers, and unlikely to tolerate even the slightest imperfection. She murmured '*Zut alors!*' and hurried off to relay the message to Monsieur Pascal in the salon.

Upstairs in Ladies' Fashions everything was immaculate, and the shop girls were fighting for a place before the looking glass to check their hair was tidy. But across the way in the Millinery Department, all was in disorder.

Minnie and Violet were rushing to and fro from the storeroom and Edith was struggling to deal with a tottering tower of boxes when Lil appeared, carrying a hat-box tied with a blue ribbon in each hand. 'I say. Where do you want these?'

'Where have those come from?' demanded Edith, crossly.

'From the mannequins' dressing rooms,' explained Lil. 'We shan't be needing them after all.'

'Well, that's all I need! Oh - just put them down anywhere.'

Lil did so, and then paused. 'You really ought to pull your socks up, you know,' she said briskly. 'The Captain is going to be walking round the store at any moment and you don't want to let him see the place looking like this.'

'I *know* that, thank you very much,' Edith snapped back angrily. As she spoke, the boxes she was holding slipped between her fingers and crashed to the ground, making several smart ladies examining a display of velvet turbans turn and frown at the sudden burst of noise. One of them shot Edith a very disapproving look through her eyeglass.

Lil helped to pile up the boxes once more. 'What's going on?' she asked. 'Where's Mrs Milton?'

'She's gone home with the toothache,' said Edith, sounding rather despairing now. 'It's been frantic all afternoon, and we're already short-handed with Sophie gone.' Then she glanced up at Lil. 'Listen - can you help me?' she blurted out.

Lil gazed at her, astonished, wondering if her ears had deceived her. 'Help you?' she repeated incredulously. 'You want *me* to help *you*?'

'Oh well, if you feel like that, you can just shove off then,' said Edith turning away, her face flaming as she carried on stacking up the hat-boxes.

Lil stood for a moment and watched thoughtfully as Edith wobbled into the storeroom and flung the boxes down. Even in its current untidy state, the little room still reminded her of Sophie. She remembered how they had sat on the floor and Sophie had told her about her father's death. It seemed unthinkable that she would never be here again.

She glanced back at Edith and made up her mind. 'Very well, I'll help you,' she said. 'What do you want me to do?'

Half an hour later, the Millinery Department was tidy again. Whilst Edith and the other girls dealt with the customers and tidied the shop floor, Lil worked in the storeroom, bundling hat-boxes on to shelves and even sweeping the floor. When she had finished, Edith muttered a few embarrassed words of thanks.

Lil looked at her for a long moment. Then she said lightly, 'You're very welcome, Edith. I'm sure you would have done the same, had it been Sophie who needed help.'

She turned on her heel and walked away, feeling that some small justice had been done, humming one of her favourite songs from the show quietly under her breath. As she went back towards the staircase, she caught sight of Sinclair, leaning over the counter in Ladies' Fashions to speak to a terrified-looking salesgirl. Behind him was Cooper, with a grim expression; then Miss Atwood, carrying her notebook and looking rather vexed. Even from a distance, it was easy to see that the two were not enjoying one another's company. The other shop girls stood nervously to attention, awaiting their turn.

But Lil felt oddly indifferent. After what had happened to Sophie, she couldn't help thinking that getting ticked off for having dirty hands or a smudged counter-top seemed awfully trifling, even if it was by the Captain himself.

She was still humming as she ran lightly down the stairs and back towards the mannequins' dressing room, her mind busy with thoughts of making her debut on a real West End stage that very evening, and all the excitement that was to come.

CHAPTER EIGHTEEN

Sophie surveyed her reflection in the looking glass. She had spent the last two weary days traipsing around the newspaper offices placing advertisements, going on foot to save even the few pennies that the omnibus would cost. When she had first arrived home that evening, she had felt so exhausted that she wished she had never told Lil that she would go to the theatre. But now that she was dressed and ready, her black mood had unexpectedly lifted. She was relieved that she would not have to spend the evening alone at the lodging house thinking about the party at Sinclair's; but more than that, simply putting on her best dress seemed to have performed a sort of magic trick. The heavy, silky fabric rustled as she swished her long skirts to and fro, making her feel like another person altogether.

The dress had been her first proper, almost-grown-up evening frock. Papa had given it to her for her last birthday. He'd hosted a dinner before he went back to South Africa and she'd been allowed to sit up for it, wearing her new frock: she could almost see him now, talking and laughing heartily, very far away from her along the long, gleaming table, until the candlelight seemed to shimmer and the illusion was gone.

Now, she saw only herself, reflected in the cracked, yellowed looking glass. She'd had to give up so many of her clothes, but she had not been able to bear the idea of parting with this dress. She felt glad to put it on again, as if she were putting her own former self back on. Lil had insisted on lending her a beaded evening bag, kitted out with a fan painted with a design of butterflies and some opera glasses, and had actually given her a dainty pair of satin slippers that no longer fitted her. Putting them on, Sophie felt transformed, as if by the wave of a fairy godmother's magic wand. But there was still something that wasn't quite right: impulsively, she pulled the pins from her hair, which she had spent so much time carefully putting up, and shook it so that it fell down her back. She added a velvet ribbon and then looked again at her reflection. Now she really looked like herself once more.

For what must have been the twentieth time that afternoon, she picked up the photograph that lay on the chair. Lil had brought it when she had dropped in earlier on her way to the theatre to bring Sophie the bag and slippers. Sophie's smile faded as she gazed at the man in the corner of the picture. His face meant nothing to her, and yet there was something about his expression – something in the unreadable dark smudges of his eyes, the line of his shoulder, the shape of his forehead – that kept drawing her back.

After contemplating it for a few moments, she propped it up on the mantelshelf – bare of her old treasures now but for the picture of Papa that she had rescued from its broken frame. The two photographs looked incongruous alongside each other. On the left, Papa, gallant in his military uniform, pinned with medals. On the right, Lil striking a pose, and behind her, almost unseen, the man they believed to be the Baron.

Sophie sighed and turned away, picking up her coat and bag. She was glad to close the door of her room and leave the Baron's face behind her. Just for tonight, she would forget about him, and forget about Sinclair's, and simply enjoy going to the theatre in her best dress to see Lil make her debut on stage.

But in the hallway she stopped short. Mrs MacDuff was standing in front of the door, her arms folded, watching Sophie with a hostile expression on her face.

'Is something the matter?' Sophie asked.

'Is something the matter?' repeated the landlady, in

a crude imitation of Sophie's voice. '"Is something the matter?" she says, artless as you please!'

She looked Sophie up and down, suspiciously taking in the frock, the slippers, the evening bag. 'Do you know what this is?' she snapped out, gesturing around her.

'A lodging house?' Sophie replied, a sharp edge in her own voice now.

'Lodgings for *working* young ladies,' said Mrs MacDuff. 'You hear that? Working. And from what I'm told, you're not working any more. And that means you're no longer welcome here.'

'I'll soon find another job,' said Sophie.

'Hmph! That's what they all say. But I know how it goes. Before you can say knife, you'll be behind on your money and I'm not having any shirkers.'

'But you can't just . . . turn me out!'

'Watch me,' said Mrs MacDuff, tapping her foot. 'I'm giving you a week's notice. If you've got no more work by then – decent, respectable work, mind you – you're out, or I'll have the Constable round. And from what I hear, you'll be wanting to steer well clear of the Law.'

'This is ridiculous,' said Sophie. 'I haven't done anything wrong.'

'No?' Mrs MacDuff laughed. She lowered her voice. 'Well what does *he* want with you then? Oh, you're a sly puss all right. Pretending that butter wouldn't melt, and all the time mixed up with the likes of him.'

'Who?'

'You know very well *who*.' Mrs MacDuff's voice became a rasping growl.

'Who are you talking about?' Sophie almost shouted, stamping her foot, frustration bubbling up within her.

'*The Baron*,' hissed Mrs MacDuff.

Sophie gazed at her for a moment, then drew herself upwards. 'I have nothing whatsoever to do with the Baron,' she said, crisply.

'That's not what I heard,' Mrs MacDuff snapped back. 'I know what people are saying. I've heard –'

'I think we should discuss this in the morning,' said Sophie, cutting her off, too angry to listen for a moment longer. 'I'm going out.'

She pushed past her landlady and went through the door, slamming it behind her, and stalked down the street, her heart bumping furiously. Turned out of the house, on top of everything else! What was she supposed to do? It wasn't as though she had any money to secure new lodgings. She shook her head. Piece by piece, the life she had been trying to build for herself was being pulled apart – and it was all because of him. The Baron – a face like a shadow in the corner of a photograph. A man whose name she didn't even know.

But at least she had Lil and the others, she thought, trying to still her trembling hands as she opened her umbrella. She remembered how eager Lil had been for her to come to the show tonight, and of all their sympathetic faces as they had determined to help her find out who was really responsible for the burglary.

Thinking of this, she stomped on through the rain towards the West End, her head held high beneath the old umbrella. She didn't notice the man in the cloth cap, his collar turned well up, who had been standing in the drizzle just outside the lodging house, and was even now walking swiftly but purposefully behind her.

CHAPTER NINETEEN

The rain was slowing just in time for the party. Miss Atwood gave a small nod of satisfaction as she looked around the Entrance Hall. The final preparations were still underway: rows of gilt chairs were being set out for the orchestra; the golden clock was being polished until it gleamed; a waiter was arranging rows of champagne glasses on a table swathed in white linen; and Claudine was placing several large floral displays, each featuring Sinclair's signature orchids, carefully into position.

Everything looked exactly as it should, and Miss Atwood began to feel increasingly pleased with herself. Cooper had blotted his copybook with the burglary, there was no doubt about that – and tonight's party would give her the chance to really prove her worth. She smoothed down her necktie as she looked over the party guest-list for what must have been the hundredth time, feeling that she was a woman on the up.

A young porter came hurrying up, an envelope in his hand. 'Message from the hospital, ma'am,' he mumbled.

Miss Atwood ripped the envelope open and stared at the note inside. For a moment, her expression of self-satisfaction wavered. Then she glanced up to see the young porter still at her side, his eyes full of curiosity. She made a little sound of annoyance and pushed the envelope into her pocket.

'Take this up to Mr Cooper in his office, at once,' she said, pushing the guest list into the young porter's hand.

Billy took the sheaf of papers that the Captain's private secretary was thrusting towards him, trying to arrange his face into a polite expression. He loathed being expected to nod and touch his cap and be deferential, no matter how rude other people were. 'Yes, ma'am, no, ma'am, three bags full, ma'am,' he muttered resentfully under his breath once he was out of Miss Atwood's earshot.

He couldn't help wondering what might have been inside that note from the hospital. Could it be news of Bert Jones? Was he finally well enough to tell the police what had happened on the night he had been shot? He longed to linger and try to find out, but he knew what would happen if he didn't follow orders, so he turned away and toiled up to the store manager's office.

The door was ajar, and Billy could hear movement inside – the sound of a chair scraping back and then footsteps –

but he hesitated on the threshold. He wasn't sure whether it was Mr Cooper himself or Sergeant Gregson, who as far as he knew was still using Cooper's office as the base for his investigations. Not particularly wanting to cross Gregson's path, he glanced through the door, saw that it was only Cooper – but then froze in astonishment as he realised what the store manager was doing.

He was standing by the bureau, polishing what Billy realised in a flash was a revolver. It gleamed, black and heavy, in Cooper's careful grasp. The store manager weighed it in his hand and then swiftly slipped it inside his jacket with all the practised ease of a man well used to handling a firearm. He locked the drawer with a precise click, and then picked up some papers from his desk before coming towards the door.

Billy jumped backwards but he was still standing just outside, looking blank, when Cooper strode out.

'What is it that you want, Parker?' he demanded sharply.

'Miss Atwood sent me to give you this, sir,' Billy managed to stammer out.

Cooper nodded and took the papers. 'Shape up, Parker,' he said tersely as he strode off down the corridor. 'On your toes this evening. And mind those hands are clean.'

Billy stood stock still in the passageway. He still couldn't believe what he had seen. What could Mr Cooper, possibly be doing with a revolver? Could it be that he knew that

Sergeant Gregson was secretly working for the Baron? The thought made him feel a rush of relief, but as quickly as it came, it evaporated again. For if Cooper was carrying a gun, it surely meant that the store, and all of them in it, were in some sort of danger.

Following a sudden impulse, Billy went swiftly down the corridor in the same direction as Cooper. At one time he would have thought that there was nothing more thrilling than trailing a man carrying a gun – it was just the sort of thing that Montgomery Baxter was always doing, usually in some sort of cunning disguise – but now that it was happening, he didn't feel excited at all. Instead there was a sick sensation steadily rising in his stomach. Careful to keep some distance behind Cooper, Billy followed him back on to the shop floor and then down to the Book Department.

Under normal circumstances, the Book Department was just about Billy's favourite place in the whole of the store. It had thick oriental rugs on the floor, dark wooden panelling on the walls, plenty of comfortable armchairs, and most importantly, books everywhere. It was wonderfully peaceful, with no sound but the low, respectful buzz of muted conversation, the soft hush of pages turning, and the occasional cough of Mr White, Head of the Book Department, who was given to a touch of bronchitis.

Mr Cooper paused for a moment beside a display of atlases and swiftly glanced around him. Billy darted behind a bookshelf, anxious not to be seen. He found himself by the shelves where the books for children were kept: fat, leather-bound volumes of fairy stories, ABC and Mother Goose books printed on shiny paper, and row after row of books by authors like Lewis Carroll and Frances Hodgson Burnett, Rudyard Kipling and E. Nesbit. Usually, nothing would have stopped him from picking up a copy of *King Solomon's Mines*, or stealing a moment to read a few pages of *Treasure Island*, but now his attention was fixed on Mr Cooper. The store manager was heading towards the doorway in the corner marked 'Staff Only' that Billy knew led out into the street. But as he was craning his neck to see what Cooper would do next, a salesman came by with a trolley piled high with books, momentarily blocking his view. He stepped back quickly, not wanting to lose sight of his quarry, but all at once there was a loud crash and he realised to his horror that he had bumped into a display table and sent a stack of books cascading to the ground.

'Oh – I say – I'm sorry,' said Billy weakly, scrabbling to pick up the fallen books. Mr White was striding towards him, looking furious. Worse still, a very familiar – and very angry – voice came from somewhere above him: 'What the devil do you think you're up to now?'

Uncle Sid grasped Billy firmly by the elbow. 'I've had just about enough of this. You're coming with me.'

The theatre was lit up like a firework in the drizzle. Huge scarlet letters blazed out FORTUNE THEATRE, and below them thronged a crowd of people in evening clothes, giddy with excitement about the first night of a new Gilbert Lloyd show. A long queue of people sheltered under umbrellas as they waited patiently to buy tickets for the cheap seats, but Lil had already given Sophie hers and she was able to make straight for the entrance.

Inside, she made her way through the crush to buy a programme for a penny. She winced slightly when she saw that the show was called *The Shop Girl*, but pushed away the uncomfortable feeling as she spotted the name *Lilian Rose* printed in small lettering at the end of the list of chorus girls. The star, Miss Kitty Shaw, had her name written in big letters at the very top of the page – even above the title of the show itself. Maybe one day Lil would have her name right at the top of the page too.

An usher in a scarlet jacket and white gloves pointed Sophie to her seat up in the curved gallery. Clusters of lamps cast pools of yellow light, and all around her was the low buzz of conversation, the rustle of silk and satin as people settled into their seats. In the boxes above her, the ladies and gentlemen in the grandest evening dress were beginning to arrive: many of the ladies took their seats as late as possible, to ensure everyone would be able to admire their outfits as they entered. It was another world up there, Sophie thought, as she watched one lady in a lavishly beaded silk evening gown and a pearl collar bowing graciously to another, dressed in rippling satin and carrying an ostrich-feather fan.

Something about all this was strangely familiar, and as she sat watching them, Sophie realised she had been to this theatre before – once, long ago, when she was quite small. A Christmas treat with Papa – *Cinderella* perhaps? She recalled the sounds of the orchestra tuning up, and the soft red plush of the seat. Even as she remembered, the lights dimmed and the orchestra struck up a waltz, and Sophie was a child again, feeling a sudden thrill as the curtain went up with a swish, and the show began.

'I always said your mother would spoil you, letting you read all those books and getting ideas above your station.' Uncle Sid's face was growing redder and redder.

Billy was sitting opposite Sid in the staff cloakroom. The head porter's huge form was folded uncomfortably on to a bench, his legs splayed out awkwardly in front of him. Billy could still scarcely believe he wasn't roaring and bellowing: he had been sure he was in for a right royal dressing down, and probably, knowing Uncle Sid, a good walloping as well. But instead his uncle had taken him down to the cloakroom and insisted they sit down for what he called 'a serious word'.

'You've got to work hard if you want to get on,' Uncle Sid was saying, his voice deep and earnest. 'Sometimes you've got to do things you might not want to do, but you've just got to knuckle down and do as you're told.'

Billy opened his mouth to try and say something, but Uncle Sid held up a hand to stop him. 'Don't answer back, don't ask why, just get on and follow your orders. That's what I've always done and it's served me well. Look, I know you think I'm too hard on you, but it's for your own good.'

There was an awkward silence as Uncle Sid took off his hat and scratched his head for a moment. Billy fixed his attention on the shiny toes of his Uncle's boots: his own, he saw guiltily, were scuffed and dusty. For once, he found himself wishing that his uncle were yelling at him. Anything would be better than this solemn lecture. But how could he possibly explain to Uncle Sid that he wasn't slacking, or playing the fool – he was simply trying to prove who was really behind the burglary, and to get Sophie her job back?

'I know you were cut up about that girl that got the sack. And we've all had our moments of . . . er . . . being sweet on a young lady,' Uncle Sid was saying awkwardly now.

Billy's cheeks turned crimson. He gazed at the floor,

thinking that he might actually die of embarrassment if Uncle Sid started talking to him about sweethearts. As he started to protest, Sid went on: 'But you can't go on like this – mooning about, making mistakes, disappearing to read those stories of yours for hours at a time. You think I don't notice you sneaking off down to the basement and who knows where else? And I'm not the only one either. I'm getting complaints about you – my own nephew!' Uncle Sid shook his head. 'I've been keeping you out of Mr Cooper's bad books, but I can't go on doing that forever. You'll have to pull your socks up. Your mum's counting on you to bring home a decent wage.'

He paused for a moment, and Billy hoped the lecture might be over, but then he went on. 'This is a grand chance for you, lad. For both of us. I've worked since I was your age for a chance at a fine place like this one – and I'm not going to stand by and watch you muck it up for us both.'

Uncle Sid's voice quavered a little as he said this, and Billy suddenly felt pricked all over by pangs of conscience. He stared repentantly up at his uncle, taking in the immaculate moustache, the carefully brushed hat, the gleaming buttons. Uncle Sid was *proud* of working at Sinclair's, he realised in a sudden rush. It meant everything to him. And he, Billy, was acting as if it was worth nothing at all.

'Well, this is your last chance. Do your best at the party

tonight. Prove to me that you're taking it seriously. Any more nonsense and I wash my hands of you. I'll report you to Cooper myself.'

With that, Uncle Sid got up and hurried out of the cloakroom, leaving Billy gazing guiltily after him.

Sophie sat fanning herself and looking around her. Many of the seats were empty now: most of the audience had hurried for refreshments at the start of the interval, but she had no money to spare for lemonade or bonbons so she stayed where she was.

She had enjoyed every minute of the first act, although Lil had been right, it was an awfully silly story, really – the tale of a beautiful young shop girl, who was happily engaged to a poor student until she was swept off her feet by a handsome millionaire who came to her counter. The millionaire had come from Colorado to seek out the orphaned daughter of an old mining chum to tell her she was due to inherit a fortune, and it was only too obvious to Sophie that the shop girl would of course turn out to be the lost daughter and would end up inheriting the fortune and marrying her poor, but deserving sweetheart. But however predictable the story might be, it was delightful to be immersed in an imaginary world where she knew the characters would be allowed a happy ending. She had enjoyed looking out for each of Lil's appearances too: there she was, pirouetting and twirling perfectly at the end of a line of chorus girls or demurely dressed in a white frock and a lace parasol, singing a jaunty song about the marvels of British trade, all the time grinning wickedly and catching everyone's eye.

Sophie decided to entertain herself until the start of the second act by looking up in the boxes. Society beauties in magnificent jewels were murmuring to each other behind their fans, whilst gentlemen lit cigars and clapped each other on the shoulder, and beside them, waiters poured out glasses of champagne. The ladies' gowns were like illustrations from the fashion papers come to life. Sophie was just trying to decide whether she would choose the pale-blue silk chiffon or the jade-green velvet, when her eye was caught by a man sitting by himself in one of the most magnificent boxes. It seemed odd to see someone sitting all alone like that: rather like herself, she thought suddenly with a wry half-smile. Then she frowned and looked again. The man's face seemed to swim before her eyes: she recognised it. She had seen it somewhere before. Remembering the opera glasses Lil had loaned her, Sophie took them out of the bag, and trying to be discreet, quickly glanced through them at the man in the box.

At first, she couldn't believe what she was seeing. She must be mistaken! But she wasn't. There could be no doubt about it. His dramatic profile and dark swept-back hair streaked with white were unmistakable. There, sitting coolly all alone, was the man whose face she had seen earlier that day in the photograph Lil had brought, the photograph that even now was sitting at home on her mantelpiece. It was the Baron.

She dropped the opera glasses in her lap as though they had burned her. She knew he couldn't possibly have seen her looking at him, but all the same her heart was pounding. For one, dizzy moment, everything seemed unreal. She glanced swiftly back up at the box. As she watched he took out a pocket-watch, glanced at it, and then leaned back in his chair to light a cigar.

She looked quickly around. No one was watching her. She clicked her fan shut abruptly and stood up, bundling the opera glasses into her evening bag, then hurried out along the row of seats, and made her way up the red-carpeted aisle towards the door.

The staff refectory was a hubbub of noise. All around him, Billy could see little huddles of shop girls talking excitedly together, and groups of salesmen, guffawing and digging each other in the ribs as they speculated about what the evening might bring. But he himself sat quietly, slowly eating the last mouthfuls of pudding and trying to listen respectfully to Uncle Sid's conversation with two of the other doormen.

Just as they were finishing the meal, Claudine came bustling over to their table, looking anxious. 'Have you seen Monsieur Cooper?' she asked Uncle Sid. 'The Captain's *boutonnière* is ready to be taken upstairs. Cooper said he wished to take it himself but I cannot find him anywhere.'

Uncle Sid wiped his moustache with his napkin. 'Well, it wouldn't do to keep the Captain waiting. Best get it dealt with. Go on, lad, if you've finished,' he added to Billy. 'Make yourself useful.'

Billy had never been near the Captain's apartments before, and felt rather nervous as he climbed up the wide, thickly carpeted stairway, carefully carrying the tray upon which rested a particularly exquisite orchid for Sinclair's buttonhole. It was beautifully quiet in the offices. He tiptoed through a wood-panelled room where several well-dressed young men were scribbling busily in ledgers, and then another, where Miss Atwood's typewriter girl was still tapping at the keys.

At last, he came into the office where Miss Atwood herself worked, which interconnected with the Captain's own, but Miss Atwood was nowhere to be seen. Billy paused for a moment, taking in the glossy leather-upholstered chairs, the shelves of books and the grand oil paintings on the walls, and thinking what a splendid room it was – more like a marvellous library than a secretary's office.

But what was he to do now? For a moment he lingered, hoping that the typist might see him and offer to take the flower in herself, but then he thought of what Uncle Sid had said, and went forward purposefully. He strode over to the door of Sinclair's office, ready to knock, but as he raised his hand, Sinclair's distinctive voice rose from inside.

'Keep this to yourself, Miss Atwood. I won't have lurid stories flying round and upsetting everyone tonight. Understand?'

'But sir – Jones is – I mean . . .'

'He's dead. It's unfortunate. Tragic, I grant you. But it won't make a difference if we tell them tomorrow. Under the circumstances, we simply daren't risk any distractions tonight.'

Billy stepped abruptly backwards, but even as he did so, Miss Atwood emerged, looking grim and pale.

'So the flowers are here at last?' she snapped. 'About time too – we've been waiting for them. Well, put them there, and be on your way.'

Billy nodded and put down the tray on the table Miss Atwood had pointed to. Then he swiftly went back out through the offices, trying to ignore the creeping cold sensation that was rising in his chest.

Sophie's satin slippers made little sound on the thick carpet as she hurried down the long passageway that led towards the boxes. She had waited until the usher's head was turned the other way to slip quickly up the stairs. Now, as a waiter carrying a tray of drinks came by, she held up her head and smiled, trying to look as if she belonged here. It must have worked, because he passed her by without a moment's hesitation. She let out a long breath and went on, counting the doors . . . one, two, three. This must be it: the Baron's box.

The door was slightly ajar, and for a moment she hovered on the threshold, uncertain now of what she meant to do. She could hardly stand here in the corridor waiting for him to come out – she would be much too conspicuous. She peered through the doorway, ready to jump back and apologise at once for being in the wrong place, should another usher appear.

She glimpsed a slice of a man's shoulder. He seemed to be quite alone, sitting perfectly still, smoking his cigar. The smoke drifted around him in a ghostly cloud. Looking to the side, she could see that there were velvet curtains around either side of the door, just inside the box. Could she slip behind one of them? The sound of footsteps approaching made up her mind, and very softly she opened the door wider, praying it would not creak – and then slid soundlessly behind the velvet drape.

Her heart was thumping even more heavily now and

her breathing seemed impossibly loud. But even as she tried to calm herself, a sick horror flooded her as, to her astonishment, the Baron began to speak.

CHAPTER TWENTY

'Sentimental rot, of course, but Lloyd's a clever fellow. He's got them eating out of the palm of his hand.'

Sophie felt dizzy with relief. For a moment she had thought the Baron had somehow realised that she was there – but there must be someone else in the box, someone who had come in while she was making her way up the stairs, that he was now speaking to. She buried herself deeper into the darkest corner behind the curtains, and peered out. Sure enough, she could see there was a gentleman sitting at the Baron's right hand. She could see the texture of his hair, greying a little at the temples, the medal that adorned his jacket, and the gold signet ring he wore on the little finger of the hand that held his cigar. His elegant evening clothes were beautifully tailored, and a silk hat was carefully placed on a chair at his side. He looked so much like any gentleman attending a society event that she found herself wondering whether Lil had been quite mistaken about the Baron's identity and these were just two quite innocent gentlemen here to enjoy the show.

'But you know we didn't ask you here to talk about musical comedy,' the Baron was saying. He had turned slightly to the left, and to Sophie's surprise, she realised he was addressing not the man she could see, but a third person who was sitting outside her eyeline altogether. She began to feel increasingly alarmed that the box accommodated not one, but three people, any of whom might have spotted her when she had slipped behind the curtain.

The sudden, sharp sound of a chair being pushed back made her freeze. But there was no further movement. Instead, the third man said something in a low voice that she could not make out, and then, to her astonishment, the Baron laughed heartily. 'Good heavens, Freddie! You worry too much. You must realise he's the type of fellow who can scarcely see beyond the end of his own nose. I'm sure he hasn't even noticed you've gone. As for being recognised here, you're more than capable of remaining unseen. Besides, you know better than anyone that the theatre is the perfect place for talking in private.' He gazed out across the auditorium for a moment, apparently surveying the figures in the boxes across the way, talking and drinking champagne. 'Just look. Not one of them is interested in anyone but themselves.'

There was a long pause in which Sophie hardly dared to

breathe, before the Baron went on. 'But after tonight we can make plans for your departure. I thought a widowed sister, living in some provincial town, who can no longer get on without her dear, devoted brother? Or perhaps you've always yearned to return to the country village of your childhood and grow prize-winning marrows? But we can work out the amusing details later. After tonight, we will begin to work on the next role you will play.'

The unseen man cleared his throat and said something else, low and urgent, but the Baron interrupted him. 'That situation has been dealt with this very afternoon. Jones is dead.'

There was an exclamation of surprise from the unseen man, but the Baron went on: 'It was inconvenient that a guard had been placed at his bedside, but of course Gregson took care of that. Jones won't be able to tell anyone what he knows now. Swaggering young fool – you must choose your associates a little more carefully in future, Freddie.'

Sophie was so shocked that she had to clutch at the curtain to steady herself. They were talking about Bert, she realised. Bert was *dead* and the men who sat before her now were somehow responsible. But before she had the chance to take it in, the Baron continued. 'But never mind that, now,' he said incisively. 'We need to talk about tonight.'

The lights were going down again, and the orchestra had

struck up a bright, lively melody: the second act was about to start. Sophie kept on listening, alert to every word.

'I shall be joining you at the party later, as you know. The papers are being handed over a little after eleven. Once everything is taken care of, I'll give you the agreed signal to confirm that you may proceed. Once we've left the building, you do your work. Do you understand?'

The other man, Freddie, spoke – this time more clearly. He had a lighter voice, with a sharpness that Sophie felt was vaguely familiar. 'Yes, absolutely,' he said.

'Good,' said the Baron, and there was approval in his tone now. 'You should know, Freddie, that we were ready to trust you alone with this business tonight. But we think it wise to be seen amongst the guests – after all, our absence might be remarked upon. Besides, our friend from Berlin is expecting to meet us, and we must not disappoint.'

Freddie murmured his agreement. Then, 'May I ask . . .' he began in a more uncertain voice, 'if it is not impertinent – what are the papers that will be handed over tonight?'

There was a long silence. The audience was laughing delightedly at the antics on stage, but in the Baron's box, Sophie sensed a prickle of tension. The Baron said nothing. He was looking at the other gentleman, who had remained silent throughout their exchange. Some kind of unspoken communication seemed to flash between them, and then the other gentleman gave a brief nod, before leaning back in his chair.

The Baron turned back towards Freddie. 'That's not really any of your business, Freddie,' he said. He waited a few moments, as if to allow his words to sink in, before he continued. 'But you have proved your worth these last few months. We can use a man with your unique skills. As such, we shall make an exception for you. Not something we often do, as you well know.'

There was another long pause and then the Baron went on: 'The papers we will be handing over to Berlin tonight contain confidential information about the British Navy. They include blueprints for their newest submarines.'

Sophie pressed a hand over her mouth. She had understood that the Baron was a criminal and a rogue, but this – this was far beyond anything she could have dreamed of. This man was passing Britain's military secrets to another country! She leaned back against the wall, feeling unsteady. Beyond the curtain, she could dimly hear Freddie murmuring something in reply, whilst below, on the stage, the performers had launched into a comic song and dance routine.

'Freddie, for such a clever fellow you are rather slow sometimes. Of course Berlin will pay well for this information, but there is a great deal more to it than that. Our relationship with them is long-standing, but now we are looking to strengthen it further. And, of course, we have Sinclair's *sparrow* to thank for that.'

Sophie's eyes widened. He was actually talking about the clockwork sparrow – and this, at last, must be its secret. But as her mind raced, trying to work out what he could possibly mean, Freddie said, in a voice full of breathless awe: 'I must confess, I still don't exactly understand the part that the sparrow has played.'

In front of Sophie, the other gentleman sighed, as though bored by the conversation. He shifted in his chair and lit another cigar. Beside him, the Baron was talking to Freddie: 'You understand the basics of a cipher or a code, yes? A set of instructions is used to generate a text that looks, to the uneducated eye, like nonsense – but if we know the system that has been used, we can translate the text and reveal its meaning. In this way, we can communicate secret information to other parties, like our friends in Germany, for example. Even if the message is intercepted, it appears to be completely innocent. You follow?'

He did not wait for an answer but went on. 'The disadvantage of this is that whilst most people would not be able to understand the message, a clever code-breaker – someone who knows what they are looking for – will be able to analyse it and crack the code, so it is not completely fail-safe.'

He paused for a moment. A drift of the gentleman's cigar smoke floated in Sophie's direction and she desperately swallowed a cough that was rising in her throat.

'So now we come to the point. The only way to create a cipher that cannot be broken by these techniques is by using a *randomly generated number* as the basis for the code. As long as the receiver has this number, this *key*, they can work out what the text really says. But there is no pattern to it, no structure, nothing that even the cleverest code-breaker can use to work out what it says.

'This method offers an unprecedented level of security. It overcomes all previous weaknesses. But true randomness is *essential* to the success of the system. You can't simply make up a random number by . . . tapping a few keys on the typewriter or dreaming one up in your head.'

Sophie sensed the Baron glancing over at the other gentleman, as if to check whether he was listening, but he was still gazing out across the auditorium. 'This is where the sparrow comes in. A musical toy, a mere trinket – but it plays a different tune each time it is wound. The clockwork mechanism is devised in such a way that the notes are played *entirely at random*. It is unique – there is no other device like it. Through acquiring the sparrow and understanding its secrets, it has been possible to develop a new system for generating completely random patterns and numbers, and thus an unbreakable cipher.' He glanced over at the gentleman again, this time bowing his head slightly as though to acknowledge him. Was this silent man, then, the one who had created this cipher, Sophie wondered? But the gentleman said nothing.

'Now, we can send messages anywhere in the world, using any network – telegraph, telephone, wireless – and no one will be able to decipher them, unless they have the key to decode them,' the Baron continued 'No one else – no government the world over – has anything to compare with it.'

'So that's why the clockmaker . . .' began the other man.

The Baron nodded. 'Mr Mendel had been working for us for a while. One of the best in his field once, poor old fellow, but even he couldn't work out how to replicate the mechanism of the sparrow. It's one of a kind. That's why we had to lay our hands it. But all the same, Mendel was useful to us for a time. Then he grew anxious, and when people grow anxious, they're apt to say things they shouldn't – have you observed that, Freddie? The Boys had to take care of him in the end – though heaven knows how they almost managed to botch such a simple task. They're a crude bunch, and not too bright, that's why we need a more subtle fellow, like you, Freddie, for the important work – like obtaining the sparrow.'

He paused reflectively for a moment, before he went on. 'We tried to buy it at first, you know – anonymously, of course – but that idiot Sinclair refused to sell at any price. *Sentimental value*, he said. The stubborn ass doubtless thought it no more than a keepsake from some sordid love affair.

'Well, Sinclair has been a thorn in our side too many times. Tonight will ensure that he does not ever get in our way again. I must say, there is a neatness to this that pleases me particularly. What could be more apt than that we dispose of a troublemaker at his own party? It is very elegantly done. You might almost say it is like clockwork.' He chuckled to himself, as if pleased with his own joke.

The smart gentleman spoke suddenly, without taking his eyes from the stage below. 'Fitz, you talk too much.' His voice was clipped and aristocratic, yet with a faint note in it that seemed unusual and which Sophie could not place. She watched, mesmerised and intrigued that after such a long silence, he had finally deigned to speak. Who could this man be, to address the Baron himself with such authority? And could 'Fitz' be a clue to the Baron's real name?

The Baron fell silent and so all was still for a few moments, as though everyone was holding their breath. At last, the gentleman wafted a silk-gloved hand, as if to indicate he would say no more, and the conversation resumed.

'Will the Berlin contact be given the system too?' Freddie was asking in a low, eager voice.

'No. We'll be keeping our knowledge to ourselves. But Berlin will be given a set of keys – randomly generated numbers we have already produced using our system – which will allow them to decipher the messages we send in the coming months. It is, of course, absolutely vital that these do not get intercepted, which is why I will hand them over in person with the other papers. Once I give you the signal that everything has gone smoothly, and we have left the building, you will activate the infernal machine. It has been set for midnight exactly, so there will be plenty of time for you to trigger the mechanism and then leave the building.'

'And are you certain it will work?'

The gentleman looked sharply across in Freddie's direction. 'The calculations are exact,' he rapped out crisply. 'There is no risk of failure so long as you play your part. Be sure that you do.'

'Yes, sir,' said Freddie, sounding more nervous than ever.

'With so many of the country's most powerful at the gala, we'll be wiping out a good proportion of the ruling parties. The chaos caused will be unprecedented,' the Baron went on. 'Some of the Society's men will then be able to step in, fill the gaps and calm the turmoil: we will be perfectly placed to take forward the next stage of our plans. And we bid farewell to Sinclair and his preposterous gin palace in the process.'

In the stuffy darkness behind the curtain, Sophie felt lightheaded. Her mind raced to make sense of everything that she had overheard. She knew what an infernal machine was: it was exactly the kind of military terminology that Papa had loved to explain to her. It was a bomb with a fuse or mechanism that could be set so that it would go off at a particular time. Freddie was activating a bomb at the party at Sinclair's, at midnight tonight. Horror ran through her: she longed to get away, but her legs were as cold and heavy as marble.

Far away from her on the stage, the second act was drawing to an end and the audience was applauding boisterously, and the chorus girls were back on the stage, bowing and kissing their hands.

The Baron and the gentleman beside him were on their feet too, smiling and applauding. But the Baron's voice sounded ice-cold as he said in a low voice: 'I don't need to tell you, Freddie, that what I have revealed to you is of the utmost secrecy. The members of the Society are not forgiving people. Any breach of this trust would be paid for with the severest of penalties. I hope you understand.'

'Of course,' said Freddie, in a respectful tone. There was something in the formality of his manner now that seemed more familiar than ever to Sophie, and she shifted her position to try and catch sight of him. Before she could stop herself, a gasp escaped her lips. For Freddie – the Baron's accomplice – was none other than Mr Cooper.

Small as it was, the sound was enough to make the Baron look round. She knew at once he had seen her. He called out in a low voice, and before she could move or do anything, the door opened behind her, and then an arm reached out and clamped her in a powerful grip, dragging her out from behind the curtain. She tried to scream, but a gloved hand holding a handkerchief was already pressed over her face. As she choked on the unbearably sickly sweet smell, she saw the men turn to look at her. Mr Cooper's expression was one of pure shock, the Baron's impassive, but it was the other man, the smart gentleman, who looked straight into her eyes, and she realised that he was smiling. His cold, amused gaze was the last thing she saw before darkness fell like a curtain all around her.

CHAPTER TWENTY-ONE

Darkness. Hands seizing her roughly, jolting her out of herself. Her head slumping backwards, terribly heavy. Falling, falling, and her head thumping painfully in the void. Her body ached. It hurt to open her eyes.

She was lying against something shiny; she could feel its slipperiness against her skin. Where was she? Everything swam, distorted. She had been at the theatre, watching Lil pirouette on the brightly lit stage, and the audience had been laughing and clapping around her – all except for the man who sat in silence and smoked a cigar . . .

Sophie struggled to pull herself upwards, feeling groggy and sick. She was conscious of a sudden shudder of fear, although she wasn't sure why. She was quite alone, after all, lying in a richly furnished room on a sofa covered in shiny leather, her little evening bag beside her. The lamps were lit, casting out a curious greenish light, but nonetheless the room seemed unusually dark. Glittering on all sides of her were strange clocks and devices, many of them displayed in glass-fronted cabinets, and twinkling with gold and silver. For a moment, confused, she thought she must be in Sinclair's Exhibition Hall, but then she remembered the robbery. Besides, these objects were so different. Sinclair's treasures had been beautiful and frivolous, but there was something sombre and serious about the whirring mechanisms that lined the walls of the Baron's room.

The Baron. Of course. Slowly the memories started to unravel, and in spite of the stuffy warmth of the room, Sophie began to shiver. She had been discovered behind the curtain. She remembered the sickly smell that had enveloped her and how everything had turned upside down and disappeared. She had been *drugged*, she realised. And they had brought her here, to this room, and left her.

Still lightheaded, she staggered to her feet. There was a door across the room, and somehow she made her way over to it and rattled at the handle. It was locked. Of course, she was locked in.

She crawled back to the sofa and dropped down, her head in her hands. The clock faces seemed to jostle and shudder before her eyes. She was such a fool! Even now, Mr Cooper and the Baron could be at Sinclair's, about to activate the infernal machine – and there was nothing she could do to stop them. Her stomach twisted as she remembered that Billy and Joe would both be in the building, and that Lil would be going to the party after the show. They had already murdered Bert, and now they were going to harm her friends, and maybe hundreds of other innocent people – and she was trapped here, forced to watch the minutes counting down to midnight on the clocks that covered every wall around her. A sob rose in her throat.

But even as despair enveloped her, something else began to well up inside her. It was unstoppable, and as it rose, she realised it had been rising for a very long time, ever since the life she had known had crumbled away. Papa, Orchard House, her old life, even Sinclair's itself, all had been wrested away from her until she was left here with nothing.

But she did have something left. It was anger, and as it flooded her, she shook her tears away and forced herself bolt upright. She'd had enough of keeping her head and keeping calm, and keeping a stiff upper lip. She'd had enough of taking it on the chin, and of all Papa's moral lessons. For she was angry with him too, she realised: angry with him for leaving her *alone* most of all. But all that mattered now was that the Baron was planning to explode a bomb at Sinclair's that night, and that she alone knew what he was planning. If anything was worth losing her head over, it was this.

She made herself stand up and walk back across the room, heaving a deep breath and rubbing her hands up and down her arms to stop herself shivering. She saw that the hands of the clocks all pointed to just after ten. That meant she hadn't been unconscious for very long, so she couldn't possibly be very far from the Fortune Theatre and the West End. There was still some time left.

Swiftly, she went over to the door and tried the handle again. Definitely locked. She knelt down to peer through the keyhole, but she could see nothing except an empty passageway. There didn't seem to be anyone outside the door.

Next she tried the window at the opposite end of the room. Pushing back the curtains, she saw that the window was not only locked, but heavily barred too. Evidently the Baron was a man concerned with security, she thought grimly. Or perhaps she wasn't the first person he had locked in this room. Standing on tiptoe, she struggled to peep through the foggy glass and get some sense of her location, but she could see nothing except for the hazy lights of some other windows in the distance.

The thing was not to panic. She smoothed her tangled hair and tried to think clearly. In front of the window was a huge desk, covered in a muddle of newspapers, letters and maps, and she began to sort through them rapidly. There were dozens of complex drawings of what looked like the workings of clocks, and page after page of figures and letters, all in the same heavy black handwriting. These must be more of the secret codes, she realised. If Billy were here, perhaps he would be able to read some meaning into them: to her, they meant nothing.

Lying amongst them was a crimson leather folder stamped in gold with the shape of a twisting serpent. There was nothing inside it, but she remembered the note that Joe had found: the black handwriting, the strange shape that they had thought looked like a snake. She traced the gilt with her fingertip – it was the same image. There was no doubt that the note had come from here – from the Baron.

And it had been *Mr Cooper* who had been his inside contact at Sinclair's all along! The Baron must have been sending him his instructions in the form of coded messages, disguised as ordinary paperwork so that no one would think twice about them. Had Bert been in on it too, then – acting as Cooper's lookout, perhaps? But if so, why had he been shot? It was no wonder that Mr Cooper had seemed so surprised to see her in the Exhibition Hall that night: she must have crossed his path only moments before he had begun to carry out the Baron's instructions. And now she was here, and if the Baron had disposed of Bert as soon as he became troublesome, she knew that he wouldn't hesitate to do the same with her.

For a moment the room wavered again, but she clenched

her fists, blew out a long breath and turned back to the table. The next thing she happened upon was an invitation card with a narrow gilt edging:

The invitation was unexpectedly plain and simple for Mr Sinclair, she thought, turning the card over to see Sinclair's monogram printed in royal blue and gold. So if the Baron was one of the favoured guests at the opening gala, that meant that Mr Sinclair must know him, she reasoned. Of course, he could not possibly know him in his capacity as 'the Baron', but perhaps he had some other, more respectable identity amongst London society? But of course they knew each other, she remembered suddenly. Fragments of the conversation in the theatre were still coming back to her, and now she recalled the Baron saying *certain absences might be remarked upon*. Then there was the way he had talked about Mr Sinclair, calling him *an idiot . . . a troublemaker*. The Baron wanted to destroy Mr Sinclair, his shop and everyone around him. The Baron didn't just know Mr Sinclair; he was out to ruin him. Sophie swallowed, and kept sorting through the papers, pushing them to one side until underneath them all she uncovered a small bunch of keys.

She hurried straight over to the door, but none of the keys fitted in the lock. She felt a sharp spear of disappointment pierce her, but of course, the Baron was scarcely going to leave her locked in a room with the keys to get out again. But one of the smaller keys did unlock the desk drawers, and she rifled through them, uncertain what she was looking for, but desperate to find anything that might help her escape.

They were crammed with more papers, account books, letters – nothing that would be of any use – until all at once, there it was. The bright, jewelled eye glinted up at her more wickedly than ever.

There, lying by itself in the bottom drawer of the desk, nestling on a white velvet cloth, was the clockwork sparrow.

Hardly daring to breathe, she drew it out and gazed at it. It felt very small and delicate and oddly cold in her palm. It was so richly jewelled, so perfect. Almost without meaning to, her fingers found the delicate key, and gently twisted it. At once the room was filled with a tinkling discordant melody. She gave a breathless laugh and sat down heavily in the chair behind the desk, still holding the bird in her hand.

It was only as she sat there, watching the key slowly unwind itself and listening as the strange tune came to a wavering halt, that she became aware that there was a second door in the room. It was a bookcase door, and she probably wouldn't have noticed it at all, except that there had been one just like it in Papa's study at Orchard House.

A small flame of hope ignited somewhere in her chest. Could it be possible that the Baron had forgotten about this other door, and maybe left it unlocked? Still holding the sparrow carefully, she went over and gave the bookcase a push, and then sank back again in disappointment. It was stuck fast. She tried the keys she had found in the desk, but it was obvious they would not fit in the lock.

She peered through the keyhole, only this time she could see nothing but blackness: probably the key had been left in the lock on the other side. She manoeuvred herself down on to the floor to put an eye to the gap at the bottom of the door. There was nothing to see, only that the parquet floor appeared to continue. There was no way out. For a moment, she found herself thinking of the day Edith had locked her in the millinery storeroom with Lil. If only the worst thing she had to worry about now was getting into Mrs Milton's bad books.

Locked in the millinery storeroom with Lil . . . It came all at once, in a burst of inspiration. Lil had been talking about that play she had seen, the one with the fearfully handsome hero who had managed to *escape from a locked room*. The trick he had used to escape wouldn't work in the storeroom because there were carpets on the floor. She looked down at the parquet: there were no carpets here. She almost laughed aloud.

Moving quickly now, she put an eye to the keyhole again. Darkness. There was no doubt that the key was on the other side of the lock, but the success of her scheme depended on there being no one in the passage outside, which she couldn't be sure of. She listened carefully: all seemed still and quiet. She would have to take a risk.

She went back to the desk and grabbed a newspaper and a silver letter-opener. She carefully placed the sparrow into the little beaded evening bag, wrapped in its white velvet cloth. Then she listened at the door again. Still nothing.

Holding her breath, Sophie unfolded the newspaper, smoothed it flat and slid it slowly through the gap at the bottom of the door. Then, clenching her teeth, she took the letter opener and prodded the narrow end into the keyhole, twisting and turning in an effort to dislodge the key. It didn't move at all, and she prodded again, more desperately. She was just beginning to feel that she would never be able to make it come loose when it fell to the floor with a horrible heavy clang that she felt sure must have alerted the whole house. Well, it was too late to stop now, she thought grimly. She slid the newspaper slowly, carefully back towards her under the door. Would the key come with it? Would it be small enough to fit through the gap?

It did – and it was! The trick had worked! Giddy with relief, Sophie grasped the key and pushed it into the lock. It turned. She had done it – she had actually done it. She was going to get out!

But first she would have to make her way alone through this strange building and find an exit. Steeling herself, Sophie grasped her bag and slowly opened the door, with no idea what she might find on the other side.

CHAPTER TWENTY-TWO

Piccadilly was thronged with carriages, horses and hooting motor cars. Outside Sinclair's was an excitable crowd, gathered to watch the guests arriving for Mr Sinclair's grand opening party. The watchers looked on enviously at those who were lucky enough to have one of the coveted invitations as they surged up the steps to the entrance in a flurry of sparkling evening gowns and smart dress suits.

The onlookers nudged each other at the sight of West End darling Kitty Shaw, arriving on the arm of Mr Gilbert Lloyd, fresh from the opening of a new show; and admired the sight of much-photographed society bride Mrs Isabel Whiteley, ascending the steps in a stunning turquoise-satin Worth gown. As the great doors swung open, music and light seemed to envelop these select few: the watchers outside caught only tantalising glimpses of the radiance within.

Inside, the guests were exclaiming at the beauty of the Entrance Hall, transformed with the light of dozens of lamps and garlanded with exotic flowers. Anyone who was anyone was there: haughty matriarchs; wide-eyed debutantes in gossamer-light dresses; smartly dressed young gentlemen; society belles posing for the benefit of the photographer. Here and there could be glimpsed a statuesque figure, clad in an extraordinary gown, but with so many celebrated beauties in attendance, it was almost impossible to tell who were the guests and who the Captain's Girls, displaying the store's most spectacular evening dresses. The cameras flashed; the ladies' jewels glittered; the light shimmered on the gleaming trumpets of the orchestra and glistened on the ornamental flourishes of the golden clock. Even the champagne glasses seemed to catch little scintillating shards of gold light and scatter them everywhere. It was a dazzling spectacle, and in the height of the excitement, more than one debutante swooned.

The room was humming with chatter about the well-known faces amongst the guests. The painter, Max Kamensky, had been seen squiring the fashionable *modiste* Miss Henrietta Beauville; and the handsome American Broadway star, Frederick Whitman, was dancing with the eldest daughter of the Duke of Beaufort; and most of the cabinet ministers seemed to be in attendance. Indeed, the only person missing was Mr Sinclair himself. Claudine had whispered to Monsieur Pascal that he was still entertaining the most important guests to drinks in his luxurious private apartments. But even without its host, there was no doubt that the Sinclair's opening gala was *a glittering occasion like no other*, as the society columnist for *The Post* jotted in his notebook with the small silver pencil he carried for such a purpose, before being swept away into the crowd once more.

Sophie tiptoed cautiously down a long, empty corridor. The room where she had been imprisoned had been richly furnished, and was obviously in regular use, but this passageway was quite different. Even in the dim light, she could see that the parquet floor had given way to bare floorboards. They creaked eerily beneath her feet as she crept forward, trying to make as little sound as possible. The ceiling was threaded with cobwebs and the windows were all heavily boarded up: only a few stray beams of light sneaked in from outside. Here and there, doors opened up on to empty rooms with yellowing wallpaper peeling off in long strips, or an old, mildew-speckled rug. Her heart was thudding and her whole body felt taut with tension. What *was* this place?

She hurried on, still a little unsteady on her feet, and once or twice stumbling on the uneven floor. In the darkest parts of the passageway, she had to feel her way through the shadow, one hand tracing the crumbling walls. All the time her thoughts were scurrying. Could the Baron or any of his men be somewhere in the building? Or had she been left here quite alone? Either way, she was in no doubt that she wanted to get out, and quickly.

At last, the passage led her to a flight of stairs that spiralled downwards into darkness. She looked back over her shoulder, but there was no other way to go. She would have to go down.

Down, down, down Sophie went, testing each stair with her toes as she did so. The staircase seemed to wind on forever, but at last she reached solid ground. She was standing in a low-ceilinged, stone-flagged passage: she could feel the coldness of the stones seeping up through her thin satin slippers. In the dim light she could see there was a lamp standing on a dusty old table, and she picked it up in relief. There was even a box of matches beside it. Without pausing to think, she struck one. Its small yellow glow in the darkness was soothing.

Her hands still trembling, she lit the lamp, glad to see the familiar warm light fill the darkness. But even as she let herself relax, she began to wonder what a new oil lamp and a fresh box of matches could be doing here, without the thick film of dust that covered everything else around her. Someone else had been here, and recently. For all she knew, that someone might be nearby at this very moment.

Trying to swallow the dread that was rising up within her, she went on, lifting the lantern high and shining it into every corner. She was in an old cellar, empty but for the occasional barrel or a rack containing a few dusty wine bottles. The cold, damp air ran over her skin and made her shiver: it smelled thick and musty. Each empty room seemed to lead on to another and another, and there was still no sign of a way out. There *had* to be one somewhere, she reasoned, trying to keep her composure. But there were only more and more empty cellars, until she could no longer remember from which direction she had originally come.

A cold panic cascaded over her, and a sob escaped her, horrifyingly loud in the dark. And that was when she heard it: a distant noise, first a shuffling and then a horrible, heavy dragging sound, like something sweeping over the floor. She wanted to scream, but no sound came out. Instead she ran, clutching the lantern tightly, stumbling over the stone flags until she hit a wall. For a second or two, she felt too dizzy to move, but then she realised that her hand was resting on something, something hard and cold. Her fingers grasped it: a handle. It was a door. She had actually found a door!

She pulled wildly at the handle, but it didn't move. The rasping sound came once more and a rush of fear swept over her. She fumbled again, and at last the handle moved with a crunch, and she dragged open the door, falling through it and dropping the lamp in her panic. The heavy door swung closed behind her, plunging her into sudden and complete blackness.

In the dark, her shaking hands found the lamp and the matchbox. Twice she dropped a match before she managed to get the lamp lit once again.

As she struggled to gather her wits, she realised that the horrible sound she had heard had vanished, to be replaced only with a heavy silence. The musty smell had gone too. She felt as if she was in some strange airtight chamber under the ocean. The lamplight revealed what appeared to be another cellar, but this time it was quite clean, free of dust and cobwebs. The walls were lined with shelves, filled with storage boxes and crates. It could almost have been one of the neatly organised storerooms at Sinclair's, she thought in confusion. Across the room was a large metal safe.

'It's a strongroom,' she whispered aloud, her voice taking on an unearthly, hollow sound.

Trying to slow her racing heart, she looked around the room, shining the lantern into all the corners. There was nothing more to be seen, but she went over to the shelves and picked up a small wooden crate at random. Lifting the lid, she saw a bed of soft straw, and nestling within it, something that sparkled brilliantly. She picked it up and examined it in the light of the lantern. It was an enormous purple gemstone. The next crate held a diamond tiara. These were the jewels, she realised, in growing amazement. Here, neatly packed away in this strongroom were the rest of the stolen goods from Sinclair's Exhibition Hall.

For a moment she hesitated, uncertain what to do, but then she replaced the lid firmly on the box. The most important thing was to get out of this place. She was the only one who knew what was going to happen at Sinclair's and the only one who could stop it. And there was only one way to do that: she would have to leave the safety of the strongroom, venture back into the empty house and try to find a way out.

She went back towards the door and cautiously drew it open, hoping against hope that she would not again hear that terrible noise in the darkness again. Gathering her courage, she made herself step outside, holding the lamp aloft. This time she went carefully along, following the wall, trying to keep track of her steps. She wished for a staircase or a ladder, anything to take her up and away from this underground labyrinth, but instead at last she came upon something quite different: a low, round brick tunnel, running away from her into pitch-blackness. The air was cold and had a swampy smell; muddy water pooled on the floor; and there was the sound of trickling water echoing somewhere in the distance.

The lantern illuminated an arrow that had been drawn on

the brick wall in white chalk. It was pointing straight down the tunnel. Making up her mind, Sophie swung the beaded evening bag over her shoulder and lifted the lantern. For a few seconds, she looked regretfully down at the swinging skirt of her best dress, and the dainty satin slippers that Lil had given her. Then she stepped down into the muddy water, and set off once again, into the dark.

CHAPTER TWENTY-THREE

As the clock struck eleven, the music suddenly halted, and the dancers paused. There was a hush, and a fizz of anticipation seemed to rise around the room. Then a spotlight snapped on, and a collective intake of breath could be heard, as Mr Sinclair himself materialised, framed in a perfect circle of light. He stood up in the gallery, high above the throng below. A champagne glass was in his hand and he wore an exquisite dress coat over a snowy white waistcoat, against which a gold watch chain gleamed.

'Ladies and gentlemen,' he announced, his distinctive, drawling voice ringing out across the Entrance Hall. 'Thank you for joining me to celebrate the opening of Sinclair's department store. I am delighted to welcome you all here tonight. As you know, Sinclair's is no ordinary shop, and as such, it is only appropriate that this is no ordinary evening. Tonight, the store is yours: explore as you will – there are all manner of surprises to be found. Lose yourselves and see what you discover. First, though, I ask you to raise your glasses and join me in a toast . . .'

Below him, a forest of champagne glasses was held aloft as the guests replied together: 'To Sinclair's!'

Billy burst out of the side door into the stable-yard. It was swelteringly hot inside the building – he could not imagine how the young gentlemen managed to look so cool and suave in their dress coats. He felt uncomfortably sticky in his uniform, and weary from hurrying about the store. The night air, full of the familiar smoky smell of the city, was pleasantly cool against his face.

The stable-yard was deserted now: all of the drivers and grooms had long gone, for they were not, of course, bothering with any deliveries tonight. Everything purchased by the party guests was to be packed and sent out on Monday morning, the boxes tied with special gold ribbons to commemorate the opening gala. Billy leaned back against the cold brick of the wall, his ears ringing with the sounds of the party and his head full of confused thoughts.

He was still struggling to take in what he had overheard in Mr Sinclair's office. He had thought that Bert was supposed to make a full recovery – and had clung to the hope that once he was well, he might confess the truth about the burglary and prove that Sophie hadn't been involved.

Now he was dead – and none of the other Sinclair's staff had the slightest idea. *Under the circumstances, we daren't risk any distractions*, he heard Mr Sinclair say again in his cool voice. He rubbed a hand over his face, feeling quite sickened, and then, unexpectedly, he experienced a wave of sorrow. He had never really liked Bert much, but it was such an awful thing to have happened.

And the shooting had been right here in the yard, he realised with a sudden shiver. It was creepy out in the dark, and for a moment he thought about going back inside and finding somewhere to read the *Boys of Empire* he carried in his pocket to distract his racing thoughts. But he knew that there wasn't really enough time: he dared not take more than a few minutes' break.

For once, he was determined to focus on the job, and nothing else, to show his uncle that he wasn't just a lazy kid who couldn't do a decent day's work. He had scrubbed his hands until they felt raw, polished his boots until they were almost as shiny as Uncle Sid's own and had even managed to flatten his unruly hair with some pomade he had borrowed from Monsieur Pascal. He had followed every instruction to the letter. As he'd gone about his duties, faces around him had appeared and melted away into the crowd again: Miss Kitty Shaw, at the centre of a group of adoring young men, raising her champagne glass as if in a toast; Miss Atwood instructing one of the waiters; Mr McDermott, standing up in the gallery, surveying the scene with a watchful expression on his face; and often Mr Cooper, slipping through the crowd like a dark shadow – but he was determined not to be distracted. Each time Billy caught sight of the store manager, he began to wonder again about the revolver and what danger might be at hand, but he forced himself to push his speculations away. He would not think any more about Bert's death either. It wasn't his job to wonder about such things: he was not, and never would be Montgomery Baxter. *Know your place. Don't ask questions*, Uncle Sid reminded him in his head.

'*Psst!*'

He thought he must have imagined the sound that came out of the dark: probably his ears playing tricks on him after the noise of the party. But then it came again, more insistent and urgent now: '*Pssst! Billy!*'

Billy looked around him, startled and uncomfortable now. As a figure loomed out of the darkness he stepped back, then he realised to his relief that it was only Joe. But what on earth was he doing out here at this time of night?

Joe jerked his head to the side, indicating that Billy should come over into the shadows where they couldn't be seen. His eyes were darting from side to side nervously, and Billy felt a prickle of apprehension.

'What's up?' he asked, trotting over to him.

'I've been looking for you,' said Joe, sounding cagey and unlike himself. 'You ought to come down to the basement.'

'I can't,' said Billy, confused. A chat in the basement would be all very well and good, but surely Joe must realise that he couldn't just wander off like that in the midst of the party? 'Uncle Sid'll throw a fit if I don't go straight back to work.'

'I think you should,' said Joe uneasily.

'I honestly can't,' Billy said. 'I don't want to get in any more trouble. I'll try and come down later, perhaps.'

'I'm telling you, you've got to come down *now*,' said Joe, his voice full of urgency.

'Why? Whatever's the matter?' he demanded.

Joe looked uncomfortable. 'There's someone who wants to see you.'

Sophie hurriedly splashed her face with water. She was shivering in her thin dress, but she didn't feel cold, only slightly numb. She was glad to feel the freshness of the water after the dank, foul-smelling air of the tunnels. She had begun to think she would be trapped down there forever. The light of her lamp had cast strange, spiky shadows and there had been no sound but the steady drip-drip-drip of water somewhere, the shuffle and splash of her own feet, and in the distance, faint skittering sounds that she told herself, over and over again, were only rats.

The end of the passageway had come out of nowhere. Even before she had seen the door chalked with a large letter S, even before she had clawed it desperately open and smelled that unmistakable perfume of rose and violet, she had known by some peculiar instinct exactly where she would emerge. She had come up damp and dirty and breathless in the darkened basement of Sinclair's department store, behind rows of glossy furs. *Deliver sparrow underground by ten.* Mr Cooper had been communicating with the Baron all along, she realised, astounded. He had been going to and fro through the underground passage that led directly from the fur storage room in the basement of Sinclair's to the cellars of the Baron's strange old house.

She had felt almost faint with relief as she stumbled forwards, her hands grasping the softness of the furs. From somewhere that seemed very far above her, she had heard the dull hum of music and voices, the faint tinkling of a piano, the sound of someone singing, and she realised these were the noises of the opening party, taking place at this very moment. As she had stood there, half-frozen, she had heard the clock in the Entrance Hall begin to strike eleven. As if the chimes had snapped a switch somewhere deep inside her, she felt more certain than ever of what she must do. There were hundreds of people in the shop upstairs who were in terrible danger – people that the Baron would cheerfully obliterate to further his own ends – amongst them, Lil and her friends. She had to stop him.

Now, she splashed her face with water again, and tried to breathe, tried to stop herself trembling. Behind her, she could hear footsteps approaching. She spun around to see Billy, baffled and indignant, with Joe hurrying behind him.

'What on earth are you doing here?' Billy demanded.

CHAPTER TWENTY-FOUR

'We have to go to the police,' Billy whispered.

'I've already told you,' hissed Sophie urgently, peering out from where the two of them were hiding behind the smooth white figures of the marble mermaids that adorned the fountain in the Entrance Hall. Around them the music of the orchestra swelled, and party guests glided to and fro. 'We can't trust them. And there isn't enough time. The Baron said he would be here just after eleven – that's *right now*.'

'Someone else then – Mr McDermott. I'm sure I saw him here earlier.'

'We *can't*,' Sophie whispered impatiently. 'Remember, for all we know he's working for the Baron too.' She was gazing out across the Entrance Hall, trying desperately to find the Baron's face somewhere amongst the blurring, shimmering crowd of guests.

Just being back here seemed unreal. She had forgotten

how extraordinarily beautiful everything was: lamps glimmered everywhere, casting a smudgy warm glow over the party guests, who laughed and smiled within their golden bubble, utterly unaware of the danger they were in. Sophie felt her stomach clench. Should she even now be yelling at them all to clear the building? Would they listen if she did?

'I don't know about all this,' said Billy. A horrible feeling of foreboding was washing over him. Part of him couldn't stop thinking about how Uncle Sid was probably already wondering where he was, and if he didn't go back soon, maybe he would make good on his threat to tell Mr Cooper. The other part was still reeling from the bombshell of what Sophie had told him about Mr Cooper himself.

He wiped a sweaty hand over his forehead. Of everything Sophie had said, that was the one thing he was still struggling to believe. It just didn't seem possible that Mr Cooper – *Mr Cooper*, who ticked him off for his dirty hands or undone bootlaces, who strode about the store making sure everyone toed the line – could really be working for the Baron. And then there was the rest of it: spies and treason, kidnapping and secret tunnels. A bomb! It sounded completely bizarre, like one of his own Montgomery Baxter daydreams come vividly to life. He looked sideways at Sophie, who was scanning the crowd intently, and couldn't help asking 'Are you *sure?*' for the dozenth time.

'How many times do I have to tell you?' she snapped back. 'There's no doubt about it. Mr Cooper has been working for the Baron all along. He set up the burglary. He took the jewels. He probably shot Bert too – and now Bert is dead. He made it look as though the thieves came in from the outside, but really it was him all the time. He took the jewels straight down that passage in the basement to the Baron's strongroom, just like the message said.'

'*Deliver sparrow underground by ten,*' Billy murmured.

'The sparrow is all the Baron really wanted. The other jewels and things didn't really matter to him – they were just a bonus. He wanted the sparrow because he knew that by studying it, he could work out this system for creating codes that couldn't be deciphered, not by anyone, even an expert code-breaker. The man's a *spy* – he's selling Britain's secrets to other countries. He's got plans of some submarines that he's planning to pass on to someone from Germany at the party tonight.'

Billy blew out a long, slow breath of air. Every *Boys of Empire* he had ever read was crammed full of tales of espionage and treason, but it was simply too extraordinary to hear Sophie talking about it happening right here, at the party that was going on in front of them.

'And then Cooper is going to activate his infernal machine and destroy Sinclair's.'

'But *why?*'

Sophie shook her head, a bewildered expression crossing her face. 'I don't know. He has something against Mr Sinclair, but it's more than that. I think perhaps because there are so many important people here. He talked about making people feel afraid, about making everything unstable. I don't understand it, but it doesn't matter. We've just got to stop him.'

'Sophie, if this is true, we simply have to tell someone *now*,' he said urgently once again.

'I know – but who? I can't see Mr Sinclair anywhere, and we can't go to anyone from the store – we can't possibly know who is working with Cooper! Half the staff could be in on it for all we know.'

Half the staff could be in on it. An image of Uncle Sid flashed suddenly and vividly into Billy's mind. With a sinking heart, he thought again of his words in the staff cloakroom that afternoon. *Sometimes you've got to do things you might not want to do, but you've just got to knuckle down and do as you're told.* Surely it couldn't be that Uncle Sid was involved in Mr Cooper's plans?

'Anyway, we don't have any time,' Sophie was saying. 'The handover must be happening any moment now. If we can prevent that, we make sure the secret papers won't fall into enemy hands.' Billy opened his mouth to speak, but she drove onwards. 'And if the handover doesn't happen, if we can delay it, Cooper won't be able to trigger the bomb because the Baron and his contact will *still be in the store*. It might just give us enough time to stop this.' She looked desperately at Billy, who was tugging on her arm now in his eagerness to interrupt. 'I know you think I'm mad, but I promise you it's all true. We can't let them do this, we just *can't*.'

'Just shut up a minute,' Billy gasped out. 'I think I can see him. The Baron. There he is – *look!*'

Joe sat and fidgeted in the darkened basement. He couldn't seem to sit still. The words *Baron* and *bomb* were still ringing in his ears like alarm bells. All his instincts were telling him to get out of Sinclair's. He wasn't about to sit around waiting to get blown to bits. Yet somehow he found himself still here.

The Baron was in the store, or so Sophie had told them. He shook his head, struggling to believe that the prim young lady who had given him a shilling less than a week ago was the same filthy, mud-splattered girl who had appeared in the basement tonight.

None of her story made any sense. After all, people did not *escape* from the Baron. He simply could not fathom how she had managed it. Could it be that they hadn't even expected a young lady like that, all lah-di-dah voice and dainty gloves, to even try to get away? After all, he himself wouldn't have guessed she had it in her. But she was tougher than she looked – and she wasn't daft, neither. If she said he should leave the shop, then he should listen.

The thought made him move forward. In her haste to get upstairs, Sophie had left behind the little bag she had been carrying. Not sure what to do with it, he scooped it up awkwardly under one arm. Putting one foot on a crate, he levered himself up and out of the window with the loose catch that he generally used as a route in and out of the basement. It opened on to the stable-yard, and once he was up and out into the dark, empty night, he felt better, suddenly more able to think things through.

The Baron was here, in the store. The thought filled him with fear, then a sharp stab of frustration. This place was supposed to be his: safe and quiet and far away from the East End, but somehow the Baron had seeped in here too. Wherever Joe went, the Baron followed like he was his own shadow.

He was sick and tired of being afraid all the time. If he only had the chink, he thought, he'd walk out of here right now and leave London behind him. He'd go to the docks and buy passage on any old ship he could find. It didn't matter where – America, perhaps. Somewhere he wouldn't know anyone, and no one would know him.

The thing was that he didn't have any money, nor was he likely to get any. Billy and the rest had been good to him, but he didn't think that any of them had cash to spare. He looked at Sophie's bag and weighed it in his hand: it felt heavy. A little guiltily, he opened it and peered inside. No money, only a few flimsy girls' things: a fan, a handkerchief, and something small and heavy wrapped up in a soft white cloth. Curiously, he pulled the cloth away.

A gleam of light ran over the object inside, making it shimmer. His mouth fell open in astonishment as he realised what it must be.

It was a sparrow all right – there was no doubt about that. Small and solid, with a slightly cocked head and a cheeky glint in its jewelled eye, it seemed so lifelike he felt it might flutter its wings and fly out of his hands. Underneath the enamel and jewels, the golden filigree of the mechanism was visible, and he touched the tiny cogs with a trembling forefinger.

He felt dazed. How had the clockwork sparrow come to be here in Sophie's bag? Had she got it back from the Baron somehow? Then it hit him – a fifty-pound reward had been offered for its safe return. He did have the chink after all; he was holding it right here in the palm of his hand.

Thoughts rushed through his head. He could go to the coppers right now, hand it in and claim the reward . . . But only an idiot would do something like that. They'd probably decide he'd nicked it himself. It would be so much easier to just go up to Drury Lane, where he knew there was a pawnbroker who didn't ask questions. With money in his pocket, he could be on his way to the docks in no time, leaving the Baron behind for good.

The idea surged through him, a fire of excitement. For a moment he thought guiltily of Billy and Sophie, trying to stop – what had she called it? – the infernal machine? But what help could he give them, really? They hadn't asked for his help after all: they'd just told him to get out, assuming he wouldn't be any use. And they were right, weren't they? You wouldn't catch him sticking his neck out to save a bunch of toffs.

As he stood there hesitating, Blackie lounged out of the shadows and bumped his head affectionately against Joe's ankles. He leaned down, but Blackie didn't seem interested in being stroked tonight, and strolled off, waving his tail. That was the way with cats, Joe thought. They were independent, solitary. They didn't get involved.

In a way, he was doing them all a favour. They wouldn't have to hide him any more. He shook away the uncomfortable thought of what Sophie would think when she found the sparrow gone, then the worse one of what Billy would say when he realised Joe had deserted them. And then there was

Lil . . . he knew for sure that wherever he went and whatever happened to him, he'd never meet another girl like her. For an instant, he wavered, but then he pulled himself together. No wonder Jem and the others had always said he was soft! Did he really think that a young lady like Lil would want anything to do with a scoundrel like him? The truth was that Lil and the others could never be his friends – not really. They lived in another world, with totally different rules: rules that made a lad like Billy risk trouble to help someone like Joe, or that sent them scurrying off, risking their own necks to try and save everyone else's. He would never be like that. Like Blackie, he had to look after himself – no one else would do it for him. It would have been nice to say thanks, but maybe it was best this way.

Resolved, he folded the sparrow back up in its cloth and pushed it into his pocket. The rest of the bag and its contents he dropped in the shadows by the staff entrance. He began walking quickly towards the entrance of the stable-yard, glancing back once at Sinclair's, and then stepping out into the side street.

Then all at once, just if she was standing beside him, he heard Lil's voice, clear as a bell in his ears, repeating the words she had said to Sophie in the park. *We can't sit back and do nothing . . . It just wouldn't be right.* He stopped, and muttered a curse under his breath. What he was just about to do was far from being right, wasn't it?

He hesitated, his instincts pulling him in opposite directions. But even as he stood there, he saw something that made his heart seem to stop in his chest. Just beside the entrance, leaning up against a smart, glossy black motor, smoking cigarettes, were three figures that he would have known anywhere. They were dressed differently now, in dark uniforms, like gentlemen's chauffeurs, but there was no mistaking them. He made a dart back towards the safety of the stable-yard, but it was too late. One of them had turned and was already looking right at him.

'Well, well, well . . . See who's here, lads. It's our long-lost pal Joey Boy. Where you been, Joey? We've been looking all over for you . . .'

CHAPTER TWENTY-FIVE

Sophie swallowed, her throat suddenly dry. Across the crowded room she could see exactly what Billy was talking about. A tall distinctive figure, wearing a violet silk scarf and smoking a cigar, was standing not far from the orchestra.

'It's him,' she said in a low voice.

'What now?' asked Billy.

A couple passed in front of them, arm-in-arm, laughing, obscuring the Baron briefly. When they had gone, they saw to their surprise that a young woman had appeared beside him. She was beautifully dressed in a green silk-taffeta gown, her hair arranged in perfect curls. It looked as though she had only just entered the store, for she was still wearing an exquisite little white fur, slung casually around her shoulders, and she carried a white fur muff.

'Who's *that?*' demanded Billy.

Sophie shook her head wonderingly. It was only as the lady turned to the Baron, as if making some passing remark to a vague acquaintance, that she realised what was happening.

'Oh no! *That's* the Berlin contact,' she murmured.

'Her?' demanded Billy, perplexed. 'But –'

But Sophie had already moved. She had no idea what she was planning to do. Even as she hurried across the room – darting past waiters with trays, stepping on ladies' trains – she didn't have a thought in her head except that she could see the Baron swiftly taking an envelope out of his jacket and reach out to hand it to the lady in the furs. Faces turned to look at Sophie in astonishment. One man's face stood out in the crowd, and his eyes flashed to hers, but there was no time to pause, or to remember who he was; she simply raced forwards, instinctively grabbing a glass of champagne from a startled waiter's tray. The lady had taken hold of the envelope. Her hand was moving – she was going to put it inside her muff – but then Sophie reached her, and threw the glass of champagne over her.

The lady flinched and gave a little scream as the cold liquid rushed down her neck. It gave Sophie the split second she needed. Faster than she had ever moved in her life, she snatched the envelope from between the lady's fingers, barely having time to register the Baron's outraged face. The she was already running as fast as she could back through the crowd, dimly aware that Billy was running frantically behind her.

*

'Good to see you again, Joey Boy.'

Jem was circling him, toying with him like a cat with a mouse. Instinctively Joe stepped backwards, but somehow, Tommy was already behind him. 'Watch yourself,' he said, grinning.

They were ranged round him now, like three points on a triangle: Jem, Tommy and Isaac, a big fellow with hands like hams, who Joe remembered was a former wrestling champion. Joe looked desperately out to where, just a few yards away, he could see the safety of Piccadilly, with lit-up motor cars going by and the sound of voices. But here on the narrow side-street that led to the staff entrance it was dark and empty, but for the shapes of Jem, Tommy and Isaac, looming closer around him.

'What are you doing here?' he managed to bluster, turning to Jem.

'What are we doing here?' Jem repeated with his familiar old jagged smile, and he looked at Tommy and then at Isaac. 'What are we doing, fellers?'

'Lending a hand,' said Tommy glibly.

'That's right,' said Jem. He eyed Joe speculatively. 'Helpful, that's what we are. I tell you what, though, what I'd like to know, and that's what *you're* doing here, Joey Boy. I thought you'd think twice before you'd cross our paths again. Not so smart of you, I'd say.'

'I'm just off – I'm on my way –' Joe began, taking a few steps back, but somehow there was always one of them behind him.

'There's no need to be in such a rush,' said Jem, so close now that Joe could see his broken teeth. 'We got a lot of catching up to do.'

'Yoo-hoo! Joe!'

The voice came out of nowhere, making them all jump. It was a girl's voice, and when he looked up, Joe saw that Lil was hustling down the street towards them. Her cheeks were flushed with excitement: it had been her first night in her show at the theatre, he realised, and now she was on her way to the party. She was wearing a hat wreathed in poppies and had a crimson scarf at her neck that deepened the red of her lips and cheeks, and made her dark hair look glossier than ever.

'I didn't expect to see you out here!' she said as she bounced up to him. Then she took in the three men. 'Good evening,' she said to them, brightly.

Joe's whole body clenched in fear as Tommy's smile grew even broader. 'Well, well, Joey Boy,' he said, his voice ringing with sly satisfaction. 'Who's this?'

Sophie had never known she could run so fast. Her slippers slid on the shiny parquet floor; her breath was heaving in her chest, but she kept on running, pushing past bemused and startled party guests.

'You there! Stop!' called out a voice behind her, but she did not pause, not even for an instant. She tore on, skidding past the counters that sold rouge and powder and scent, dodging a porter with a stack of boxes. Through the Flower Department, where a crowd of people had gathered to watch a ballerina clad in petal-pink perform a solo. Up and out, up the stairs, she kept on running, holding the envelope to her chest, Billy running beside her. There were heavy footsteps behind them, coming closer. Her mind was racing as she tried to work out which way they could go. Along the gallery, through the Reading Room, up the back stairs. Perhaps they could lose them on the third floor.

They burst into the Millinery Department. It looked exactly as it always did, though Sophie was dimly conscious of Minnie and Violet shrieking as they rushed through, sending a display of hats cascading to the ground. 'What are you *doing* here?' Edith demanded incredulously, her hands on her hips, blocking her path; but Sophie pushed her aside and kept on running. This was no time to let Edith, or anyone, slow her down.

They were back on the stairs now: she strained her ears for footsteps coming after them, but she could only hear the sound of her own breath, her feet hitting the ground, and Billy's, following behind her. Spots danced before her eyes and she could scarcely breathe inside her corset, but she kept on running, knowing that somewhere below them, the clock was counting down the minutes towards midnight.

'Not this way!' Billy was gasping behind her. 'It goes to the roof!'

'I know – there's another way down – through the roof garden. A staircase on the other side,' she panted out.

They crashed through the doors and out on to the roof terrace. After the fizzy exuberance of the party, it seemed oddly still, with no sound but the leaves of the young trees quivering in the breeze. Here and there they could see the distant figures of one or two couples taking a romantic stroll along the gravel paths. Taking a sharp right turn, Sophie dashed away from the main path and into the undergrowth, darting through the black shapes of the trees, like spiky paper cut-outs in the dark.

The door was ahead of her, just beyond the goldfish pond. From here they would be able to go all the way down and get out on to the street, where surely they could lose their pursuers amongst the people outside. Her fingers closed on the door handle in relief, but it wouldn't open: her body slammed uselessly against it. She shook the handle impatiently. 'Oh gosh – it's locked,' gasped Billy in her ear.

CHAPTER TWENTY-SIX

Sophie stood on the rooftop, clutching the precious envelope close to her chest, her heart thumping, with no idea of where to go.

The wind buffeted her, blowing out her hair, her muddy skirts. From up here, she could see London spread out before her like a counterpane: a doll's-house landscape, glittering with tiny lights. She could see all sorts of things that were usually hidden: the shapes of chimney pots and crooked rooftops; secret attic windows, as small as postage stamps; the scratchy lines of the scaffolding that supported the letters stretched across the tops of buildings around Piccadilly Circus, spelling out words like *CIGARS* or *BOVRIL*. She saw all this in a flash, and down below, the people – tiny figures, no more than wind-up toys moving along the streets.

The lights blurred and smeared, and she felt dizzy. The voices and the footsteps were coming nearer, faster, and there was no escape left for them now.

'I've got an idea!' came Billy's voice suddenly, through the dark. 'Quick – come on! This way!'

They were running again, her feet pounding and her breath catching in her chest as they raced across the roof. They dashed through the gardens, between the shadow shapes of the trees, towards the pond. There was a sort of summerhouse there – a place intended for elegant ladies to sit and drink iced tea on hot summer afternoons, out of the glare of the sun. Now, of course, it was dark and empty, but they pushed their way inside, pulling the door closed behind them. Then, silence. Billy took the envelope from Sophie's hands, his eyes darting wildly around as if looking for somewhere to hide it, but she motioned to him to be still.

Together, they crouched low in the shadows, trying to hold in their gasping breaths.

Slow footsteps crunched across the gravel. Then they stopped.

A cool voice came from outside. 'I commend you on your efforts. Really I do. You have surprised me, and that does not happen very often. But this is no time for a game of hide and seek. Come out at once, and bring my envelope. I have your friends here, and I'm afraid they are already looking rather unhappy. They will soon be much more so, unless you do exactly as I say.'

*

Sophie and Billy stood side-by-side at the edge of the pond. Sophie had taken the envelope back and was holding it close to her chest.

Opposite them stood the Baron, tapping his foot impatiently. Just behind him was Cooper, holding his revolver. Billy's eyes widened at the sight of the store manager, but Sophie barely saw him: instead, she was gazing in horror at Lil, whom Cooper held tightly with his other arm. Her hair had come down, and her face was white with fear.

On the Baron's other side, two big men in chauffeur's uniforms were holding Joe, who had blood trickling down the side of his face and was struggling frantically in their grasp. A third stood just behind them, carrying a piece of lead pipe, weighing it heavily in his hands as if he was enjoying himself.

Seeing Billy staring at him, Cooper flashed him a sudden and unlikely grin. 'In trouble again, Parker? Mind not on the job as usual, I see.' His voice sounded exactly as it always did: crisp, precise and impossibly familiar.

'It was you,' Billy blurted out, his voice wavering. 'You stole the jewels. You shot Bert Jones.'

Cooper looked indifferent. 'Poor Bert,' he said casually, tightening his grip around Lil's shoulders. 'He was so proud I'd placed my trust in him. But I picked the wrong fellow to rely on. He couldn't resist the chance to brag about all the secrets he knew. Bad luck for him.' He glanced over at Sophie for a moment. 'Perhaps I should have chosen you to help me, Sophie,' he said, teasingly. 'You've certainly proved yourself very . . . *capable.*'

Billy threw him a disgusted look. 'You were working for the Baron all along, weren't you?' he demanded, gesturing to Cooper's companion, who was beginning to look impatient. But to Billy's astonishment, Cooper began to laugh.

'Oh dear, oh dear.' he said. 'I always knew you were a young fool, Parker. Do you really think the Baron himself would trouble with the likes of *you?*'

Sophie stood stock-still. She could see from the triumphant expression on Cooper's face that it was true: the man facing them down on the rooftop with his white-streaked hair and silver-topped cane was not the Baron at all. How stupid they had been to think that they were the ones who had finally learned what the Baron looked like. For a moment she was back in the theatre box, looking down on the stage where the tiny figures moved like marionettes. *You talk too much, Fitz.* And then all at once, the shattered pieces seemed to fly together: the smart gentleman, his face cast half in shadow, half in light, his strange smile. The face in the crowd that had turned to look at her, their eyes meeting for a split second as she raced through the party. In one clear, sharp moment, she saw the truth.

'That's enough!' The voice of Fitz – the man who until now she had believed was the Baron – snapped through the still air. 'Hold your tongue, Freddie.'

He turned to Sophie and held out a hand. 'The papers, if you please. There are important people waiting. Hand them over, Miss Taylor, and you and your friends here go free. The alternative will not be at all pleasant.' He gave her a long, measured glance across the pool, and her body seemed to fill with ice. Her mind raced desperately: could she fling the papers off the roof into the street below, or dash them into the pond before her?

But his black eyes were boring into hers. 'And please don't try to be clever,' he said. 'You move a muscle, you make so much as a whimper to alert anyone to our presence here, and your friends will feel the consequences.'

Sophie stood motionless on the rooftop for a long moment, a small figure in a tattered evening dress. The wind streamed her hair across her face, and she pushed it back. She gazed at Joe, captured by the Baron's Boys, the very people that he had been trying so hard to escape. She gazed at Lil, who was shaking visibly. Sophie had never seen her look afraid before, not even for a second. The thought made a sob begin to rise in her throat. There was only one thing she could do now.

'No time to think about it, Miss Taylor. Help her make her mind up, please, Freddie.'

Cooper grinned and shoved the gun hard against Lil's ribs. She screamed, and Sophie darted forward. 'Take it,' she cried, pushing the envelope into Fitz's outstretched hand. One of the other men immediately grabbed her arm, jerking her roughly back and then pushing her to the ground.

Fitz tucked the envelope inside his jacket, before sneering at Sophie. 'Come on. We mustn't keep him waiting,' he remarked to Cooper, turning and heading back towards the stairway. Over his shoulder he called: 'Lock them up in that little place there, and then for God's sake, get ready to activate the mechanism, Freddie. It's not long now until midnight.'

'But – you said you'd let us go!' gasped Billy angrily.

He laughed. 'I did, didn't I? Unfortunately for you I'm not known for being a man of my word.' He strode away, a black and white shape disappearing into the dark.

Cooper shoved Lil roughly towards the summerhouse. Joe struggled hopelessly in the arms of his captors, who just grinned at each other at the sight of his agitation. 'Always knew you'd come to a sticky end, Joey Boy,' said Jem in his ear.

Desperately, Billy made a dash forwards to try and get

away, but one of the Baron's Boys caught his shoulder in a savage grip, and shoved him hard to the ground. He opened his mouth to yell, but the man pushed him forward so his face was stifled in the dirt. Above him, he heard Sophie call out, but the sound was cut off abruptly. He scrabbled vainly, the only thought left in his mind that this couldn't possibly be happening to them. This wasn't right: this wasn't how any of the stories ended.

Someone rolled him over. Cooper's face loomed above him, large and pale in the darkness. 'Time to follow orders for once, Parker,' he said, and then the lights went out.

Uncle Sid stormed angrily up the back staircase, his temper rapidly gathering a head of steam. He had really thought that he'd finally got the message into his nephew's thick head. For the first time it seemed like he was actually listening, instead of just looking away with that dreamy expression on his face. He had made a good start on the evening's work too; he had seemed to be actually making an effort. But then he'd given the boy a five-minute break, and he'd scooted off for half an hour or more. Sid had gone down to the basement where he always seemed to be hanging around, but there was no sign of him there. Then Edith up in Millinery, of all people, had told him some yarn about him running off to the roof gardens with that girl that he'd been mooning after, the one that Cooper had given the boot. What she could be doing back here he didn't know. Anyway, he'd taken that with a pinch of salt because everyone knew that Edith was a bit of a spiteful madam.

But whatever Billy was up to, he would put a stop to it once and for all. He'd have him up on the carpet before Cooper, if it came to it, he thought bitterly. Either that or he'd finally give his nephew the good hiding he deserved. Monkeying around the store during Mr Sinclair's opening party, indeed! Whatever did the boy think that he was playing at?

'Oh do hurry – we simply must get out!'

Billy groaned. Sophie's voice sounded like it was coming from somewhere very far away from him. In a daze, he pushed himself upright. He was inside the summerhouse, sitting on the ground. In front of him, he could see Joe crouching down beside the door, examining the lock, with Sophie close beside him.

Lil was leaning against the summerhouse wall. Her face was very white, but she seemed unhurt. 'I say – they've only gone and ruined my best hat,' she said, though her voice was only a weak imitation of its usual bright sound.

He could feel something dripping down his forehead.

He put up a hand and then saw that his fingers were wet with blood. Everything seemed to tilt unpleasantly, then Lil was beside him, holding something soft against his head. 'I think you'll pull through,' she was saying, beginning to sound more matter-of-fact and like herself now. 'Here. Just hold on to this.'

'Pass me that hair-pin,' Joe muttered to Sophie. He was trying to pick the lock, Billy realised as he pressed Lil's handkerchief to his forehead.

'Quickly,' Sophie was saying. 'There must be almost no time left.'

'I'm going as fast as I can,' Joe snapped back, but even as he spoke, there was a sharp clicking sound, and the door opened. 'Jem should have remembered he taught me how to do that himself,' he said, a note of pride creeping into his voice.

Sophie was out of the door in a moment, Joe close behind her. Lil pulled Billy to his feet. The men had gone: the roof garden was deserted, the sound of their feet loud as they stumbled out of the summerhouse and across the gravel.

'What's happening?' Billy gasped, still half-dazed.

'We have to find the bomb – and stop the mechanism,' said Sophie.

'But how can we?' Billy cried in horror. 'There's no time left – and the bomb could be anywhere in the shop! We've no idea where to find it.'

'I think I do,' said Sophie grimly. She didn't stop to explain what she meant, but instead began to race back towards the stairway.

Back inside the store, the light seemed dazzlingly bright, the colours intense. Everything blurred before Billy's eyes, as he stumbled down the stairs after the others. There was no thought of a roundabout route now, no time to remain unseen. Instead Sophie led them resolutely downwards, straight as an arrow speeding towards its mark. But Billy's head was pounding; he was falling behind. The colours began to spin and spiral, and he jumped at the sharp scream and a crash as they tore past a waitress, upsetting the tray of ices she carried. Behind him, he could hear someone crying out: 'They're here, Mr Parker! I can see them!'

It was Edith's voice. Hands reached out to stop him, caught him off balance. He tried to push them away, but everything swirled around him again.

'Let go of me!' he tried to say. 'You don't understand!'

But it was already too late. Before him, he saw Uncle Sid's enormous hand settling on Joe's collar, dragging him backwards. Joe was struggling, trying to wriggle away, but as a porter ran up to help, Billy saw that it was no good. 'You stupid idiot,' he muttered resentfully to Edith as he found himself sinking downwards, and for the second time that evening, everything blurred into darkness.

Lil and Sophie were still running. 'Stop them!' boomed Uncle Sid.

A porter leaped into their path: Sophie swerved to avoid him, twisting along the passage, through a door and out on to the main staircase that led down into the Entrance Hall. The porter made as if to grab at Lil, but seeing who she was, he stepped back, as if he didn't quite dare to lay a finger on one of the Captain's Girls. The few seconds' hesitation was all she needed and Lil surged forwards after Sophie.

They were back, lost amongst the crowds of the party now. No one seemed to notice them as they flew onwards, snaking their way through the people standing on the staircase. As she ran, Lil felt filled with a sudden, peculiar sense of exhilaration: those horrible moments on the rooftop began to melt away. She had almost outpaced Sophie now. 'Where are we going?' she managed to gasp out as she drew level with her.

'We have to get to Mr Sinclair. We have to tell him that the bomb's *inside the clock*,' Sophie exclaimed, pointing ahead to the enormous golden structure before them. But even as she spoke, Uncle Sid's figure loomed behind her, and he grasped her arm, yanking her away.

'*Run!*' shrieked Sophie – and Lil did. She dodged this way and that through the crowd, pirouetting around a waiter with a tray of drinks. She could see the clock directly before her, gleaming with the reflected light of a dozen lamps. The hands stood just a minute away from midnight. Time seemed to slow down. It was all up to her. She was the only one left now and Sophie was counting on her. Behind her, a waiter was racing through the crowd to get to her. Uncle Sid was shouting. Two porters were closing in.

There was only one way left to go. Using a *jeté* she'd learned for one of the dance routines for the show, she leaped, flying down the last few stairs and landed, not ungracefully, right at the feet of Edward Sinclair himself. He was standing amongst a group of smartly dressed guests, raising a glass of champagne in the direction of Miss Kitty Shaw, who was wearing a golden evening gown that glittered as seductively as the great clock behind them. For an instant, Lil froze, but it was only for a moment. Then everything happened at once.

'I'm terribly sorry to bother you,' she announced breathlessly to the astonished group. 'But I'm afraid that there's a bomb in your clock and it's going to go off at midnight.'

The words came out of her mouth meaning nothing. She could see the faces around her: bemused, astonished, confused. A society hostess raised her eyebrows in shocked disapproval. Kitty Shaw looked furious. 'What in heaven's name do you mean by this?' Lil heard her say in disgust.

Sinclair was merely staring at her, his head tilted slightly to the side, as if she were a strange curiosity he was trying to understand. But it was the figure behind them, whom Lil had barely noticed – the detective, Mr McDermott – who sprang towards the clock just as the doors opened, with a clunking, whirring sound, and the small golden figures emerged, signalling that midnight was about to strike.

PART V
'At Repose'

This dainty silk boudoir cap in an oriental style is intended for relaxed home wear. The perfect complement to a tea gown, it will both protect the coiffure and ensure elegance whilst relaxing in the boudoir – whether writing letters, reclining on the chaise-longue to overcome a tiresome headache, embroidering or simply resting at the close of a busy day . . .

CHAPTER TWENTY-SEVEN

It was a little after two o'clock in the morning, and Elsie, the new parlour maid, was trying to stifle a yawn as she climbed the stairs up to the master's study, carefully balancing a tray of tea. She wasn't used to being awake in the middle of the night, and she felt as if she could easily still be dreaming. Surely the housekeeper hadn't really just awoken her from a deep slumber and instructed her to serve tea and sandwiches to guests in the master's study, in the dead of night?

As she unloaded the teapot and the cups from the tray, she tried not to stare around her. The doctor was one thing – she could understand how someone might need the doctor at this time. But who were the rest of the master's guests? She was sure she'd never set eyes on any of them in her life, and they were a rum bunch, too: a lad with a great bandage fastened around his head; a shabby young fellow who looked as though he'd been in a fist-fight; two young ladies wearing evening dresses, but with big shawls wrapped round their shoulders; and a big handsome fellow in a smart uniform. Elsie lingered as she passed him his tea. She'd always been a bit partial to a man in uniform.

'Thank you Elsie, that will be all,' said the master in his usual matter-of-fact voice.

'What d'you reckon that's all about?' she demanded of Daisy, the housemaid, who had helped with the trays, the second the door had closed behind them.

But Daisy merely shrugged. 'Oh, search me if I know,' she said carelessly. Daisy had been working for Mr McDermott for over two years now, and she wasn't surprised by much any more. The master could entertain a monkey to tea in the middle of the night, she thought sagely, and she wouldn't turn a hair.

Back inside McDermott's study, the doctor had finished attending to Billy's head. 'You'll feel a little uncomfortable for a day or two, but there shouldn't be any scarring. Just make sure you take plenty of rest,' he was saying cheerfully, as he packed his instruments back inside his bag and made ready to leave. Opposite them, Lil was curled up in a big leather armchair, helping herself from a plate of Gentleman's Relish sandwiches and close beside her, Joe, who had a large bruise blooming across one side of his face, was deep in conversation with McDermott himself.

Joe thought that it was the strangest thing to be here in this cosy, comfortable room. He leaned back into the cushioned chair and sipped the hot cup of tea that he had been handed. When McDermott had first brought them here, he'd still been shaking all over. He couldn't stop reliving the terrible moment when Jem had taken hold of Lil and he knew there was nothing he could do to stop him. He still couldn't help glancing at her every now and again. It was a relief to see her with her mouth stuffed full of sandwich, leaning forward in her chair to say something to Billy.

It had been even stranger when McDermott had come to sit beside him, and had begun asking him questions. He'd never expected to find himself in conversation with a private detective, and at first he had been cagey, unsure what the fellow was trying to get him to say. But as McDermott had listened intently – pausing now and then to scribble a note, and once even to go over to the telephone to place a call – Joe had found himself talking more naturally. He didn't think anyone had ever listened so seriously to anything he had to say in his life. Gradually his hands had stopped trembling and before long he was sitting back easily in his chair, swigging his tea and accepting a second slice of fruit cake as if he were quite at home.

Across from him, Billy and Uncle Sid, side-by-side on the Chesterfield sofa, were looking a good deal less relaxed.

Uncle Sid kept clearing his throat and taking little sips of tea, whilst Billy shuffled his boots and fiddled with the bandage that had been fastened around his head.

Billy's mind kept jumping back to different moments. He couldn't think what had been the most peculiar part of it all: the mad chase through the store; Lil being held at gunpoint by Cooper; coming round, woozy-headed in the Entrance Hall, to hear how McDermott had grabbed the clock hands with mere seconds to spare; or simply this, sitting here, sipping tea at two o'clock in the morning, with Uncle Sid beside him. A muddle of different emotions was sweeping over him: anger that his uncle had persisted in treating him like a waste of space wrestled with a strange desire to explain everything and be forgiven. Mostly though there was just an impossible awkwardness that left him dumb.

He looked sidelong at his uncle and saw that Sid's face wore an uncomfortable expression of reticence and confusion and could it be – pride?

Billy cleared his throat. 'Sandwich?' he stammered, holding the plate out to his uncle.

The gesture hung in the air between them for a moment, and then, after a pause. 'Well now, I don't mind if I do,' said Uncle Sid, picking one up daintily in his enormous hand.

The telephone shrilled and McDermott answered it. After

a few short words, he replaced the receiver and addressed them all.

'That was Scotland Yard,' he said briskly. 'They've been examining the clock. They have confirmed that there was enough dynamite in there to cause very extensive damage. They've also completed a search of the building and confirmed that there are no other devices to be found.'

He turned to Sophie, who was sitting quietly in an armchair to one side. 'I must say I'm very curious to know how you knew the bomb would be inside the clock.'

Sophie had not touched any of the sandwiches. She had been given the chance to wash, and to tidy her hair, and someone had brought her a shawl to wrap around her shoulders, but although she was now outwardly tidy, inside she was in turmoil.

Looking up at McDermott, she shook her head. 'It was a guess,' she admitted. 'I didn't know anything. But it seemed like the sort of thing that he – the Baron, I mean – would do. He's obviously fascinated by clocks. There were dozens of them in that room where they had me locked up. And there was something I overheard that man Fitz say too, something about the plan being *like clockwork* . . .'

Her voice faded away. She couldn't stop thinking about how terrible it would have been if her instinct had been wrong, or if Lil hadn't managed to get the message to

Mr McDermott before it was too late. She stared around at the others, feeling sick at the danger she had put them in. 'I should have come to you straight away,' she said to McDermott in a voice heavy with remorse.

The detective looked back at her keenly. 'I can understand why you didn't,' he said. 'You'd found out you couldn't trust Cooper or Gregson – how would you know I was any different?' He sat back down in a chair beside her and took out his pipe. 'Actually, part of the reason I was there is because there had been some questions raised about Sergeant Gregson – well, that and the fact that Mr Sinclair does like to do things in his own way. But Scotland Yard have had their suspicions of Gregson for some time.'

'What – you mean they knew all along that he was up to no good?' Joe asked.

'Well, not for certain, but they had an inkling. And they had asked me to watch him carefully. Although I am a private agent, I have been working closely with the Yard for a long time. We knew that there was more going on at Sinclair's than merely a simple robbery, and we even had a few of our men stationed at the party, on the alert for anything else suspicious that might take place – but I must admit that none of our intelligence work prepared us for what happened.'

'Can you tell us how the infernal machine worked?' Billy asked curiously.

'I'm far from being an expert in explosives – but as I understand it, the bomb was concealed within the body of the clock,' McDermott explained. 'A long electrical fuse was connected to the clock hands, which had previously been fitted with special copper contacts. Once the Baron's business was done and his safety assured, Cooper's job was to connect the fuse, so that when the two hands came together at midnight, and the contacts touched, the current would detonate the bomb. Happily for all of us, Miss Rose gave the warning in time, and so I was able to stop the clock hands and prevent the connection being made. And as you know, Scotland Yard at once sent some of their experts to disconnect the fuse and take apart the mechanism.'

Billy was listening in fascination, but Lil, uninterested in the workings of machinery, had other questions. 'Tell us about Mr Cooper. Did you already know he was involved?'

'Not exactly,' said McDermott, a note of regret in his voice. 'He was very smart about concealing his secrets. But I had been keeping an eye on him. We suspected all along that the robbery had been an inside job, and there was something about the way he cut Miss Taylor loose so fast, on so little real evidence, that struck me as peculiar. After that, I had a man tailing him, watching his movements when he left the store. But everything seemed perfectly above board. Of course, we had no idea then about the tunnels. He was doing the Baron's business all along, right under our very noses.' He shook his head, as if a little disgusted with himself.

'Shocking business. Never would have believed it!' Uncle Sid was heard to mutter, apparently to himself.

'They must have been jolly pleased with themselves when they found those tunnels,' said Lil.

McDermott nodded, leaning back in his chair and taking a puff of his pipe. 'Though they're not nearly as uncommon as you might think. We've known for some time that there are vast networks of tunnels under the whole of central London, many of them very old, which are being used by criminals as a way to travel the city in secret. Cooper may have already known about the tunnels when the store was being built. It may even have been him who instructed the workmen to fit the door that leads into them. It certainly wasn't part of any of the official store plans.'

'And I suppose the Baron bought that old house because of its proximity to the underground route,' said Sophie, working it out. 'He must have had that strongroom built himself.'

'Very probably,' said McDermott, nodding. 'Anyway, for a while we thought we must have been wrong about Cooper.

But as a matter of fact, I must confess I had a man following you too, Miss Taylor. We had our eye on all sorts of people – even Miss Rose here aroused my suspicions when I found her in Cooper's office.' Here, Billy gave Lil a very meaning look, and she smothered a laugh.

'That's the thing about the Baron – he has a habit of recruiting the most unlikely of people.' McDermott went on. 'But tonight the man watching Miss Taylor told me that he had seen someone fitting Cooper's description and another fellow manhandling her into a carriage. That certainly set all the alarm bells ringing. But then just a short while later, he was seen at the store, so we thought it must have been somebody else. He knows how to cover his tracks, that's for sure.'

'So he was never really an ordinary store manager?' Lil asked. 'He was working for the Baron all along?'

'So we believe. John Cooper was certainly a false name – an alias. We'll probably never know who he really is, except for the fact that he's known as "Freddie". I only wish he hadn't slipped through our fingers tonight.'

Uncle Sid nodded vehemently at this. 'Playing us all for a set of fools,' he muttered bitterly. 'And all the time a snake in the grass!'

'And what about the *Baron*?' asked Lil. 'Who is he? We know he wasn't that fellow from the roof.'

'Yes – from what you've told us, Scotland Yard have been able to identify "Fitz" as Mr Raymond Fitzwilliam, a former actor. We believe he has been acting as a front man for the Baron, at times actually impersonating his master. You can see how the Baron is adept at surrounding himself with a whole structure of people who do his work at different levels, keeping his own identity a carefully guarded secret.'

'Did you already know that the Baron was the one behind the burglary?' asked Billy curiously.

McDermott shook his head. 'We didn't – but we could have guessed he had a hand in it,' he went on, taking a puff on his pipe. 'You'd be surprised how much of the crime in this city can be traced back to him, one way or another.'

'So who is he – really?' Lil asked again, leaning forward.

McDermott shrugged. 'We don't know for sure. But what we do know is that there is someone very smart, with considerable resources, masterminding much of the large-scale criminal activity taking place in the East End. There's been a shift in the past years away from petty crime – pick-pocketing, protection rackets, smuggling around the docks – to something far more organised and comprehensive. We know there's someone clever driving it forward, the man they call 'the Baron'. But whoever he is, he is very skilled at concealing his tracks. We've certainly never set eyes on him.'

'But I have,' said Sophie. 'I've seen him twice, I'm quite sure of it, though I didn't know then that he was really the Baron. Once in the box at the theatre, and then at the party at Sinclair's, I saw him in the crowd. It was only for a second, but I'm certain he was there, among the guests.'

'And you're probably right. We've long since speculated that the Baron has another, very different identity in London's polite circles, and you may be sure we shall be taking a thorough look over the guest-list for Mr Sinclair's party. We believe that's why he is always so careful that those who work for him in the East End don't see his face – and makes sure that they don't know him by any other name.'

'But now Sophie has seen him and she knows what he looks like!' exclaimed Lil excitedly.

'And I'm afraid that makes your position a rather dangerous one,' said McDermott soberly, turning to Sophie. 'We will be taking good care of you over the next few weeks while the investigations continue. But for now, is there anything else you can tell us about him? No matter how small.'

Sophie thought for a moment. 'He was very smartly dressed,' she said, trying to picture the man she remembered. 'Much more elegant than the other man, Fitzwilliam – he made him look showy by contrast. And I believe – no, I'm sure of it – he was wearing a military medal with his evening dress.'

'A medal? Do you remember what it looked like?'

'It had a striped ribbon – green, white and orange, I think,' said Sophie slowly. 'I noticed it because Papa had one like it.'

'Green, white and orange?' repeated McDermott, looking at Sophie with bird-bright eyes. 'Are you sure? That's the King's South Africa Medal. Not many of them were awarded.'

'So that would mean . . .'

'It would mean that the Baron – whoever he is – served in the Boer War. That's very interesting. Anything else you can tell me?'

Sophie thought for a long moment, then shook her head. 'I've already told you about all the clocks. The only other thing I remember is that when I was listening to Fitz, he kept talking about a society of some sort. He said something like "the people in the Society are not very forgiving".'

'A society?' McDermott looked at her with interest. Then he gave her a rare smile. 'You've done very well, Miss Taylor. What with the description you've given us, and that of the lady they called 'the Berlin contact', you've already provided us with a great deal of useful information.' He contemplated her for a moment or two. 'I must admit, it's intriguing,' he went on, almost to himself. 'He's usually so cautious . . .'

Sophie looked at him, uncertain of exactly what he

meant, but Joe was nodding. 'That's what I thought. I mean – begging your pardon – but he's not exactly a feller that'd baulk at, well, you know, doing away with anyone who got in his way. But he didn't.'

McDermott nodded. 'And he took you to his own private study, filled with his personal effects. Why?'

Sophie shook her head. She was thinking again of the strange room full of whirring instruments, and of the extraordinary way he had looked at her, in that moment in the box at the theatre. He hadn't looked shocked or even angry, but only amused. It was as if he hadn't been surprised to see her at all, as if she was someone he knew quite well. Thinking of it, she shivered.

'But what about that Sergeant Gregson fellow?' interjected Uncle Sid unexpectedly. 'That crooked police chap, the one who did for poor young Jones. Couldn't he spill the beans?'

'If he's got any sense, he'll be very far away by now,' said McDermott, turning to Uncle Sid. 'I haven't seen him since before the party. He must have realised that he'd been discovered. But in any case, he may never have come face-to-face with the Baron himself. In the past, even when we have been able to get hold of one of the Baron's men, they've never been willing to tell us much.'

'None of them are going to peach on the Baron,' said Joe. 'They'd know what to say, all right. *I ain't seen nothing, I ain't done nothing, I don't know nothing.* That's how they tell you to deal with the rozzers – I mean, the police,' he corrected himself awkwardly.

'So, you mean that we still have no idea who the Baron is?' asked Billy, rather sadly. The detective stories he read always ended with the dramatic unmasking of the villain, and he couldn't help feeling disappointed that after everything, Mr Cooper, Sergeant Gregson and Fitz had all managed to escape scot-free – and the Baron's true identity was just as mysterious as ever.

'No, but we're creeping nearer,' said McDermott. 'With the information Miss Taylor has given us tonight, and what Joe here has been able to tell us about the Baron's Boys, we're a good deal closer to understanding his operations. And thankfully we have the clockwork sparrow safely back.' He gestured to the bird, which was now sitting on his desk, resting on its white velvet cloth. 'It's going to prove extremely useful to Scotland Yard. What's more, I've just heard that they've made a thorough exploration of the tunnels and found the strongroom you spoke of, Miss Taylor – and the rest of the jewels will soon be restored to their rightful owner.'

'But I'd have thought the Baron would've had them well away by now!' said Joe in surprise.

'I don't think he would have considered it worth the risk,'

said McDermott. 'Remember he is a ruthlessly pragmatic fellow, and those jewels were just a means to an end. What he was really interested in was the sparrow – he only took the other treasures to make it look like a more straightforward robbery, and throw us off track.'

'If only we had been able to stop them handing over those secret documents,' said Sophie. 'I know we ought to just be thankful that everyone is safe – but I do wish they hadn't got away with those.'

Billy glanced quickly up at McDermott, and McDermott gave him a quick nod in return. Then, Billy took a deep breath and grinned around at the others. 'Actually,' he said, in a voice that was trying very hard to be casual, but couldn't quite conceal its jubilation. 'They didn't get away with those documents, you know.'

'What do you mean? Sophie handed them over when that hateful man came at me with his beastly revolver,' said Lil, puzzled.

'Except she didn't. I mean, she did hand over the envelope of course, but the papers weren't inside it. I took them out and stuffed them in my pocket. I don't really know *why*, it just seemed the thing to do. But then it felt too empty, so I put in the only other thing I had to hand, just so they wouldn't know the papers were gone.'

'And what was that?' asked Sophie, her eyes beginning to

shine. She thought she might already know the answer.

'My *Boys of Empire*,' said Billy, grinning back at her. 'I s'pose I'll never finish that Montgomery Baxter story now.'

The others exploded with exclamations of surprise and delight. 'But Billy – that's *marvellous!*' exclaimed Lil.

Joe struck the arm of the chair with his fist. 'By gum! Just imagine their faces when they open that envelope and find your story paper in there instead!'

'These are the real documents,' McDermott said, tapping a pile of sheets covered in diagrams and numbers, which were on the desk at his side. 'Top secret and incredibly dangerous in the wrong hands. We may not have been able to prevent the Baron learning how to create these coded messages, but we're delighted that you managed to stop these papers leaving the country. Scotland Yard will be taking them straight back to where they belong tonight.'

'Montgomery Baxter himself couldn't have done it better,' said Sophie, giving Billy such a delighted smile that he felt his face turning a brilliant crimson. Uncle Sid was gazing at him in speechless astonishment. Billy had to look swiftly down at his boots, mumbling something about it being nothing that any of the others wouldn't have done, as Lil thumped him on the back so vigorously that he would surely end up black and blue tomorrow.

To Billy's relief, at that moment the door opened and

the maid came in, followed by Miss Atwood with Lucky, Mr Sinclair's pug, on a lead. She looked weary, but there was a triumphant gleam in her eyes.

'Oh good, you're all still here,' she began, and then continued more formally, 'Good evening. Er – Mr Sinclair has asked me to convey to you his sincere thanks for your efforts tonight. He deeply regrets he cannot pass them on in person, but he is busy entertaining some of his most important guests to a late supper at The Ritz, since the party had to finish so . . . *abruptly*. However, he has asked me to convey some messages to you.'

McDermott nodded and gestured to a chair. Miss Atwood sat down rather rigidly, waving away the offer of a cup of tea. 'With the exception of Parker here and a few other senior employees who must, by necessity, know, Mr Sinclair has asked me to request that you keep the full details of what happened this evening to yourselves. We have, of course, had to give a brief explanation to the staff and party guests, to make clear why the store had to be evacuated, but we would prefer it if the – er – full extent of the situation remained confidential. We do not, after all, wish to create a sense of public *panic*,' she said, glancing over at McDermott as she spoke.

'But – there was such a commotion,' said Lil, screwing up her face in disbelief. 'Running – and shouting – and all the goings-on with the clock. Surely people will have questions about all that?'

McDermott shrugged. 'You'd be surprised how unquestioning people can be, Miss Rose. And I think that, for once, this is the kind of publicity that Mr Sinclair will feel his store could do without – is that right, Miss Atwood?'

Miss Atwood nodded, looking a little uncomfortable, and swiftly went on: 'Mr Sinclair is also delighted to hear that his jewels are being returned to him, and he has asked me to tell you that he considers the reward for finding them belongs to the four of you . . . young persons. He has also asked me to make some recommendations about your futures.'

'Our futures?' repeated Billy, confused and a little anxious. Surely Mr Sinclair wasn't going to turn round and give them the sack now, after everything – was he?

Miss Atwood turned to Uncle Sid and made a small bow. 'Mr Sinclair feels that your nephew does not have the best opportunity to perform to his full potential in his current position.'

'Eh?' asked Uncle Sid, looking even more confused than Billy himself.

'I think what Miss Atwood is trying to tell you is that after what young Billy here has done tonight and over the last few days, he's proved he's well qualified to be more than an apprentice porter,' explained McDermott crisply.

'He would like to propose to you that Master Parker transfers his apprenticeship to work in the office,' said Miss Atwood, looking as if the idea pained her slightly. 'We are in need of a – er – bright young man, to train up. We would arrange full tuition in typing, shorthand, accounting and so forth. You would be reporting directly to me, Master Parker. It is a demanding position, but Mr Sinclair appears to have a great deal of faith in you.'

Billy's eyes were round with astonishment. He looked from Miss Atwood to Uncle Sid to McDermott to Sophie, and back to Miss Atwood again. 'The Captain wants me to work in the office?' he repeated, in disbelief. 'Do you mean it?'

Miss Atwood did her best, but was unable to entirely restrain a smile. 'Yes, I do,' she said.

'Well – *gosh!*' said Billy in amazement. Uncle Sid clapped him on the shoulder, himself apparently struck dumb that a nephew of his should be deemed worthy of such an honour – and by the Captain himself, too.

'Mr Sinclair also wishes to extend an offer of some suitable employment to you,' Miss Atwood went on, turning swiftly to Joe, who had been sitting nervously throughout the conversation, gently smoothing the silky ears of Lucky the pug, who had immediately gravitated to his side. Now he looked up quickly, anxious and uncertain what the private secretary could be driving at.

Lil however, grasped her meaning at once: 'Oh, jolly good! You could work in the stables!' she exclaimed excitedly, turning to Miss Atwood. 'He's awfully good with animals – especially horses,' she explained.

'I'm sure Sinclair's could always use another groom, eh Miss Atwood?' said McDermott with a grin. He added to Joe: 'It could be a fresh start for you, young man – and you'll have somewhere better to sleep than the store basement, too.'

Billy's mouth fell open. 'You *knew* about that?' he demanded incredulously.

McDermott laughed, but Joe barely heard him. A decent, honest job working in a real stable . . . it was everything he had ever dreamed of. And he'd be able to stay at Sinclair's, with Lil and the rest! He sat back in his chair, trying to take it in.

Miss Atwood had turned to Sophie, who was only half-listening to the conversation going on around her. She was gazing at the secret papers spread out on the table, her eyes gleaming. Impossible as it had seemed in those last few desperate moments, they had actually done it. Between them, they had saved Sinclair's and stopped the Baron carrying out his plan. They had stopped British secrets falling into enemy hands.

Suddenly she felt so tired that she thought she could almost have laid her head down on the desk and fallen asleep amongst the blotting paper. But Miss Atwood was speaking to her directly now:

'Mr Sinclair is particularly keen for me to speak with you, Miss Taylor,' she said. 'He has asked me to give you his gravest personal apologies for your dismissal. He asks respectfully if you would be willing to return to Sinclair's.' Miss Atwood gave a small, slightly embarrassed cough. 'In fact, he asked me to tell you that there is no one he would rather have on his staff.'

Sophie's face flushed as she realised that the others were all staring at her. She thought of all that going back to Sinclair's would mean: of the hustle and bustle of the corridors, of Uncle Sid sweeping the great doors open on to an excited crowd. She thought of the elevators surging up and down, of Claudine creating her lavish window displays while the porters swung by with their trolleys loaded with immaculate blue-and-gold boxes. Then she thought of the Millinery Department, the long hours on her feet, Mrs Milton's scolding, Edith with her nasty remarks, and of herself, standing up in the window, looking down at the street below. She thought of all the people at Sinclair's who had been so quick to believe she was guilty – and then she thought of the alternatives available to her.

Finally, she looked around at the others: Joe, watchful and quiet; Billy, with an anxious look in his eyes; even Uncle Sid, watching her earnestly, awaiting her response. And last of all there was Lil, who could barely keep still in her seat, she was so desperate for Sophie's reply. 'Oh *do* say you will!' she burst out at last. 'Sinclair's isn't half as much fun without you.'

Sophie grinned at Lil and then turned to Miss Atwood. 'All right,' she said at last, nodding slowly. 'I'll come back.'

A few hours later, Sophie was sitting in a motor taxi, gazing out of the window as it drove her through empty streets towards the lodging house. Soon, the sun would be rising; an edge of fiery pink was already becoming visible around the dark, cutout shapes of the buildings.

Piccadilly was deserted now, but on Monday morning, these streets would be thronged once more with cars and motor buses, with business men and typewriter girls, with beggars and flower sellers, bootblacks and newsboys. The shoppers would be there as well, of course, surging in and out of the great doors of Sinclair's. Quite soon she would be back there too, going about her business in the Millinery Department just as if everything was exactly the same as before. But, she reminded herself, it would not be quite the same. For one thing, she didn't think she would have to worry about the other girls calling her 'Your Ladyship' or 'Sour-milk Sophie' any more.

She yawned and leaned her head against the window, thinking dimly how extraordinary it was to be driving through the streets of the city at five o'clock in the morning. But even that wasn't nearly so extraordinary as what Mr McDermott had said to her and to Lil, as he showed them out to the motor taxis that Miss Atwood had insisted on providing to take them all back to their homes. Behind them, they could see Uncle Sid clapping Billy on the shoulder as the two of them clambered into another cab, and Joe, waving from the doorway. Instead of the basement of Sinclair's, he would be spending the night in the comfort of Mr McDermott's guest bedroom.

'The two of you make rather a resourceful pair, you know,' Mr McDermott had said to them, as he opened the door to Sophie's cab and helped her inside. 'Mr Sinclair is inclined to see young ladies such as yourselves as . . . shall we say, *decorative*, first and foremost? But I am different. I know intelligence and courage when I see it. You have first-rate instincts Miss Taylor – and with Miss Rose here to help you act on them, I suspect you would be a formidable team. If you ever find yourselves tired of Sinclair's, come and find me. I think there could be quite a different sort of career out there for a couple of young ladies like you.'

She looked now at the card he had handed her: simple and smart, dark blue print on a plain white ground. In neat lettering it read *Anthony McDermott, Private Detective*. Even reading it brought a smile to her lips. Herself – a detective! Whatever would Papa have made of that? She grinned to herself as she gazed out of the window, across the empty streets of London, where the first rays of the sun were turning the rooftops to gold and silver, and another day was about to begin.

DEPARTMENT STORE MYSTERY SOLVED!

MILLIONAIRE'S JEWELS RECOVERED BY POLICE

Mr Edward Sinclair's priceless collection of jewellery, stolen from Sinclair's department store last week, was rediscovered by police on Saturday night in a raid on a house in the West End of London. The raid took place even as Mr Sinclair's invited guests toasted the store at a reception to celebrate its opening (*see Page 8*). Detective Inspector Eager of Scotland Yard told us: 'The jewels were locked in a strong room in the basement of the building, which was found to be otherwise derelict and abandoned.'

Speaking to our reporter, Mr Sinclair said: 'Words cannot express my delight that my jewels have been returned. I plan to reinstate the exhibition as soon as possible so that all of London will have the chance to see these treasures for themselves . . . *Story continued on Page 2*

———◆———

Scotland Yard launch investigation into corruption amongst London's police force – Page 6

Sinclair's Opening Gala disrupted by safety concerns – Page 8

Society photographs: London's most elegant in attendance at Lord Beaucastle's annual spring ball – Page 13

———◆———

AUTHOR'S NOTE

Sinclair's department store is fictional, but this book was partly inspired by the real history of London's department stores. In particular, it owes much to the story of Selfridges, which was opened by Harry Gordon Selfridge in 1909, but it also takes inspiration from Liberty, Harrods, Fortnum & Mason, and many other famous stores that you can still visit in London today. You will not find a department store at Piccadilly Circus, where Sinclair's is supposed to be situated, but imagine it roughly in the position of Waterstones Piccadilly, which itself was once home to the department store Simpson's.

ACKNOWLEDGEMENTS

I am so grateful to Ali Dougal, Hannah Sandford, and everyone at Egmont for giving *The Mystery of the Clockwork Sparrow* such a fantastic home, including Benjamin Hughes for the beautiful design and Júlia Sardà for her gorgeous artwork. Enormous thanks to my wonderful friend and agent Louise Lamont, and to all those who supported and encouraged me in writing this book, including Nikesh Shukla and Anna McKerrow for advice, motivation and keeping me going; the Booktrust gang, especially Hannah Davies, Claire Shanahan and Katie Webber for all their enthusiasm; and my dear friends Leah Cox, Amy Merrick and Hazel Wigginton, who were excited about this book from the start.

Most of all, special thanks to my parents for all their love and support, and to Duncan for everything, especially the many hours spent walking London's streets with me, helping to imagine the world of *The Mystery of the Clockwork Sparrow* into life.

SINCLAIR's

Sophie and Lil will return
in another thrilling adventure:

The Mystery of

THE JEWELLED
MOTH

Follow our brave heroines from the
bright lights of the West End to
London's dark heart.
Marvel as they don *cunning disguises,*
attend a *fancy dress ball*, uncover
terrible secrets and face their
most *dangerous challenge* yet . . .

Coming spring 2016

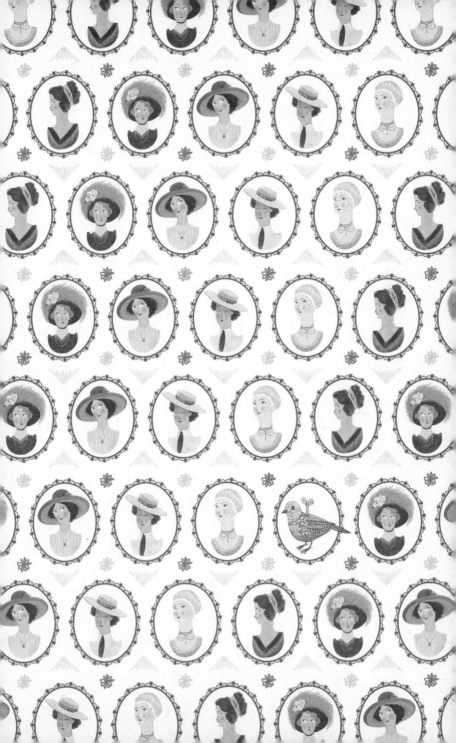

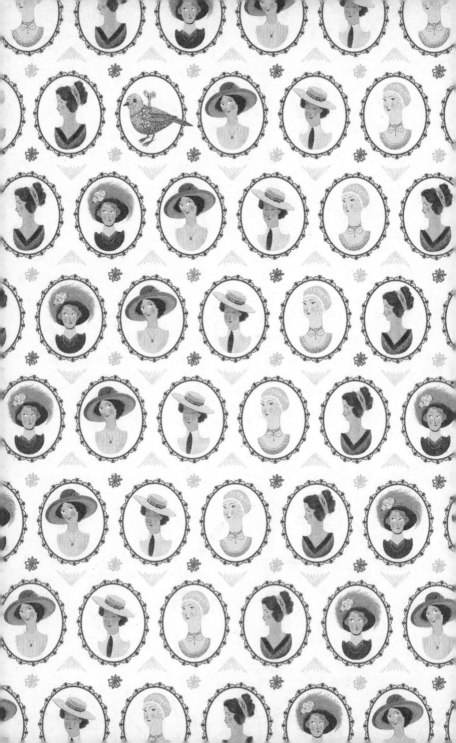